THE FANTASIES OF FUTURE THINGS

||||||||||||||||||||

DOUG JONES

SIMON & SCHUSTER

New York Amsterdam/Antwerp London
Toronto Sydney/Melbourne New Delhi

Simon & Schuster
1230 Avenue of the Americas
New York, NY 10020

For my Father:
Clarence E. Jones, Jr.
1947–2023

Maggie screamed and the winds grew stronger, and a voice, gentle and sweet, not thunderous as she expected, spoke to her from the whirlwind: *Who is this that darkeneth counsel by words without knowledge? Gird up now thy loins like a man; for I will demand of thee, and answer thou me. Where wast thou when I laid the foundations of the earth? Declare if thou hast understanding. . . .*

"The Foundations of the Earth" from
Let the Dead Bury Their Dead
Stories by Randall Kenan

ANGER

ONE

JACOB

There is this boy.
Small.
Dark.
Floating.
Floating in a pool of crystal blue water.
His arms spin, his legs kick,
his breath comes quick and short.
Swimming.
This dark boy floating, arms flailing,
legs churning, is swimming.
His muscles stretch and contract,
moving his small body forward.
It is gleeful for him to feel the water.
To feel his forehead part the liquid,
feel the liquid against his face, pass his ears,

cross his back, down his arms, around his torso,
over his butt, and along each leg.
Small boy blows bubbles.
Dark boy enjoys the water.

Jacob grew up believing Atlanta was a Black Disneyland. A mystical, magical fairyland where Black people lived in a different America. It was on every page he read about Atlanta in *Black Enterprise*. Stories in *Ebony* about the Big Peach of the South read like love letters to the city. The summers Jacob spent there visiting his grandmother were proof of Atlanta's special enchantment. Neighborhoods like Cascade Heights, Collier Heights, and Loch Lomond Estates were the wizardry that made you forget Jim Crow ever existed. Atlanta was synonymous with Martin Luther King, Jr., and Morehouse and Spelman. That was the city Jacob fell in love with, the city to which he declared his undying allegiance. That was the city he knew before the Olympics, his baptism by fire.

Jacob wasn't naive. He didn't grow up some brown-skinned boy playing in open fields, smelling daisies with his head stuck in the clouds, believing in God and the fundamental righteousness of people. He grew up in New York, Bed–Stuy, to be specific. At a time when graffiti wasn't a headline attraction in a museum, it was a neighborhood brand plastered on subway cars roaring through the city. He grew up in a New York where the murder of sixty-six-year-old Eleanor Bumpurs by a white cop for being four hundred dollars late on the rent of her Bronx public housing apartment was declared a justified result of an eviction gone wrong. Where a mob of south Brooklyn Italian white boys murdered an unarmed Yusef Hawkins, thinking he and his friends had come to plunder the fair white maidens of their village. Where the institutional machinery of New York City itself—from city hall to One Police Plaza to the *New York Post*—convicted five brown-skinned boys for an assault on the persona and personhood of white womanhood they never committed. Where the musical lyricism of De La Soul, A Tribe Called Quest, and Queen Latifah made heads nod and booties shake, capturing anxieties, passions, and aspirations in heart-pumping rhythms.

Atlanta seemed like an escape from all that—or at least a respite. Like things in "The City Too Busy to Hate" might be just a little more careful than everywhere else. Like the balance of power was tilted a little bit in Black people's favor. Jacob didn't think Atlanta would always be the cozy, comfortable, charming southern cityish type town of his childhood summers, but he wasn't prepared for the abrupt transformation that heralded Atlanta's Olympic announcement. No one was. Most people were just trying to find a livable median between the Atlanta-that-was and the Atlanta-that-was-soon-to-be. Jacob had graduated from Morehouse, settled with his roommates in an expansive three-bedroom apartment in Little Five Points, a cute neighborhood of turn-of-the-century Shaker-style houses and Craftsman bungalows. Flowering dogwoods, towering maples, and massive hickories lorded over gardens teeming with rosemary, black-eyed Susans, and azaleas. Morning dew clinging to blades of grass could easily send an unwary foot askew. Birdsong floated in the air, excited and aimless, its only purpose to invite smiles of appreciation from all who listened. Unobstructed sunlight filled a cloudless blue sky, a beacon toward a bright and beaming future. Jacob and his roommates could not have afforded that apartment in Brooklyn. They could not have afforded that apartment in Buckhead or somewhere off West Paces Ferry. At that time, Little Five Points was a hip, coming-of-age neighborhood populated by professionals very early in their careers and young creative types. Think the early days of Fort Greene and Spike's Joint just after *She's Gotta Have It.* The neighborhood was poised for takeoff into gentrification; a hand held over it would sweat from the heat rising from it. After the Olympics, people widened their eyes when they heard "Little Five Points," and thought "Inman Park." Another impact of the Olympics—the way some neighborhoods had to grow up quick, transforming overnight from "emerging" to "established."

After four years of Morehouse, Jacob could have returned to Brooklyn. He could have taken four years of Booker T. Washington versus W. E. B. Du Bois, of Malcolm X versus Dr. King; four years of discoveries on a campus full of men that proved his early flirtations with the same sex were evidence of something deeper and scarier; four years of the explorations and development of friendships; four years of finding the beginnings of independence. Jacob could have taken those four years, gone back to Brooklyn, set up residence in Fort Greene boheme, five train stops away from the brownstone where he grew up and all that was familiar in his world. But Atlanta was calling. Beyond summer visits to Grandma's. Beyond the protective cocoon of his parents' brownstone. Beyond the bubble of his reality at Morehouse.

Back home on breaks, Jacob had secretly begun explorations of his same-sex fascinations. A quick walk from the A train

Nostrand Avenue station sat the Starlite Lounge. The South Oxford Tennis Club was three stops from there at Lafayette Avenue. And across the East River at the end of Christopher Street, worlds away from Bed–Stuy, on the edge of the West Side Highway was Keller's. Clean-cut, mustached brothers in close-cut fades or rocking high-tops coupled with perfectly trimmed goatees. Stomping in Timbs or Air Jordans, Adidas tracksuits or the latest gear from Cross Colours. Jacob was spellbound. He watched brothers dance together; some were lip-locked or just hugged up, showing the kind of intimacy that was supposed to be forbidden between Black men. The mystery was intoxicating, like discovering a world hidden in plain sight. By day, Jacob moved around the city, going about his daily life with family or school or work— for Jacob, summer breaks usually meant working a Wall Street internship or bagging grunt-level work at a real estate firm. In the evenings after work or on the weekends, Jacob found those places where he could uncover with other brothers, where they could unload the weight of the secrecy in which they lived—careful about their presentation, the concealed revelations, the pronouns tailored to fit conversations with family or friends or colleagues. Their gatherings were an ecstatic release. It was in the way they moved together, the passion of furtive kisses, the reluctant lingering to let go of each other until the next time. Returned to the anonymity of unseen lives, their temporary high always ended in a crash. In Atlanta, Loretta's, Traxx, and the Pearl Garden were every bit the equivalent of their New York counterparts. Their plentiful offerings of tasty eye candy came with the added bonus of actual physical satisfaction for Jacob—he was too scared to go home with anyone from a club in New York. His imagination rife with nightmares over the various scenarios that could ensue, all of them ending with his parents finding out about his secret life because he'd been maimed or murdered.

Freshman year became sophomore year then junior year, and Jacob was suddenly a senior facing graduation, confronting how to make sense of this new world in which he found himself in his post-college life. Friendships became a collective safety net, a web of familiarity in which Jacob and his boys learned to navigate what had become their lives. Atlanta felt like a realistic possibility of a life different from New York. Where Jacob crafted something sturdy, molded a version of life that, ultimately, he'd be proud to share with his parents. He graduated, worked retail, and couch surfed a few months before he found a job that looked like it was headed in the direction he was supposed to be traveling.

The day Jacob discovered what it meant to live in a place and not just visit was the day fantasy undressed itself and replaced idealism with reality. His alarm clock buzzed. He yawned, stretched, turned on the TV. Monica Kaufman talked about the rioting downtown after the Rodney King verdict. Stories about lynchings always seemed to belong to a different era. Even the tragedies of Eleanor Bumpurs, Yusef Hawkins, and the Central Park Five were stories that were told after they happened. But the video of four cops pummeling an unarmed Rodney King on the ground was a modern lynching caught in real time. Their acquittal was the same as pictures of white mobs standing next to burnt Black bodies hanging in trees. Cities erupted across the country. Mayor Jackson stood in front of Dr. King's statue at Morehouse, expressed shock and outrage at the verdict. He urged students to remain calm, to remember the tenets of nonviolent protest. He and the city council discussed instituting a curfew, but that never happened. To determine if King's civil rights had been violated, President Bush announced the Department of Justice and Attorney General Bill Barr would investigate the four cops. He admonished citizens across the nation about the loss of life and the destruction of property. On channel after channel, politicians and community leaders spoke in detached, somber overtones about the respect we should all have for one another, our collective calm, our national patience, that the government should be allowed to pursue its investigation. Jacob turned the television off, rolled back over.

Cozily protected from the chill of the air conditioner, he lingered in bed underneath the comforter. Yawned again, stretched deeper, extended arms, wiggled toes, muscles tingling a bright, invigorating sensation. Jacob's pillow whispered, *Don't get out of bed yet.*

With neither of his roommates awake yet, Jacob lay in bed that morning in the quiet of the apartment. Neighbors moved in the apartments around his. The familiar sounds of footsteps and muffled voices, creaking floors, shutting doors, running water, things dropping on floors. All part of their daily organization, their movement toward priorities, goals, destinations, the lives people imagined for themselves: Natural. Typical. Expected. Jacob eventually made his way to the bathroom. His roommates—Sean, his best friend since their freshman year at Morehouse, and Rodney, Sean's boyfriend—woke up. And the organization of their worlds found them exchanging dismay but not surprise over the Rodney King verdict. They discussed expectations for the day, mused about the night, the next day, the one after that, and even the weekend. Safe. Tidy. Normal.

Later that morning, the past and the future collided on a construction site in Summerhill, where there were no fresh, dewy blades of grass, only the hardness of concrete, packed dirt, and exhausted houses. If it was ever present, all birdsong was now dead, and the beaming full richness of the sun had transformed into a hot, blazing glare hailing down. All organization had collapsed into the raw disorganization of undelivered promises as a neighborhood being erased fought against the savagery it took to make forgotten people disappear. Summerhill had missed out on southwest Atlanta's good fortune. The houses were livable but not grand, the little plots of land on which they sat were manageable but unimpressive. Once upon a time, Georgia Avenue was probably a bustling commercial corridor knitting together the fabric of Summerhill block by block, just like Fulton Street back in Bed–Stuy. Groceries might have been purchased on one block; another two or three blocks down Georgia might have been a butcher who catered to the precise cuts of meats customers desired; the neighborhood bakery, just a few more steps away, scented the air with the doughy temptations of freshly baked delights; a tailor; a cobbler; all the familiar things daily life required. Sprinkled down Hill Street, across Bass Street, dotted all over Connally would have been neat little two- and three-bedroom Shaker-style houses, painted the friendliest of blues, the heartiest of reds, the warmest of yellows. Tidy front yards, just large enough to contain the aspirations of a dedicated gardener who understood the different times of year for different plantings, who adhered to watering schedules, saw the symmetry and symphony of colors, their shapes and textures, where others could see only dirt. Summerhill was probably a neighborhood of dreams, where families emerged every day from those orderly compact houses on their way to work or school, then stopped along Georgia Avenue each evening before starting all over again the next day. Summerhill was not Cascade Heights. Or Collier Heights. Nor Loch Lomond Estates.

That morning, seven short, squat, one-story houses on Connally Street confronted Jacob. The houses sat on lots that were narrow and long, one tired building butting up against another. To witness them was to wonder that people had ever lived in them. Jacob stood with his colleague, Daniel, behind police barricades in front of the houses, and watched as officers paced in front of a crowd. An officer shouted through a bullhorn. The people in the crowd were connected in various ways to the houses. Jacob watched as young children clung to their parents' legs, looking up. Looking up for answers to what was happening. Looking up because they were hot, they were overwhelmed and scared, like their parents. But their parents refused to look down at them. Their parents were looking at bulldozers and loaders and backhoes that had been assembled for the press conference. Looking at reporters and camera crews and VIPs beginning to arrive. Looking at the future, trying to see what was about to happen. Looking at Jacob and Daniel looking back at them. There were couples gathered, or maybe they were groups of friends— that is to say, people who stood in twos, threes, and fours—who observed the activity a few yards away from them on Jacob's side of the barricades, with the police in between, dividing one side from the other. A haggard collection of tents had sprouted up, an indictment against the work he and Daniel were supposed to be doing. Their boss said the tents were a result of their incompetence, their failure to patrol the site day and night, and their inability to foster relationships with alert neighbors to prevent the tents from happening. The scene was surreal: tents pitched on asphalt and concrete like an urban adventurer's vision of a campsite. Wires threaded between the tents, upon which ragged clothing or bedding or newspapers were draped, blowing in the wind. People cooked over fires. The police and fire department extinguished the fires, removed the canisters and grills, but new flames sparked up elsewhere in the campsite, again and again, until the police and firemen simply stopped. The tent city was instigated by Elsie Grace Boone, a local activist. Her organization, People for Social Justice and a Grassroots Movement—PSGM, or Prism—corralled local organizations, neighbors, community activists, artists, students, the homeless, anyone, into setting up shop at the tent city. Clusters of people grouped around folding tables and chairs, circulated with clipboards, wearing T-shirts that had the Olympic emblem crossed out on the front and read NOT IN SUMMERHILL in bright red lettering on the back. They passed out flyers, talked and scribbled on their clipboards as they went. The police were agitated. The officer with the bullhorn paced menacingly back and forth, shouted for people to keep clear of the barricades by two feet. He held the bullhorn in his left hand, his right thumb hooked casually in his utility belt, too close to his gun. Jacob felt anxiety rising.

He introduced himself and Daniel to another officer as part of the developer's staff, confirmed the officer knew about the looting downtown. They had a quick exchange, during which the officer said that the entire APD was aware of the verdict, and the GBI was on standby. Jacob and the officer assessed each other: two brown faces roughly the same age, an operative of a corporation seeking to protect its dominion over property versus an agent of the state menacing its authority over the people.

"Officer, you think that bullhorn is a good idea?"

"What's your suggestion?"

"It's tense out here. The press conference is about to start, then folks will have somewhere to focus their attention. Maybe just let the situation ride."

The officer snorted. "That officer is making sure you'll be able to have your press conference."

Jacob tried to protest, but the officer just waved. "Thank you, step back."

Somewhere, Flavor Flav's lyrics bumped loud—*911 is a joke in yo town*—rivaling the volume of the bullhorn. The police did their best to locate the source of the music, but it kept jumping from spot to spot, just like the fires. Jacob took a step toward the houses, looked past Daniel, who stood, stared at him. Jacob gazed at the reporters with their microphones and cameras, stared at the backs of the police standing in front of the barricades separating them from the crowd. Started toward the houses.

"Where are you going?" Daniel called out.

Jacob's foot rested on the bottom step of the closest house.

"Jacob."

The air between them wrinkled with uncertainty and caution, hesitation plain in Daniel's voice. Jacob surveyed the area again, watched as their boss concentrated on the microphone of a reporter standing in front of her. The reporter stood at the lowest point of a sloping sidewalk, and Beth stared down at him, waited hungrily for his next question. She had one hand cocked under her chin, the other resting on her hip. She nodded curtly, then both hands came up as she described the width of the scale of the project, the depth of its impact, encompassing all of Atlanta, delivering revitalization to this underserved, underdeveloped part of the city. Jacob surveyed the crowd again. The tent city. The people with clipboards started putting up signs. Poster boards proclaimed illegal use of eminent domain. Declared Atlanta favored development at the expense of hardworking people. Foretold of social conflict. Beth finished her answer, looked to where Jacob and Daniel stood, gestured, and the reporter followed her motion.

Finally responding to Daniel, Jacob walked up the steps, "I just want one last look inside."

Daniel glanced over his shoulder, saw the reporter heading their way. "Don't let that reporter in here after us," he said to another officer.

Between the house's small rooms, the air was trapped and unmoving. Jacob imagined a family living there—what little privacy there was for a mother and father, the limited space for children to roam and grow. He closed his eyes, thought about the Brooklyn brownstone he called home—its staircases from one floor to the next, its long hallways, its big, cavernous rooms.

"You looking for anything in particular?" Daniel asked.

Jacob shook his head. "Not really. It's just too much outside. Needed to step in here. Listen to what these houses might tell me."

Behind the reddest of cherry-puckered lips, Daniel smiled, bright pink gums and white teeth flashing. He sported a close-cut fade and his goatee was a well-cultivated bush surrounding those lips. Jacob thought about what Daniel would look like with his hair grown out, thick and curly and shining, a lush black color against the light melon tone of his skin. He reminded Jacob of his best childhood buddy, Alexis Jimenez, a light-skinned, curly-haired Dominican kid. He lived across the street from Jacob and didn't speak any Spanish because of too much time spent living in various non-Spanish-speaking foster homes. His own name, "Alexis," embarrassed him—he said it sounded like a girl's name, so he shortened it to Alex. Said as soon as he was able to legally change his surname, "Jimenez" would become "James." Alex James. He was happy it didn't sound Dominican.

"But you still look Dominican," Jacob had teased. "Although all of y'all kinda do look Black."

"You can suck my Black Dominican dick," he'd shot back.

"You ain't got no black dick, light as you are."

"Why you worried about how my dick look?"

Jacob tried not to smile. Daniel made Jacob wonder where Alex was and what he looked like as a grown man. Reminded him about things he had yet to tell his parents. Jacob watched Daniel, reminded himself that work wasn't a place to make friends, wasn't a place to make declarations about life outside the office.

Daniel snapped his fingers to get Jacob's attention. "Hello, hello? Still there?"

"Calm down. I'm standing right here."

"Yeah, but you just went somewhere. Still don't know why you got us walking through here again."

"Are you paying attention to what's happening? You heard about the Rodney King verdict? About the riots downtown?"

"Who hasn't?"

Jacob waited for Daniel to offer a deeper, more meaningful revelation. Jacob wasn't expecting a dissertation, but the conflict he was experiencing made him doubt the honesty of their paychecks. He wanted to know if Daniel felt the same. But Daniel only stared ahead blankly, offered nothing. Jacob just shook his head.

The pine floors creaked with each step as Jacob wandered from one room to the next, went from one house to another, and Daniel followed. They used the back doors to avoid the crowd and reporters in front. Jacob thought the houses would be larger with no furniture, but the emptiness only proved how little space there was to begin with: cramped kitchens; bedrooms where entire families slept; toilets and showers shoved into what should have been closets. Each house was just as tiny and spare as the one before it and the houses were so close together that they all would fall if one collapsed. Jacob walked and listened as Daniel followed behind. A porch rattle spoke of a boy's daredevil stunts jumping from one house to the next. It was in the shake of a rail. In a missing banister. In a plank of wood, cracked and upturned from where the boy landed and that was never fixed. There was wear that spoke of one generation to the next. It was in the dip of steps that carried the weight. In rusting nails used to hold loose floorboards in place. In weathered paint, cracked and peeling with age. There were secrets among them—a hiding place around a corner, tucked away from watchful eyes where bodies experimented with each other. A broken screen door hanging away from a doorjamb, evidence of a parent speaking to a child once too often. Or maybe a fight between lovers. Out back, laundry had dried in the bright light of the sun on clotheslines stretched across the yard. There were cookouts—loud, raucous affairs with music and cussing and drinking and fingers that grew sticky late into the night with more than just barbecue. Once upon a time, fathers and mothers, sons and daughters, sisters and brothers, aunts and uncles, grandparents and cousins, worked and loved and fought in and through the bare windows and silent doors surrounding Jacob and Daniel. All that had ended, and now those seven houses, leaning into each other, stood still and empty, like impotent sentinels guarding an unremarkable history.

Finished with their walk-through, Daniel and Jacob stood on the front porch of the last house, just outside the doorway. The police pulled back the barricades surrounding the houses, so the swelling crowd stood just off the sidewalk instead of in the middle of the street. A few more reporters conducted interviews. A few more signs appeared: OLYMPICS VS. AFFORDABLE HOUSING, WHO PAYS FOR LOCAL DEVELOPMENT? OLYMPICS = JOBS FOR ATLANTA. Public Enemy was replaced by Arrested Development, a few people chanted "It's raining revolution!" in sync with the music. The cop with the bullhorn was nowhere in sight.

"So," Jacob tried again with Daniel, "what you think of all this?"

"Think of what?"

"All this." Jacob waved a hand over everything—the houses, the people, even the two of them.

Daniel looked down, then back up at Jacob, lifted his hand, shading his eyes from the sun. He took in the crowd. People poured in from Georgia Avenue and Cherokee Place. Reporters were everywhere, and Beth had latched on to another one. From his perch on the porch steps, Jacob saw the bulk of the Atlanta–Fulton County Stadium a few blocks away. Beyond that, cars raced along the Interstate 75⊠85 corridor. Northbound traffic snaked its way past the capitol, city hall, and the glittering hotels of downtown toward Buckhead, home to good, rich, southern, country-club living. Places of fabled gated communities with pool houses bigger than all seven of these houses put together. Southbound traffic wound its way past Hartsfield International Airport toward southwest Atlanta. It went to places equally as storied, but less the prototypical good, rich, southern, country-club living than what was on the northern side of town. Still, the darker occupants of southwest Atlanta had done their best to weave the lore and poetry of Atlanta into their own mecca. Yet surrounding them stood examples of the misplaced trust that had broken a neighborhood. Life turned inside out and upside down in the name of progress. The empty houses echoed the reflections of the lives that once occupied the windows and porches that were tattered and barren and about to be torn down. They were the forgotten, living between the fantasies of Buckhead and southwest Atlanta.

"All this?" Daniel shrugged, a thoughtless, reckless dismissal, as casual and unbothered as tearing down these houses.

Jacob closed his eyes and inhaled the heat in the stillness of the air, the asphalt and tar of the street where they stood, the sweat of the people in the crowd. There were too many people smiling, too many teeth showing, too many voices chattering at a pitch that was too loud, too unconcerned, too careless. When Jacob opened his eyes, Daniel was at the bottom of the porch. He stood turned toward the people staring at them from the other side of the barricades. Daniel listened to the bombardment of noises and emotions around them then turned back toward Jacob, waited until he was certain he had Jacob's attention.

"I think this is an opportunity. I think this is progress. This whole neighborhood has been an eyesore since before you were in your mama's belly, thinking about Morehouse." Daniel sneered the word "Morehouse," and Jacob heard derision against legions. What an unsophisticated, untutored, inexperienced, high yellow nobody. The air between them flickered.

"You're a dumb fucker."

"What?"

"You heard me. Worry about who was thinking what in your own mama's goddam belly. You don't know nothing about me." How could he know the different parts Jacob kept separate in himself? Those parts Jacob kept hidden from everyone else. A small gathering of sturdy brown faces stood firmly rooted in place, staring at them from across the street. Jacob felt them watching, and it made his stomach churn. He closed his eyes again and he was there among them, in the crowd of bodies and blackness as familiar as his own skin. His parents stood with him, talking, just like the ghosts in these houses. Jacob's father was the memory of trees stretching from one side of their block to the other. He was the comfort and security of their home. Jacob learned to ride a bike going up and down their block, training wheels sitting higher than the two tires touching the ground. His father trotted along beside him, held his seat, coached, "Balance, Jacob, *balance.*" Jacob heard his father's warning about being on his knees in the street, playing bottle-top skelly whenever cars drove by. Jacob's mother was the reminder about being inside before the streetlamps came on. She was the watchful eye at the window, always instructing Jacob and his brother how to present themselves to the world. If Jacob concentrated harder, maybe he would have heard them tell him why he was there at that time.

Daniel and Jacob moved in opposite directions: Daniel closer to the group of people in front of the first house, Jacob toward the back.

Behind the houses the trees were cut down, sawdust sprinkling the dirt like evidence of a bloodless murder. When the trunks and branches had been chopped and stacked into neat piles, ready to be mulched, and when Jacob had completed his first inspection—to be sure all the rooms had been cleaned out, that no memory of the former inhabitants had been left behind—he counted the variegated lines of the tree rings, to see how many years had been ended by the hack of a chain saw. He stopped when he got to twenty-seven, six years older than he was then. A backhoe sat nearby for after the press conference ended, to dig up the tree stumps and strike the first blow of demolition.

Daniel found Jacob standing behind the houses; he said Beth was ready to start the press conference. Jacob regarded Daniel silently, still feeling his flippant dismissal, and Jacob wondered if his accusations were having a similar effect on Daniel. They stared at each other. Neither of them could see over the other one's head, but they stared directly into each other's faces. Were they standing a few inches closer, they'd have each felt the other's breath. Jacob was the color of richly tilled soil. His blackness looked like the smoothness of satin. Daniel's face glistened with droplets of sweat reflecting bits of light, like wet grains of sand twinkling in sunlight on a beach. Squared shoulders and flat stomachs revealed the athleticism of their high school years. A fight between them would have probably ended in a draw. Finding out would have been as easy as one of them taking a swing. Their standoff another assessment, just like Jacob's talking to that officer.

Deciding not to swing, Daniel spoke first. "You think too much."

"You don't think enough."

"You just called me stupid."

"No. You opened your mouth."

Jacob's calves tensed; he balanced on the balls of his feet, ready to box, his arms loose and flexing, ready for action, to dodge and strike should Daniel swing. There was so much moving around them—those seven houses and the lives that lived there, moved where? doing what? surviving how?—the agitation of the future, the verdict and the riots, their hopes for tomorrow. Jacob wanted to hit something. Strike body blows, short jabs and fancy footwork to propel himself forward. The static of a loudspeaker sounding out front disrupted their confrontation. Faces sweaty from heat and anger, they gathered their stuff and walked around front.

"Where have you two been?" Beth stood in the middle of a little crowd, exasperated.

"Around back," Jacob answered. "Last-minute details."

Beth looked unsatisfied with that answer, which meant there would be a conversation later—if only to emphasize better preparation, insurance they were an efficient, coordinated unit; in the meantime, there were reporters and cameras, politicians and guests, spectators and microphones that required attention. Concentrating on the immediacy of the press conference, Beth refocused. She told the small crowd that this project represented the first step in Atlanta's hosting the 1996 Olympics: to ensure the surrounding neighborhoods could support dynamic, international programming and development. Jacob watched her audience watch her, transfixed. Beth's conversation flowed smoothly, uninterrupted. She talked about her first actions when it was announced Atlanta would make a bid to host the 1996 Olympics; she talked about the full scale of this project and the investments she'd secured once Atlanta was actually named the host city; she detailed the project's benefits—not just for the Olympics, but also for its contributions to the future health and evolution of Atlanta. The project would initially house athletes during the Olympics, with places nearby for them to relax and recharge on days they weren't competing. After the Olympics, it would be the neighborhood's anchor development, paving the way for new housing and shopping in the area. Those seven houses were only the beginning; after that, the neighborhood, then onward to find another forgotten corner of the city. People laughed. Beth smiled. The sun, shining bright and sitting high, beamed a little warmer.

"Now, after that brief preview," she said, "let's start the press conference for *this* project."

The small group dispersed; the reporters and cameramen took up positions in front of the podium. Beth pulled Jacob and Daniel aside, apologized to a group for interrupting their conversation with the neighborhood's council member, Cornelius Jackson. He was her VIP for the event and the key to getting the project done. It was his vote in the city council that would give her control of the project. The group she interrupted was clearly annoyed, but Beth forged ahead anyway and introduced Jacob and Daniel to Cornelius. He was thick around the middle, the kind of thick people referenced when talking about the South: ham hocks and cornbread and platters of fried chicken. Smoked ribs and brisket with barely enough room for mac and cheese and collard greens on the table. Cornelius looked like he ate a first helping, then returned for seconds and thirds. His most prominent feature was his shiny bald head. It reminded Jacob of a chestnut—brownish red, smooth all over, probably felt as solid as it looked. Cornelius shone so brightly he was loud—his pupils were deep black orbs sitting in the startling whites of his eyes. His teeth gleamed as though he'd brushed them just minutes before he started smiling. And he had a big voice, which could easily pinpoint him in a crowd of people. He shook hands with Jacob and Daniel, grinned and talked in that way politicians did when meeting a new person—they listened more than they spoke, they measured and assessed, beginning arithmetic for a future transaction. Cornelius said he had represented this district for the past decade and, finally, it looked as though there was going to be some progress. He remarked, "Atlanta needs the Olympics, and this neighborhood needs Beth." She smiled back, her lips pursed in a thin line, her eyelids almost closed to slits.

"Oh, Cornelius. Stop," and then Beth was all teeth and charm and hands on shoulders, steering the conversation. She told Cornelius that Jacob was a product of Morehouse, that Daniel grew up in Atlanta—what better project managers could there be? One, a graduate from an institution known for advocating social advancement, the other having a vested interest in seeing the growth and development of the city in which he grew up. With her vision and Cornelius's support, this project was just the beginning. Together they would make Atlanta the twenty-first-century city it was poised to become. His torso shaking from his gut to his shoulders, Cornelius laughed hard and loud, sounding like a suspect St. Nicholas.

"I love this woman's energy."

"Vision, Cornelius. *Vision.*"

"Okay." He sounded dismissive. "When is this press conference starting? I have a meeting at city hall."

"Soon—we have quite the crowd. Is the mayor coming?"

Cornelius erupted again, told Beth they should have a joint staff meeting about the project, then he started for the podium. Beth insisted that Jacob and Daniel separate. "Meet people you don't already know." She repeated what she just said in front of Cornelius and the small gathering of people, reminding Jacob and Daniel that the goal was to make Summerhill a better neighborhood for the future. In that would be the beginning of the transformation of Atlanta: build the right houses and find the right families to put in them. Daniel was to shadow her and the council member and Jacob was to go off to meet the council member's staff.

With Beth casting a spell over the audience, the press conference started. Her southern accent drifted through the speakers like a hex. Her hands moved for emphasis, and her head swayed to the rhythm of her words. She told a tale of a Summerhill that was the birthplace of Atlanta's most influential leaders.

"Imagine small and orderly houses in a bustling, energetic community out of which erupted the passion to fuel the growth of an entire city." She stepped in front of the podium, giving photographers a clear shot of her next to the Olympic flag waving lightly in the breeze. "Together we can capitalize on this moment and see again a shining Summerhill built from the glory of Atlanta's legacy—Dr. King, the multifaceted entrepreneur Herman E. Perry, and Alonzo Herndon, Atlanta's first African American millionaire!" Beth's blond bob was a halo, her face reddened from the heat and the sun and the fervor of her movement. "Summerhill, the welcome center of Atlanta! Summerhill, the host neighborhood in the host city of the Olympics! Summerhill and Atlanta and the twenty-first century!"

She finished to scattered applause, introduced Cornelius, who began talking with the low, steady cadence of a minister. He was the warlock to Beth's witchery, painting a picture of an efficient little Black community murdered by greed, blight, and poor planning.

"The Olympics will not be the Atlanta–Fulton County Stadium again." He recalled the past while warning about the future. Shouts of agreement erupted from the crowd. Cornelius promised the watchfulness of a savvier community that understood the importance of Summerhill in promoting Atlanta as a city of integration and progress. He reminded everyone that E. P. Johnson Elementary School, the first public school for Black children in Atlanta, started in Summerhill. His voice ascended in pitch and tempo, mentioning the jobs for Summerhill residents that this project would create. Cornelius endorsed Beth, her hand raised high in his. He said she was committed to redeveloping the houses while also helping the families who lived in the neighborhood. And while his voice boomed and their hands clasped together, arms raised in victory over their heads, Jacob saw a vision of a red-faced Beth, her blond bob thrown back, riding the jellied mass of Cornelius. He laughed as she concentrated, ground hard in his lap, his large Black mitts marking her ass with smacks. Glass broke beyond the police barricade and someone shouted, "How's the pussy taste, you Uncle Tom sonofabitch!" Then more glass shattered, and the crowd overwhelmed the barricades, as Cornelius and Beth started running for cover inside the houses. Daniel disappeared and the flow of people surged around Jacob, carrying him in a swell of bodies. He heard shouts, then fists landed on his head and his shoulders. Four years of Morehouse, the legendary prowess of King and Jackson, Young and Lewis; mythic civic lessons that ignited dreams of socioeconomic parity were as distant as the differences between Du Bois and Washington. Those kids looking at their parents, their parents looking at him, this was just that basic: food on the table; clothes on backs; shelter. The Talented Tenth would have to wait. Jacob fought to stay on his feet, ducked and swung back, felt his knuckles connect with flesh. Hands grabbed him, yanked off his tie, pulled his blazer over his head. Then it was just Jacob in a wrinkled white shirt and nondescript khakis, shielding his face, swinging and kicking his way through bodies.

TWO

DANIEL

MAY 8, 1992
VIA REGISTERED MAIL TO
SUE ELLEN MILTON
C/O DANIEL MILTON
354 GILCREST AVE SE, APT. 2
ATLANTA, GA 30316

Dear Tenant,

Lease of these premises expires October 31, 1992. This will serve as notice that the landlord is exercising its right not to renew the lease. Please remove all personal items and property from the premises and return all keys, including the mailbox key, to the management office by 5pm on that date. Please provide a forwarding address, and upon completion of a satisfactory inspection of the premises after it has been vacated, any remaining security deposit will be forwarded. Your cooperation is appreciated.

Sincerely,
Management

Daniel reread the letter tacked to the apartment door. The whole of Atlanta was so obsessed with the Olympics, this landlord was anticipating the increased rent he could get. Daniel thought he'd be able to stay longer after his mother's death. The letter was a reminder that he would be allowed to stay only for as long as it took the landlord to kick him out. Rent was $350 a month when his mother leased the ground floor two-bedroom, one-bathroom apartment six years ago. By the time of her death, the rent had increased to $400 a month. Daniel walked from the living room, down the hall, into each bedroom. He heard the laughter of stories they remembered from times living in their shotgun house. Remembered the heaviness of Mama's tears as she grieved for her husband, Ray. Felt again the helplessness as he and his sister, Lilah, watched Mama waste away on her deathbed. Daniel stared at the letter. Listened to Mama recount the number of times they'd moved. Zigzagged their way across Atlanta from one neighborhood to the next in pursuit of cheaper rent for a bigger apartment in a location where Mama didn't have to travel so far to work. Where the landlord was just a little more understanding of the costliness of life. A landlord possessed of a willingness to ignore the next-new-something-for-someone-else.

This cold letter addressed to his dead mother was proof of the fruitlessness of their quest.

The air had quickly changed at the construction site. Mama always said show up early to something important so you can see what's happening. That's how she scored the best stuff at church giveaways and secondhand stores. Fluffy cushioned couches, color still vibrant, threading not so bare. Plates, glasses, and cookware that looked brand-new. No chipped edges. No scratches or dents. She always found not-so-out-of-date fashions. A few times she even discovered clothes with the original DAVISON's tags still attached. Mama knew when the Gibraltar Christ Community Church's Community Connection store in Vine City and the Salvation Army in Peoplestown accepted donations. She went once a month to each one, got in good with the folks handling donations. *Spying out the good stuff,* Mama called it. Figure out what you want, then go get it.

Daniel felt the tension as soon as he had arrived at the construction site. He watched people move around the tent city. They weren't all homeless—some of them came that morning, lugging props, changed from what they wore into costumes assumed for a performance. The props were rags, tattered lawn chairs, coolers blackened with smudge marks, overstuffed plastic bags. He watched the prop masters embed themselves in the crowd. They brought containers of food that they shared with people. They handed out wet wipes. Water. And socks. There was something hypocritical about that, about protestors who arrived from somewhere else and changed their clothes to fit in among the people already there. Perhaps they came from the sturdiness of four walls and a floor below a ceiling that wasn't the sky, in a place where they had a bathroom with running water, electricity, and a stove on which to cook food eaten off a plate at a table surrounded by chairs. But then again, wasn't it all a performance? Just like the Olympics itself, the best from all over the world, leaping, running, swimming, vaulting, competing for some future vision of their own loftiness on the backs of the dispossessed who'd been dislocated from the possibilities of their dreams. So Daniel watched as Jacob and Beth directed contractors to move construction equipment to places that made the site look active from different camera angles. The media arrived. Then politicians. As if to do battle, the police showed up, outfitted in shields and helmets. Their presence heightened tensions as they waited and watched. The way Beth moved around didn't help. One moment she stood in front of the houses, chatting, the next she vanished only to reappear next to a bulldozer, pointing for it to be moved somewhere else. She didn't seem like a woman in control. A short, blond woman from Richmond, Virginia, she bragged about being self-made, about how she didn't need an MBA or JD to get to where she was. Her undergraduate degree was enough—that and grit and focus along with some connections. But Daniel watched as she stood still several times, looking around, as if unsure about what to do next, and he decided that's how Beth looked—like a woman caught up in a larger moment.

Jacob glided around the site more smoothly. Showed an officer where barricades should be set up; suggested to a cameraman the best position for a tripod; deflected an inquiry from a reporter for an interview, nodded toward Beth instead.

Daniel helped the contractors direct the flow of people away from the bulldozers and backhoes. He watched the folks from PSGM. They handed out T-shirts, talked to people about a petition. More than a few times they pointed to Jacob and Beth. Black man. White woman. Black neighborhood. PSGM had made the news when it tried unsuccessfully to stop the Georgia Dome project. The Dome would have its ribbon cutting in August, but PSGM managed to create a few headaches. Their leader, Elsie Grace Boone, helped PSGM secure money to relocate small businesses that closed because of the Dome project. PSGM also ensured the state paid market-rate prices for all the property it took. They negotiated a community-benefits agreement that would be monitored by a not-for-profit funded by the project. Elsie Grace wasn't at the site, but PSGM looked to be in charge. More people arrived. Tensions heightened further. Public Enemy blasted, Arrested Development chanted, the discontent was tangible by the time Daniel finished walking through the houses with Jacob. Daniel listened as Beth spun her fantastical tale from the podium. He stayed just long enough to see the police hustle Beth and Cornelius into the houses as the bottles flew. Just long enough to watch Jacob swinging wildly through the crowd.

Now Daniel stood surrounded by plastic bags, secondhand furniture, and knickknacks. That's the legacy Mama left. She never knew if she was at the brink of a sinkhole or had footing on solid rock, if she was at the beginning of a steep incline or a flat plateau. That uncertainty was her life. It was the best place they ever lived, the ground-floor apartment with a front porch and a small terrace off the back bedroom. A step up from the shotgun houses. It always felt like they ended up in the apartment because Mama was running from something else. In his memory, Daniel traced it back to the shotgun house owned by Ralph Reid. Lilah said that shotgun house was at least a decent place, better than all the ones before it. And Ralph Reid was a responsive landlord. He made repairs quickly. Winters in the house weren't so cold. Dead bolts were installed on the front and back doors. The only problem was Ray and his objection to Ralph Reid's being Black. Their brother, Marty, said it was because Ralph Reid reminded Ray that he was white and what that looked like in 1975, a Black man more successful than a white man in a southern city like Atlanta. Mama didn't care; she admired Ralph Reid, talked so much about how he was so busy adding to all his real estate holdings that Ray would tell her to shut up.

Daniel looked around the apartment again, wondered how Ray managed to convince Mama to trade that place for this one. He thought about the tent city, about the people behind the barricades. Jacob thought Daniel indifferent to what they saw, that Daniel didn't feel the anxiety that surrounded them. But what Jacob didn't know was that Daniel didn't need to stand in an empty room to imagine life in a tiny house crammed with hope and fear, wondering about tomorrow. That was his life. Digging through the past, searching for an explanation of his existence, Daniel was an interloper in his own family. Stuck in a ramshackle apartment shoved in the corner of a dirty beige brick building wedged in a place between east Atlanta and south Decatur, a no-man's-land of tilting homes and gas station convenience stores where grass kissed the edge of paved roads.

It had been months since Mama's death, and Daniel took his time wrapping, boxing, and discarding remnants of her life. Not that there was much worth saving, but he didn't want to miss any possible clues. Mama was always so secretive, the search exhausted him. The difference between how hard Mama worked and how sparsely they lived was humorous. Their little family lurched through existence, from one moment to the next. Mama used to remark, "God has disappointed me. Look at my life." That was Mama thinking backward, retracing moments, shuffling through memories, asking where she misstepped, ended up wrong. *God has disappointed me.* Marty and Lilah never knew if by "disappointment" Mama meant the failure to attain some long-hoped-for dream or if she meant that no matter how hard she worked, how much faith she had, how much she planned and plotted and sacrificed, she could never escape the circumstances from which she started. Maybe she meant it to be more a question as to why the good luck that happened every day to everyone else seemed to avoid her: *Why* has God disappointed me? Maybe her *God has disappointed me* was just loud enough, just blasphemous enough that God decided her whole life would be proof that he had.

Of all the things Mama had wished for, the most she ever wanted was to sleep late on her one day off. In red-eyed delirium she'd declare the night before: "I'm gonna sleep late in the morning. Don't bother me. Y'all take care of yourselves." And then she'd stumble off to bed where, for a time, she slept. If Lilah and Marty were good and dutiful children, they would have kept quiet, allowed Mama to dream and languish in bed well past the break of dawn, to forget about waking up even when the sun dipped toward the western horizon, and still then to only toy with the idea of getting up. Good and dutiful children would have said, "Mama needs her rest," and allowed their mother to dream. Forget about work. About kids. About a husband who helped her with nothing. Forget about the tiny house they lived in, how for something so small it was always so dirty. Forget about her own mama, who lived in the living room, cramped in a corner that could barely contain a cot and chair. Forget about money that did not exist and space they didn't have.

But even good and dutiful children have their limits. They forget. Get hungry. Sounds would reach Mama deep down in the depths of her slumber. Drag her back to the present. It was always some familiar ruckus that robbed Mama of this one desired pleasure. Some recognized noise. Some common racket. A garbage truck going by. A siren. A slammed door. Mama listened from her suspended place of dormancy, tried to return to the dreamland where she'd just been instead of coming back to an impertinent present. As Lilah and Marty kept at it, Mama's wish of sleeping late had returned to being just a prospect. She got pissed, moaned, furrowed tighter into her knotty, worn blanket, and hid her head under a pillow that was flat and limp. More sounds disturbed her. The television was too loud, played cartoon music of some roundabout chase: a flute's frantic whistle followed by high notes on a piano wound into the screech of a violin overwhelmed by the loud, crashing thump of a drum. Maybe a bird being chased by a cat being chased by a dog being clobbered by an old woman's umbrella for bothering her kitty. That's what Mama felt like: outwitted time and again whenever she got so close to what she wanted she could feel it. Foolish.

Screams.

That was the sound. Not a garbage truck or fire engine or slammed door this time, but screams. Not terror-laden howls, but the joyful, careless shrieking of children playing with reckless abandon. Fucking noisy children. What had she told them when she went off to bed? Now Mama was fully awake, everything she had dreamed about was gone and she was left only with stuff that haunted her, made her tired all over, as if she had just crawled into bed. How could two kids—*just two*—keep up such a racket? And what in hell was Ray doing? Too busy doing nothing, too busy sitting on his fat ass to even mind the children to keep quiet so she could sleep on her one day off.

Mama should have known better.

She sat up in bed, swung her feet toward the floor and groaned as they hit the cold, hard wood. The floor protested her weight as she leaned forward and crouched down, peeking underneath the bed to drag out her slippers. Daylight drained through the brown sheet that hung across the window. Mama didn't even bother with the light. She shuffled toward the bathroom before making her way into the kitchen.

"The hell is this?"

The seconds ticked away, and that's when Lilah and Marty remembered: *Be quiet.* They were squatting on the floor, huddled over pieces of a mixing bowl, its unstirred contents inching between their toes and disappearing under the peeling linoleum.

Flour. Who knew how many eggs. And half a gallon of milk. The rest of the kitchen was worse: Three empty cans of sausages were in the sink, the once-pink links blackening in a pan on the stove. Syrup, pooled on the table, dripped in long, gooey bands to the floor. Two bowls of cereal in more milk sat, half-eaten, on the counter. Mama snatched up each child by an arm and shook.

"What the hell is this?"

Lilah heard the click of Marty's teeth gnashing as Mama shook him. Between his own head moving and Lilah writhing, trying to get away, all Marty saw was his sister's mass of brown locks bouncing and shaking, covering her face.

"We was hungry," Marty managed.

Mama looked at him, thought, this was punishment, that's what this was, punishment for staying in bed past the break of day. The kitchen was reason enough to get up: The remains of last night's meal. The trash can full and smelly. Dishes stacked along the edge of the sink in her hopes that Ray would get to them—why? He hadn't even bothered with the plastic covering for the window she kept nagging him about. And now this. Behind her, the TV flipped channels.

"Ray? Ray!" She stomped into the living room. "Ray, you heard these kids in there; why you ain't help them?"

Ray sat up and stared at her, a pale, skinny woman in a nightgown, swinging a child from each arm. The veins in her hands bulged as each child strained to get away, and her hair stood out like dark threads against her forehead where she'd begun to sweat from wrestling with them. Ray rubbed a hand against his fleshy belly, scratched. He didn't bother twisting around to see into the kitchen. He turned back to the TV, dragged on his cigarette. Held it. Exhaled. "I told them to wait for you." The chair creaked. Mama looked past him toward her mama, a body covered in a heap of clothes and sheets, sitting in a corner, staring out the window.

"Shit." Mama had whirled around, stomped back into the kitchen, shoved Lilah and Marty ahead of her. "Clean this shit. Clean this shit up *now*."

The way Lilah told it, it was an accident. But you could never tell with Mama. Maybe. Maybe not. Afterward, Mama cried and tried to hold Marty, but he crawled away, shaken. Mama said she'd wanted to hit Ray. Wanted to beat him. Beat him into moving—from in front of that television to fixing the window, taking out the garbage, getting a job, something. Sitting in front of the television Ray had had the audacity to chuckle at the program he watched, an invisible "Fuck you" that floated through the air. Mama stood at the sink, choked back anger, drew water for the dishes, and thought about the number of meals on the floor, in the pan, on the counter. Five days' worth of breakfasts, at least. Two days of dinners. And one more week until she got paid. Somehow, she'd have to make up for what was lost here and still have money for what was to come. Thoughts cycled through Mama's head: *I told them to wait for you. The hell he think he was, after I busted my ass all this week long, and all I want is a few extra hours sleep and he has yet to stir himself from in front of that goddam TV, has yet to get up and find himself a job? Motherfucker. White-trash motherfucker. Lazy white-trash motherfucker.* Mama had grabbed the skillet with the shrunken black links sticking to the bottom and she had meant to carry herself over to Ray's chair and swing. But she didn't. By the time her arm swung, launching the skillet and its burnt contents through the air, it was arcing not toward Ray, but Marty. The little boy howled, grabbed his leg, a bluish-purple bruise spreading across his thigh. Lilah screamed and folded herself into a corner the farthest away from Mama she could get.

Mama's stuff had been sorted into different piles in her bedroom. She liked to be fashionable, but never wanted to seem like she tried too hard. And there was always the issue of how much to spend on herself when there were always her children to consider. "Fuck Ray. He can walk around in his drawers." Mama said her outfits had to do double time—look good enough for her to go to work, but still be comfortable enough to wear every day. She loved billboards showing models in dramatically printed flare pants, wearing midriff blouses. That translated into pairs of flared jeans, coupled with the smallest men's shirts she could find. The extra cloth of the shirts created extra warmth under her winter coat. In the spring and summer, she'd tie the shirttails around her waist—"I may have kids, but I still got it!"—a nod to those midriff blouses. There were a few pants suits. Dark blue. White. Cream-colored. They looked like petite-sized men's military uniforms, but with feminine touches: tapered jackets, high-waisted pants, dramatically detailed buttons. "Just because we're poor, don't mean we have to look like it. People think there's nothing but junk in those secondhand places. Ha." Amusing irony—clothes donated back to Gibraltar and the Salvation Army that Mama bought from there in the first place.

Daniel piled her shoes in different heaps: sporty, professional-looking Thom McAn oxfords Mama wore to work or whenever she was out running errands. She'd scope out the shoe departments at Sears and Woolworth's for trends in sneakers and Top-Siders. Kept on the lookout for similar styles. Hard to tell that nearly every pair of shoes she wore or bought for the children came from those secondhand places. A shoe cobbler near her job worked wonders. Mama said he knew how to make sure feet didn't look raggedy. Said his work was magic for the sole—laughed at her joke—then paraded about her latest purchase, instantly her favorite. Mama wasn't embarrassed by her well-publicized, endless trips to the secondhand store, her tales of the bargains to be found, the money she saved, the styles she reintroduced to the world. Daniel divided her shoes according to their remaining usefulness: a box for those with tread on the soles, minimal wear to the heels, few scuff marks. Those would go back to Gibraltar. Atlanta had gotten so expensive, and things would only get worse with the coming of the Olympics. Somewhere there was a mother with mouths to feed and bodies to clothe, arriving home to a similar note from her landlord tacked to the door. The brands that Mama wore weren't current anymore, but that mother wouldn't care. All she'd see was a way. Just like Mama.

Shoes with the toes turned up, creased across the top, heels just beginning to lean to the side from too much wear would go back to the Salvation Army along with bags of clothes. Shoes too beat-up, stained by rain and the red dirt of Georgia, the heels gone and soles flapping away from the uppers would be thrown in the dumpster out back.

Months of stuffing clothes into bags revealed nothing. Searching through pockets, ripping through coat linings, inspecting the space between flapping soles and leather uppers revealed even less. Daniel raided all of Mama's hiding spots: a hole in the wall behind her vanity mirror; another hole in the wall behind her bed's headboard; a loose floorboard in the closet that covered one more place she thought secret between her and God alone. Nothing. Nothing. Nothing.

Daniel tore through the apartment—emptied drawers, toppled the shelving of closets, peeled back carpeting, and pried loose other floorboards. In his wake, a trail of madness: Fingerprints and spots of toothpaste turned hard white, staining the bathroom mirror. The counter was a mess of water spots and dried soap marks. A dried, thin string of goo dripped along the side of a can of shaving cream. Hair clogged the sink drain. The kitchen was filthy from neglect, plates crusted with bits of food rose from a sink full of stagnant water. Flies, attracted to the foul-smelling fumes, hovered from plate to plate, danced above growths of watery molds. What dishes weren't in the sink or scattered on the counter, littered the cheap linoleum floor. Dumped with them were soup cans and spices, boxes of pasta, bags of flour, sugar, and cornmeal. The bare cabinets stood open, their empty shelves illuminated by cold fluorescent light. Stains and skid marks streaked the floor Mama used to keep so clean. Grime caked at the base of the counter, and who knew what feasted on the crumbs underneath the oven.

In the dining area, Daniel cleared the secondhand buffet of stoneware and pots, and stacked them on the table that was propped against the wall, to hold its weak leg up. The table shook whenever he walked by and one of the stoneware cups had crashed to the floor. He hadn't bothered to clean it up. The hollows of the pots and stoneware harbored no secrets. No pieces of paper were tucked in the corners of the buffet.

The living room was thoroughly rummaged, the couch stripped bare, cushion covers and cushions separated, thrown in a corner. The few books and dolls and framed pictures on the bookshelves strewn across the carpet. The shelving's discolored gold tint flaked and peeled with age. He cleared the end tables, the knickknacks on top of them added to the junk on the floor. Half-filled boxes were everywhere, lids flapped in the wake of his movement. The landlord's letter transformed their half-filled emptiness into urgent decisions waiting. The windows were opened, curtains knotted in the hopes that light and air found their way into the room. But the screens were caked with feathers, leaves, and the dried carcasses of bugs caught in the mesh. They hadn't been cleaned in at least a year. The apartment was on the southwest side of the building, turned away from any breeze. And a conglomeration of trees hid it from the sun. Daniel examined every photo album he found, removed pictures from behind the protective film, and searched unknown faces for signs of full lips, curly hair, and skin a darker hue than Lilah's and Marty's. He found nothing, living in this apartment, bits of Mama's past scattered through his present.

A radio blasted next door. In the apartment above, footsteps pounded across the ceiling. Children screeched, playing ball out in the hall. Their discordant cacophony was an endless sound that wound its way into the single note of a mother who cooed at Daniel, forever placating him with half-truths and partial answers, who always kept him at bay before she finally escaped into eternity. Mama was dead, and all Daniel had were a patchwork of memories and pieces of stories that threaded their way into nothing.

|| THREE ||

JACOB

Two weeks after the construction-site riot, the cops had four people in custody. Cornelius flexed his political muscle. Said the city wouldn't stand for such lawlessness. Protest was one thing. Stating objections, making a public record of opposition was part of the process. Physical conflict was entirely different. And no one would stand for property damage. Jacob didn't think property damage mattered since the entire site—houses included— was being demolished. Beth commented that she would not be dictated to by community thuggery. No way in hell she was going to let maniac agitators hold her project hostage.

"You need to watch those kinds of comments." The flat, even, unmodulated sound of Cornelius's voice came at them from where he sat at the other end of the conference table. He had called Beth's office with an update on the police report

Jacob had filed. Now they sat in his conference room and listened to the update. Two detectives stood behind Cornelius, his chief of staff and an assistant flanked each side. The length of the conference table, the arrangement around Cornelius, the four seats on either side of the table that separated Cornelius's and Beth's staffs—it all had a magnifying effect: Cornelius seemed larger, more imposing, like on the podium at the press conference.

"Excuse me?" Beth didn't expect his reproach.

"Remember where you are, who you are, and with whom you're doing business." One of the detectives had been leaning over Cornelius, one hand resting on the table, his other hand pointing to something they'd been discussing. He stood up as Cornelius spoke, his hands clasped in front of him, his attention focused on Beth. The chief of staff cleared his throat. Cornelius's assistant scooted his chair backward.

"My employee was attacked. We're working on an open site with no security—"

"Stop."

"Who do you—"

"Which of you two is Jacob?" Cornelius pointed to Jacob and Daniel.

Beth's face flushed; she started to stand up. Jacob remembered the way Cornelius had laughed at her during the press conference, then ignored her question about the mayor. He remembered Beth interrupted the group of people with whom Cornelius had been talking. They were in his office now, away from the public, away from the media, away from the pretenses of public decorum. Displaying allegiance to the woman who paid his salary, Jacob hesitated answering Cornelius's question. Cornelius turned to his chief of staff.

"Jacob is that one," he answered, pointing.

"These detectives will escort you to the precinct where they're holding the people who attacked you."

"Cornelius—"

"Council member Jackson," the assistant corrected Jacob.

Jacob nodded acknowledgment before he continued. "I said in the police report that I couldn't see any of the faces of the people who assaulted me."

"The four they're holding are suspected of assaulting other people and doing property damage to other projects around the city. Have a look. If nothing comes of it, so be it."

"But—"

"Just do it," Beth snapped. The color of her face had returned to normal, but she was still perched on the edge of her chair. "I'll come with you, since this happened while you were working."

Again, the entire room paused, faces turned in her direction.

"Thomas, you go with them." Cornelius motioned to his chief of staff.

"We don't need your help," Beth barked at Cornelius.

"My presence at that press conference made it an event of the Atlanta city council. Jacob was assaulted at that event, and he is my constituent."

Silence.

"And there is no project on that site—not yours or any other—until I advise my colleagues on the city council as to what I'd like to see happen there."

After escaping the mob, Jacob had made it to his car by cutting down Connally, across Georgia, down Grant Terrace, and over to Bass before finally getting to where he'd parked on Hill Street. His heart pounded, the sound of blood rushed in his ears, and he breathed hard as he gulped down air. He checked to make sure he wasn't followed. He sat, dazed, and thought about what happened. A few buttons were gone from his shirt, and he didn't miss the tie, but it was too bad about the blazer. That blazer and the two suits he'd bought with his first paycheck had been his first adult purchases. He'd applied all the suit-buying lessons learned from shopping trips with his father. Even spent more money to make sure the tailoring would pass his father's examination. Jacob shook his head, flipped down the driver's-side mirror. A bruise swelled above his right eye. His hands hurt, skin torn and bleeding from punching wildly, and cuts were beginning to welt from where he'd shielded himself from bottles. He was sweaty and sticky—could feel his T-shirt stuck to the small of his back, the sweat soaked through to his collared shirt. Droplets of blood dotted his shoulders.

Jacob sat in his car, listened to glass bottles breaking, voices shouting, and sirens wailing. His breathing slowed; his pulse returned to normal. Heat hammered at him through the windows. He started the engine, turned on the air conditioner, gripped the steering wheel firm and tight, his knuckles pronounced where each finger curved around the steering wheel. The air conditioner did its work, and soon there was a nice chill in the car. His shirt was still uncomfortably sticky, but the sweat was dissipating. He checked himself in the mirror again, dabbed at a few remaining blotches of sweat. The swelling above his eye began to hurt, and as the minutes passed, he wondered if Daniel had escaped. What happened to Beth and Cornelius? Should he go back? It would have been so easy for him to remain there, secreted away in that overlooked and ignored corner of the city. He folded the sun visors down, turned the radio on. Jamiroquai blasted through the speakers. Morse code, violins, bass, and percussion in a sym-, phonic plea to the universe: *Is anybody out there? Oh, we got emergency on planet Earth.* Indeed. Witnessing this world, would anybody out there even care? Jacob sat, still processing that he'd been assaulted in a riot while at work. Of course, he'd been in fights before—little lunchtime schoolyard altercations about whatever was important to elementary school children at that moment. This was different. This fight was beyond a schoolyard tussle that would be forgotten in a few hours. This was a fight for a way of life being lost. Jacob sucked in air, exhaled, tried to calm himself. He had parked in front of more dilapidated, abandoned houses. The somber emptiness of their presence made it seem eerily bright in the car. The car became frigid from blasting the cold air. Jacob began to shiver, the anxiety and cold tightening his belly. He adjusted the temperature, turned the volume on the stereo up a bit higher. The music clashed with the stoic inquisition of the houses, their bare windows, their blank doorways, their porches sagging toward the ground. He wished for tinted windows to craft a barrier between himself and inanimate objects that measured, assessed, evaluated, but could not shield him from judgmental histories and suspicious futures. Then he wouldn't feel so silly, playing music so loudly to such a solemn audience. Or maybe he was being rude—a disturbance to their overly burdensome silence. *Emergency on planet Earth.* Jacob turned the radio off.

It wasn't like on television, where people sat in a dimly lit uncomfortable interrogation room. The room was bright, fluorescent light bounced off cinder blocks painted a glossy beige. The ceiling was at least nine feet high, oblong windows at the top of one wall. The windows were too high to see outside, and they didn't open, but they did let in a good amount of light. Most of the floor space was occupied by a single laminate-top rectangular table. Four steel-bottomed plastic chairs were arranged along its longer sides, and the shorter sides had two chairs each. The room was unusually quiet—Beth startled when an officer entered suddenly without warning.

"Soundproofing foam sprayed in the cinder blocks and inside the door," the officer apologized.

The door, solid metal and painted the same glossy beige, had a single pane of one-way glass—to see into the room.

"Why are we in this room? Where are the perpetrators? Are we going to see a lineup?" The officer responded slowly to Beth, explained that the detectives at the councilman's office would join them shortly.

Beth repeated her questions when one of the detectives finally arrived, but he ignored her. Jacob and Daniel remained quiet. Everything about Beth said she was a woman out of her depth. The pitch of her voice was too high, the rapid-fire nature of one question after another made her sound on the brink of panic. Thomas dragged one of the chairs from the table and withdrew to a corner. In the quiet, the sound of metal against linoleum was harsh and loud.

"I don't like how we're being treated. I feel like we're the criminals." Beth watched the detective who sat across from the three of them. She thought of ways to make herself look bigger—adjusted the way she sat in her chair, went from sitting on the edge to sitting back, slightly more relaxed. She crossed her legs, right over left, folded her arms in her lap. She exhaled.

"Officer. What's your name?"

The detective looked up, the thick black waves of his short hair sparkled in the light as he moved. His skin was a little darker than yellow rose petals, with hints of red undertones. Jacob found himself admiring the dramatic contrast between the detective's jet-black hair, his eyebrows, his goatee, and the softer, lighter color of his body. He'd been writing. He stared at Beth for a moment longer than necessary before he responded to her question.

"It's 'detective,' not 'officer.'" Another pause. "Wilson." He glanced at Thomas, then Jacob, then Daniel, then Beth. Then went back to writing.

Beth didn't miss a beat. "How long is this going to take?"

Detective Wilson shuffled through the papers. "I'm looking for the report you filed. I have this one from"—he flipped to the first page—"Mr. Jacob Jenkins. But nothing from you or—" He looked questioningly at Daniel.

"Daniel Milton. I didn't make one. I managed to get out of there before the riot started."

"Mr. Milton." He turned back to Beth. "My colleague is reviewing the statements of the four people we're holding. He'll join us after he's finished." He returned to the paper he was reading.

"I didn't make one either. A report."

Detective Wilson didn't look up immediately. When he did, furrows wrinkled his forehead, his eyes opened wide, the arch of his eyebrows lifted high in exaggerated irritation. "I know."

A year prior to that sit-down at the precinct, Jacob interviewed with Beth for his job. Part of their talk included a tour around Summerhill. Beth drove a Ford Taurus, hair up in a blond ponytail, specs riding her nose; she wore loose-fitting jeans and sported a pair of weathered Red Wings. She pointed out spot renovations. Said that was a sign the neighborhood was ready for a larger development. Along the route she stopped to talk to some locals; lone white woman in earnest conversation with the people. Jacob had been impressed. He didn't find out that interview was a performance until after he was hired. Her entire outfit had been a costume. Beth's standard uniform was a navy-blue pants suit paired with a silk blouse. The ponytail became a pageboy that stopped just south of earlobes where fantastic diamond studs sparkled. That Ford Taurus was a rental; Beth pushed a gunmetal-gray Mercedes S 500. Even her talk with the locals was part of the show: What was happening in the neighborhood? Did people know the Olympics were coming? Did anyone know anybody who wanted to sell property now? That was the work for which she was hiring. She wanted Jacob and Daniel to be her street team—build relationships with neighbors; find interested sellers before they spoke with real estate agents; make cash offers to immediate prospects; manage acquisitions quickly and quietly. That's how she found the houses for the project for which she needed Cornelius's approval. Her conversation with the detective was different: his Black face to her white one; his detective's shield to her business suit. Watching them watch each other, Jacob wondered what they saw—a young Black man and a middle-aged white woman? Did they see each other from the different places in history to which they each belonged? How he looked at her and did not see deference. How she looked at him and did not see intelligence. Each of them confident in the authority of their own vision, the comfort they took in the contrasting scopes of their experience. In the corner, Thomas coughed, breaking their silent confrontation.

Detective Wilson smirked at Beth, then put both hands flat on the table. "Lookit, where are my manners?" He took his time pushing himself up from the table. He was handsome. At least six foot three, with the solid physique of a running back. Jacob tried not to stare at the towering height of him. Clad in an Atlanta Falcons jersey falling casually over deep-blue denim jeans. His detective's shield swung from a chain around his neck. Gun holstered on his hip. The smirk evolved into a smile that seemed perfunctory, laced with the slightest bit of arrogance. He stayed focused on Beth. Jacob concentrated to keep from smiling admiringly. "Can I offer any of you some water?"

Daniel and Thomas said no, and Beth mumbled something that didn't sound like yes.

"What about you?" He startled Jacob out of his admiration, who may well have been daydreaming about the allure of a six-foot-three-inch body belonging to a handsome Atlanta Police Department detective, but who was also thinking about what it meant to mount a protest, to fight for life itself; thinking about the effort required to struggle against being rendered invisible; thinking about how particular lives lived in recognized ways took existence for granted. Everyone stared at Jacob, waited for his response. He coughed, hand to his mouth, looked down quickly to recompose himself, and when he looked up again, he tried to assume the same casual regard with which the detective looked down on them.

"I'm good. Thanks."

"Okay. Well, let me go see what's taking my colleague so long."

"What in the entire fuck?" Sean had exclaimed when Jacob walked through the door of his retail shop after the riot. Jacob ignored the stab of pain above his right eye, shrugged to reassure Sean.

"It looks worse than it is."

He told Sean about the press conference, how the riot started, and that he'd been jumped. Sean listened intently to Jacob's escape from flying fists and breaking bottles before he made it to his car. Jacob winced at the pain in his ankle, which he tried to disguise by slowly walking to a stool at the counter.

Sean wasn't fooled. "One of two things is about to happen: We're about to go to the emergency room so a doctor can look at you before you file a police report. Or you can go to the back while we wait for an ambulance and the police to come here. Choose."

Jacob opted for the emergency room. Luckily, he hadn't suffered anything serious. The emergency room physician said the cuts and bruises would heal in a few weeks. All the media at the press conference translated into citywide coverage of the riot. Jacob provided as much detail as he could to the police, who showed up after the emergency room staff contacted them. No one answered the phone at his office. The police said they'd check with the council member's office to find out what happened with Daniel and Beth.

"You'll be fine. Just rest for the next few days. Here's a prescription for the pain."

Jacob and Sean had been tight since Freshman Week, when Sean taught Jacob how to dress for the August heat of Atlanta. They sat next to each other in Sale Hall. Jacob was stifling in a white cotton shirt and dark, tropical-weight wool slacks. His throat swelled against his top button and his tie had him choking.

"You look hot."

If Sean was being funny, Jacob had been too irritated to laugh.

"I'm Sean. You're from somewhere up North. Chicago? Detroit? New York?"

The first thing Jacob noticed about Sean was that he was pretty. His face was a collection of pleasantly arranged shapes: square jawline, rounded cheekbones, pointed nose, flat chin. He was a deep, rich cream color, darker than eggshell white, but not quite beige. Face smooth all over, no blemishes. Jacob had never met a man with such a smooth complexion. Sean's wavy hair and bushy eyebrows complemented his heavy, sweeping eyelashes. His prettiness made Jacob immediately suspicious. His father said to always be careful around pretty men—they talked too fast, as if the extent of their experience was far beyond other people's. A bunch of slick-ass know-it-alls in love with their own razzle-dazzle. As Sean waited for Jacob to introduce himself, the upperclassman onstage told the freshmen class to look left, look right, that some of them wouldn't make it.

"Jacob. New York—Brooklyn."

"Cool. 124 Hubert Hall." Sean's voice was an octave or two higher than Jacob expected.

"208 Thurman."

"Great. I'll come find you after dinner. Give you some fashion tips so you make it through the rest of the week without all that chocolate melting."

By his freshman year in college, Jacob already knew he liked boys, but he had yet to manage what happened after *like*. And he really didn't know how to react to another brother flirting with him—especially in public settings. He was also annoyed Sean had clocked him so quickly. He checked his posture and the way he held his hands, looked around to see if anyone had overheard.

"Relax. I just have a good sense of who's who. My two brothers went here."

"You're out of line."

"Trust me when I tell you no one cares, except for the administration. And parents." It was so cavalier the way he said that, so dismissive of the rules of nature the way Jacob understood them. Sean Dumont from Gretna, Louisiana. Third son in his family to matriculate at Morehouse, all of them following their father and grandfather before them. A third-generation Morehouse legacy.

Jacob's grandmother was a nurse, and after his mother finished undergraduate school, she went immediately to Long Island University to get her master's in education. Jacob's father was the first person in his family to attend college. He told Jacob and his brother, Darrel, stories of the odd jobs he worked to supplement the scholarship he was awarded. The wee hours of mornings before class spent packing ice and fish under the Brooklyn Bridge on the East River at the Fulton Fish Market. Weekends doing homework and research papers in between slinging carcasses of cows and pigs along the West Side Highway in the meatpacking district. Working in the meatpacking district meant getting up at three a.m. to get to work by four. Transvestites, male hustlers, and prostitutes catcalled workers as they hooked sides of cows and pigs to bring in off delivery trucks. Teenage boys in parked cars with grown men too early in the morning. His father shook his head at the things he saw. Eventually he found a job close to campus and in line with his major, working in a lab at Long Island University Hospital. Jacob's father reminded his sons that higher education wasn't a guarantee. Success was hard work, determination, and a commitment to provide a better future for your family. Jacob's parents established considerable momentum for their children, who only had to keep up the momentum, with no room for fuckups or stumbles.

Jacob listened to what Sean said. Of course what happened behind closed doors mattered, one Morehouse brother to another. Otherwise, they all would be running around campus holding hands and lying around campus with their heads in one another's laps. But they weren't. For some brothers, it was simple curiosity, questions about another man's body, whether or not the physical satisfaction one felt being with a woman was similar. Curiosity satisfied, their same-sex dalliances would transition into futures of wives and houses filled with children. Jacob belonged to the group of brothers for whom same-sex desire was an absolute collision. They didn't have a road map on how two Black men might live together. They learned too early the kind of desire they felt was unmentionable. It left them charting unknown paths on how to manage life, develop friendships, and make romantic connections. Maybe a spouse one day, along with the house and the white picket fence plus kids. It certainly wasn't as casual as Sean's comment suggested. It involved too much: the right perception conveyed in an appropriately packaged presentation made to secure the correct employment, all part of the long game for the administration's fundraising objectives to ensure the survival of a small, liberal arts college, exclusively for Black men. The attention was too great, the stakes too high, any deviations from the norms not an option. If Jacob knew this—felt this—as the elder of his parents' two children, as the first of his extended network of cousins to lead his generation into the hallowed halls of higher education, then Sean—a third-generation Morehouse matriculant—surely knew this too, just as they both knew the casual nature of his comment to be a complete falsehood. However, what definitely was true was that some brothers were riskier than others, and Jacob preferred to fly under the radar. Sean and Jacob eventually became best friends. They did connect in Jacob's dorm room after dinner later that night. Riffling through his closet, Sean advised that the trick to dressing for Freshman Week was managing the August humidity of Atlanta. Starched cotton shirts were like walking around in sweatshirts. He instructed Jacob to wear linen ones instead—roll up the sleeves to just below the el-bows and never ever button all the way to the top. Use the tie knot instead to hold the collars together, and keep a loose knot. Someone would tell him if his collars started to spread. Tropical-weight wool was laughable—Sean asked if Jacob had ever been to the Caribbean? In the summer? It was too bad he didn't have seersucker pants, but khakis would do. Save the wool for the air-conditioning in King Chapel.

After thirty minutes, Detective Wilson returned with his col-league, Detective Kennedy. As soon as they sat down Beth im-mediately started with her questions, but the detectives were interested only in Jacob.

"I see PSGM has been actively protesting this project."

In frustration Beth sighed, looked at Jacob and Daniel, then responded before either of them had a chance to open his mouth. "So, they've gone beyond petitions and signs now and graduated to being thugs?"

Detective Kennedy shot her a look. "No. Some of their peo-ple just get overzealous. This woman named Elsie Grace Boone heads them up. She's a real firebrand. Politically connected. Sharp. Work in this neighborhood, you're going to have to figure out how to work with them."

"Not if these are the tactics they use."

Detective Kennedy leaned back in his chair. Stared at Beth. He wasn't as tall as Detective Wilson, nor as good-looking, but his presence was commanding. He was dressed differently than Wilson: short-sleeved collared shirt, detective's shield swinging over a knit tie, gun, the hem of tailored slacks resting atop comfortable walking shoes versus Wilson's high-top Jordan's. The white of his shirt against the brown of his skin made him that much darker against the beige backdrop of the wall behind him. He continued to stare at Beth. The intensity of his gaze searched her face. The potency of silence overwhelmed the spartan room in which the six of them sat, reducing Beth to the smallest, pettiest of women. Thomas finally came to her rescue.

"Detective Kennedy makes an important point. If we're to see a successful project here, we will have to contend with PSGM. I'll speak to the council member about setting up a meeting. Right now, Jacob must decide how to proceed with these four people."

"*He* has to decide?" Beth was incredulous.

Detective Wilson responded. "He was the one assaulted. He was the one who filed a police report."

Beth didn't hesitate. "He wants to proceed with pressing charges." She looked expectantly at Jacob, nodded for him to confirm her decision, even made shoving motions with her hands, as if to push him along. "We need to send a message."

"Jacob?"

Jacob looked around the room and considered what Beth asked him to do: press charges against four people based on the suspicion that they'd been the ones who assaulted him. Four people he'd never seen but whom, given the neighborhood and the project, he assumed looked like him. The day of his interview with Beth, Jacob was a year out of college, still working a retail job while he searched for an entry-level position with a real estate development firm. Beth's position looked like the difference between crunching numbers in front of a computer while cold-calling potential property sellers and hitting the ground immediately in the middle of all the action. He was hooked by the end of their interview. It didn't matter the annual salary was ten thousand dollars less than a similar one with a name-brand developer.

Detectives Wilson and Kennedy seemed benign enough. Maybe that was because of Cornelius. Maybe not. But the record of police interacting with Black bodies is an American nightmare. Detainment. Interrogation. Prosecution. The physical and emotional expense, the length of time and financial cost. Afterward, possible incarceration. All based on a maybe. Jacob's head was down while he swung like hell at everything in front of him. The bruise above his eye pulsed. He felt a twinge in his ankle. Beth stared at him; everyone in the room waited for a response. That's when Jacob knew he'd be leaving that job. He just had to figure out how.

FOUR

DANIEL

Daniel stood at the entrance to Westview Cemetery. Death was caught here, trapped in headstones and stone monuments like arrested dreams. Birds didn't chirp and the wind barely stirred. Occasionally a car rolled by, slow and steady, maybe reflective of the mourners inside or else scared that speed and a revving engine might upset those buried. Even the greenery looked frozen in time, halted in the motion of life: grass so green and perfectly cut it could be Astroturf. Trees were scattered throughout the landscape; great, massive brown trunks at least nine feet in girth. They were solitary figures towering over tombstones and placed just so. Burdened with the weight of dense green branches, their limbs were heavy, and it was so quiet Daniel wondered again how such lushness wasn't a sanctuary for birds. Visitors marked the tombstones of loved ones with bunches of flowers. Bursts of colorful wreaths. Purple blooming crosses. Ordinary, pastel-hued bouquets sitting at the heads of graves. Daniel was empty-handed.

Mama is dead. Still haven't heard from Marty.

That was how Lilah delivered the news of Mama's passing. Daniel suspected it, that morning call from her so early, so soon after he'd just left the two of them—Mama, bedridden and mumbling, barely moving and incoherent; Lilah taking over while Daniel went to work. Daniel and Lilah couldn't afford the part-time nurse any longer, nor could they manage any more changes in their work schedules to care for her. Guilt haunted them at first, thinking they had willed Mama's death. Relief came later—freedom, finally. Later still, anger. At Mama. At Marty. At Ray. The two of them at each other.

Mama is dead. Still haven't heard from Marty.

They knew she wouldn't get better, but they had hoped. Daniel hoped, so he could get answers about his father. Lilah hoped, so he would stop bothering her. Neither of them knew what had happened to Marty. All the while, Mama slipped further and further away. Gone from standing bolt straight, striding around the neighborhood, righteous, looking whomever she encountered full in the face and greeting them with a loud word to shuffling between living room and front porch, between kitchen and back porch, losing her hair, bent from time and weathered by Ray's death. Whenever he thought Mama might be lucid, Daniel slipped in a few questions. Always about the mystery of his father: about the differences between him, Lilah, and Marty; why

Mama made him think his birth was an accident; what happened between her and Ray? Mama was dead and Daniel was back to when he was ten and dreamed of his father, a man too big to fit in his world. Fantasized about baseball mornings, afternoon football, hoop shoots and layups and slam dunks. A little boy's desire for arms more muscular and longer, for larger feet and wider hands, for legs like his but thicker, for a face that mimicked his only bigger, all of it stronger and harder and older. How he'd look decades into the future, a model, an example. A ten-year-old's fantasies of a defender of the home and protector of the family. Someone who beat back the unknown with fists and squashed fear with laughter.

Daniel remembered the first time he'd asked. Reached down into his ten-year-old gut, mustered up what courage he could, and demanded, "Where is my father?"

Mama had looked up from a bowl of green beans, surprised. She couldn't decide if it was his tone or the question that caught her attention. Ardent. Strident. Purposeful. He'd come to find something and meant to have it at all of ten with a voice barely distinguishable from a girl's and making demands of his mother, a woman more than three times his age. Deciding if she was amused or disgusted, Mama stared back at him.

"Who knows where he is? Probably out drinking. Said he'd be back for dinner, though." She grabbed a few green beans, bent them to snapping. Dropped them into a bowl of cold water.

"Not that slob. *My* father."

Hearing the accusation in his voice, Mama recognized the question then. She was sitting, Daniel looking directly in her face. Mama saw her son—his curly hair, his light eyes, bushy eyebrows, thick lips, dusky skin—and confronted the past come back to haunt her. He stared, brazen and unflinching. Insolent little bastard that he was, he repeated the question.

"Where is my father?"

That's when Mama backhanded him, a slap more stinging because of wet skin and cold water.

"Boy, you'd best watch your mouth."

Heat spread across Daniel's face. A tingling sensation swept through his body. It wasn't the first time Mama had hit him, but it was the first time she hit him so that he felt the force of her purpose. He stared back at Mama. Didn't move. Didn't stumble. His eyes were clear and bright, not clouding over.

"You going to answer my question?"

Mama slapped him again. Harder—his neck bent, his head tilted as air left his mouth. His ears popped, he staggered backward but managed to keep standing. He straightened up. Swallowed. Looked back at Mama.

"Still isn't an answer."

She hit him even harder. Daniel got lightheaded. His legs wobbled. He felt something running from his nose. "Who the hell do you think you are?" Mama stood up. "Come on." Her hand closed into a fist.

Daniel's face throbbed, tears streamed down his cheeks. He steadied himself, closed his eyes and opened his mouth. Mama raised her fist.

"Stop it." He heard his sister's voice.

Daniel opened his eyes. Lilah stood in front of him, held Mama back.

"Just stop it," she repeated.

"Girl, you best let me go unless you want some too."

Lilah didn't move. "You do what you have to, but look at him. I'm not going to stand here and let you beat him." Mama heard accusation in Lilah's voice too, colored by experience and the things she understood could happen between men and women.

Mama shook herself from Lilah's grip. "I'm not going to stand here being insulted by my own goddam children."

Mama looked past her daughter. Daniel wasn't crying so much as tears silently streaked his face. He looked back at her, his mouth set tight and grim, his eyes the hard stare of a declaration he didn't have to say out loud. It was in his stance, indictment plastered across his face: he wanted her to admit the wrong he knew she committed. Mama moved toward Daniel, but Lilah blocked her again.

"Hit me, Mama. I'm big as you. Hit me."

Marty came into the kitchen then, saw the three of them standing there: Lilah in between Mama and Daniel. Daniel a mess.

"What the hell is going on here?"

Lilah looked over Daniel's head at their older brother. "He asked."

Marty looked at Mama. "What'd you tell him?"

Mama looked at Marty, then Lilah, then Daniel. The same tone of unvoiced knowing echoed in Marty's voice. It was the third insult she'd endured from her children that day. As if mothers were beyond human weaknesses, incapable of mistakes, deserving of damnation at the slightest revelation of failing. They'd turned her mistake into an accusation. And their absolute disrespect for the sacrifices she'd made, not even regard for her experience. Mama had had enough. She looked at each one of them, disgusted.

"Y'all get the hell out my face *now*!"

Mama is dead. Still haven't heard from Marty.

Not that they heard from Marty that often, but it had been months of Mama laid up on her back since Marty had vanished. Always so solitary and limited to whatever thoughts he was thinking, his whole life long, Marty was a reminder of what Lilah and Daniel were not. Mama always saved the best part of herself for him. Left her other two children wondering what he had that they didn't. Daniel and Lilah tending her, gone from working overtime to pay for the nurse to cursing when overtime ran out, forcing them to remember the routine the part-time nurse had established: cleaning bedpans, changing sheets, wiping spittle, washing her with sponges. Gone from being occupied with their own lives to being plagued with hers. Learning which gestures meant what—a turned head, grunts, or blank stares for how she was feeling; pretending to sleep when she didn't want to eat; pushing pillows off the bed when she wanted to sit up; thrashing and twisting, barking utter nonsense:

Darkness hurts my insides . . . Ray, you petrified shit . . . Marty, my best boy Marty, be quiet . . . I need water, soft, clean water for his birth.

When they tried to get her to explain, she'd either go quiet or make a shushing sound until they left her alone.

It wore Lilah out first. Daniel had arrived one day to hear

Mama screeching. Lilah was sitting in the living room, staring at the television.

"Scratch me, I'm disappearing!" called Mama from the bedroom.

He looked at Lilah. "What's going on?"

"Scratch me, I'm disappearing!"

"I can't take this anymore. There must be another way. A state home. Group care. Something."

"Those things cost money, Lilah."

"I don't care. Anything is better than this."

"Scratch! Scratch! Scratch! Disappearing!" Mama was hysterical. They looked at each other, their faces a mix of panic, grief, and anger.

"I'm not doing this anymore. I've got my own life, my own bills, my own shit to do."

They listened to Mama moaning in the bedroom, neither of them bothered to move. Finally, "She's our mother, Lilah."

"Yeah, what a mom. What has she done for us? No money. No future. Not even health insurance so she can take care of herself. Nothing. Her and that sorry-ass Ray. Could barely take care of themselves, much less us. And now we're stuck with her? Supposed to put our lives on hold for hers? Some kind of mother."

Daniel left Lilah in the living room, went to see about Mama. She had pushed the covers off the bed; the pillows were on the floor with them. Stench clogged the room—an uneaten breakfast; piss where she had wet the bed; shit, but there was nothing on the bed and he couldn't see the source of the smell.

Mama snaked and wiggled in her nightgown. It had rolled up, revealing flattened, wrinkled breasts. Knowing how much she needed him, Daniel felt an overwhelming sense of satisfaction. *Honor thy father and thy mother.* Lilah out on the couch, refusing to touch her, and Marty who-knows-where. He was the only one left to care for her. How she mistreated Daniel from the very beginning: Smothered him with distractions from the questions to which she would not provide answers. Devised anything to occupy his attention. Manufactured fights and petty competitions between him and Marty. Invented obsessions about Lilah; all designed to keep Daniel away from her and from getting closer to himself. And there she lay, in bed, writhing, finally caught and overtaken by the guilt of her actions.

"Scratch me! Itch! Disappear!"

Daniel walked to the closet for a clean set of sheets and nearly kicked over the source of the shit smell: Mama's unemptied bedpan. Daniel's skin tingled; he forced himself to stand still in order not to go beat Lilah. He cleaned Mama, changed the sheets, emptied her bedpan, dumped the breakfast, aired out the room, and tried to make sense of what she was saying. He took a comb and scratched her scalp, stroking what little of her hair remained. Mama lay quietly on clean sheets, in a fresh nightgown, scratching her breasts, moaning.

"Somehow, she managed to pay out the lease on this apartment. With everything else, that is something." He rejoined Lilah in the living room. "I'm here most of the time anyway. Just going to break my lease and stay here. Then we won't have to alternate nights, just work out the days."

"She's not getting any better, Daniel."

"So what?"

"So, I'm not doing it."

"Yes, you are. Because of that bedpan, you'll do it." Coupled with the hard glare Daniel leveled at his sister, the threat in his voice was unmistakable.

Lilah looked at her brother the way she faced off with Mama that day in the kitchen when Daniel asked about his father. She measured the depth of her brother's resolve. It wasn't the violence he threatened; it was the debt they owed this woman who had toiled daily in ways that they knew, and more that they didn't. Mama had made sure there was shelter over their heads, clothes on their backs, food in their bellies. That debt meant something. The look on Daniel's face meant they would both fulfill that obligation.

"You still think you're going to find out something. We can't even understand her."

Daniel didn't bother to answer.

Lilah watched him, shook her head. After a few moments she said, "That fucking goddam Marty."

"What? What about him?"

"He's just so fucked-up. Us needing him, and he ups and disappears."

"He knows something."

"How do you know that?"

Daniel looked at his sister, his eyes focused on her but staring at someplace not there. "Why else would he run away? Especially with Mama so sick?" he finally asked.

"'Cause he's a selfish little prick and she made him that way."

The grass made a soft sound bending under Daniel's footsteps. He wasn't surprised to hear Marty's voice on the phone. "Meet me at her grave tomorrow at one thirty." Daniel expected that Marty would eventually call. It was Marty's tone that annoyed him. They didn't exchange pleasantries or inquiries as to how the other was doing. As if Marty had never left, had not deserted them for almost a year. As if they should just accept his return and pick up where he'd left off. What also surprised Daniel was that Marty knew where Mama was buried—knew enough to find his way there and order his brother to meet him. Surprised Daniel to the point of irritation, and that's when he decided to be late. At first, thirty minutes was enough. That stretched into three hours. When Marty called again, Daniel was on the couch, flipping through channels. "You coming or what?" Daniel liked the exasperated sound in Marty's voice. "Yeah . . . I'm on my way."

Daniel picked his way over to Mama's grave, while Marty watched his brother approach. Daniel stopped a few feet short of the headstone. *Sue Ellen Milton. April 30, 1942–September 17, 1991. Beloved Mother.* Lilah and Daniel fought over that word, "Beloved." Marty turned, bent down and brushed at the headstone's lettering. Bunched up the flowers he planted.

"Y'all should do a better job of keeping this up," he mumbled.

"The cemetery's doing just fine. You back to stay?"

Marty looked up, squinted against the sun. "You usually come here without flowers?"

"I usually don't come."

"You saying you don't love your mama?"

Daniel smirked. "I'm not the one who turned tail and ran."

Marty picked at a rock, dislodged it from the earth, and left a dirt brown spot in the short green grass. He aimed, threw it at a tree. A loud crack cut through the quiet, and a scar marred the place where the rock hit the tree bark.

"Jesus. Dick. I'm going."

"Who's running now? Took you long enough to get here. You can't handle this?"

"Handle what? Maybe you should just say something instead of doing whatever this is."

Silence. Marty kneeled again. Picked at the dirt.

"You could start with why you left."

"'Cause she made me."

"She made you?" Daniel snorted. "She was on her deathbed, Marty."

"She did. Told me a story, gave me some stuff, then said go. Told me to leave, said not to come back until she was dead."

Daniel listened to Marty, tried to decide if his brother was lying. Marty was taller than Daniel and leaner, with sharper features—a pointed nose; hard, flat chin; and bones detailing the sides of his face. He had wide shoulders, long arms and legs, just short of being lanky. Clothes rested on his frame in an elegant, almost graceful manner, and he looked as though he would have had wild success as a dancer. But he moved with a slow swagger, a ponderous, halting gait. The combination of his lean build, sharp features, and deliberately thoughtful movements made him look foreboding, almost severe. That severity informed Daniel he wasn't lying.

"Why? Why would she do that?"

"Because she didn't want you to know about your father—not before she died. She wanted you to know eventually, but she didn't want to tell you."

"And you did it? Did it and didn't say nothing?"

Marty hunched near the tombstone, his back to his brother, eyes focused on the grave.

"You knew what this meant to me, Marty. You knew."

"It was her dying wish. Honor her last request."

Daniel looked from Marty to the purple and yellow tulips he tended. A slight breeze caught their flowering petals, stirred them like colorful underscoring to "Beloved Mother." He watched Marty, feeling duped and foolish. How he had cared for Mama, thought that he was lessening her ache at Marty's abandonment. Marty stood. Turned. Watched his brother and waited. When it was clear Daniel had nothing more to say, Marty turned back around, traced his hand longingly over the lettering of "Beloved Mother." Minutes passed like this, one brother with his back to the other, the two of them standing on the grave of their mother.

"Well?" Waiting for his brother to start talking again proved too much for Daniel. His voice cracked. Too high, too whiny, too nasal. He concentrated to get himself back under control.

Marty turned slowly. Barely raised his voice, only slightly tilted his head in Daniel's direction. "You already know what you need to. We all do."

"I don't know shit," Daniel wheezed. "I don't know one motherfucking thing."

"Have some respect." Marty stood with shoulders squared, chin jutting aggressively toward Daniel. He glared. "How'd she look?"

"What?"

"I want to know how she looked. She was always talking about you. Everywhere we went, that was the most she ever did—talk about you. I couldn't even be here when she died because of you. You talk about not knowing nothing. I don't know if she was in pain. Don't know if she was scared or at peace or what. Before I tell you anything else, you tell me how she looked in that coffin."

Daniel wanted to tell his brother that their mother was dust and bones in that coffin. That she withered away and didn't mention his name. Daniel shifted his weight from one foot to the other. He watched Marty arrange and dig and throw and kneel and stand and sit and listened to him talk. All he wanted was for Marty to utter a phrase, yield an answer that would rest some of his questions. And all Marty said was that he'd been Mama's fool. Daniel watched Marty, waited for him to smile, offer an excuse and apologize, disclaim what was just said as an act of grief. When it was clear no apology was coming, Daniel closed the few steps between them, ducked, avoiding Marty's first swing, gathered the tulips in both hands and yanked. He stood to Marty rushing him, caught a blow to the stomach as he returned a punch to the jaw. Their momentum carried them backward over Mama's headstone in a mess of purple and yellow petals and flailing arms and legs.

|| FIVE ||

JACOB

Thursday nights were for family fun—Jacob plus Sean and Rodney. Sometimes a friend joined them. It was a time to check in: about work, about the folks at home, about one another. Beyond the friendship Jacob and Sean had cultivated while at Morehouse, there was the additional benefit of living in Atlanta, the opportunities the city offered hormonally driven young Black men attracted to each other. The club scene and nightlife, the apartments of friends who lived off-campus were places where they connected and relaxed in one another's company. They lived two parallels at once: one visible life known to family and peers, filled with the familiarity everyone expected; a second, more discrete life, filled with unexpected discoveries they worked to understand, building different identities, forming a separate community.

Jacob called home weekly to check in with his parents. After their usual discussion about work, his parents asked about his dating life. He listened to the expectation in their voices—his father's quips about finding a supportive woman. A modern woman, yes, in the way his father understood the differences in dating between their generations, but a woman who was also mature enough to understand the balance required in how a family made decisions. His father paused long enough to acknowledge the paternalistic leanings of the advice he provided before he kept going about how life changed, how objectives evolved, how the person he was at twenty-one with a wife and newborn son was very different from the mid-career professional he was at fifty, a financially stable family man with an expansive range of options.

"Make sure you allow for growth and flexibility—for you and your wife," he said, forecasting the life he thought his son would live.

Jacob's mother tried to lighten the tone. "What your father is trying to say—"

"I'm not trying, I said it. He heard me."

"—is that we understand times have changed from when we were dating. There is much more emphasis on establishing an equitable partnership. Take your time until you find exactly what you want. No rush."

Knowing the limits on the types of relationships his parents were ready to acknowledge, Jacob listened, grunted affirmatively when and where required. He was apprehensive about their reaction to this part of his life, knew that they wouldn't understand he was still the same person. Added to that would be their concerns about HIV and AIDS—Magic Johnson's 1991 HIV disclosure a cautionary warning, but that epidemic had yet to sweep in Jacob's direction.

Jacob didn't consider himself "in the closet," but he didn't want colleagues or people with whom he had to do business to assume they knew him based on one fact. And he didn't want that to affect his job or count against future prospects. He learned to navigate various transitions, the different rules governing different spaces, how multiple situations dictated various terms and conditions. He noted the Black men who tried to piggyback off the momentum the white boys made—waving flags, holding hands, making public declarations. But those kinds of risks were too early for most Black men, who, unaware of where there might be cliffs, or steep inclines or sharp twists, or terrain that was rocky and uneven, plotted pathways through an uncharted map.

Jacob and Sean matriculated through Morehouse—schoolwork occupied weekdays and the weekends started Friday nights with loud music, rum-and-Cokes, vodka tonics, or margaritas at Loretta's or Traxx, and carried all the way through Sunday afternoons with cards and chips at a friend's off-campus apartment. Junior year their duo became a trio when Rodney and Sean started dating. Jacob was anxious and scared at first, worried that the two of them would exclude him, but it was Rodney who proposed the idea of their being roommates after Jacob and Sean graduated. Rodney was putting himself through graduate school at Emory. Jacob and Sean were unemployed and penniless, except for graduation gifts. The three of them as roommates were perfect—a new family Jacob made away from Brooklyn. They understood their collective struggle, the reasons for the silent compromises made with parents; the sacrifices made at work in service to the survival of careers; their shared quest to identify times and places where they didn't have to sabotage one part of themselves for another. Jacob loved their buffer zone of brotherhood and support and togetherness in a world that for the men they were was anything but. And he loved Sean and Rodney as a couple. Thursday nights were for spending time with the family they created. Dinner. They watched *A Different World*. Some conversation. However different it was from what his parents expected, the two of them made Jacob think about the kind of relationship he wanted. Sean said it took getting together with Rodney for that part of him to surface—a "focused monogamist," he called it. After the craziness of work, he looked forward to coming home to the comfortable embrace of Rodney's arms. The consistency of that, the settling, the reminder that there was more than the daily hustle—that life itself was more, the goal for which they all strived. Jacob watched them cheerfully, if a bit uncertain about when the same would happen for him.

"That's all you need, Jacob," Sean would tell him. "Just one brother. *One*. And forget all that other nonsense at the club."

"Yes, ma'am," he always responded.

And that's how Jacob met Sherman—at one of their Thursday family-night dinners.

———

Beth was furious Jacob didn't press charges against the people the police caught.

"If you're not willing to protect the interests of this project, I'll have to reevaluate if I have the right man for the job." Her voice was as sterile as the interrogation room at the police precinct. The detectives left Jacob, Beth, Daniel, and Thomas to discuss why he didn't want to press charges. As Beth chastised him, Jacob felt like he was back in the riot. His breath quickened; he got lightheaded; the fluorescent light beamed as brightly as the sun.

"Beth, just like I said to those detectives, I didn't see who hit me. There were just too many people, and it was so chaotic. My head was down and I was swinging. As soon as I got clear, I ran to my car."

Beth tilted her head backward, her nose higher in the air. "Who cares? Someone attacked *you*. Pressing charges is the start of finding out who. I can't believe you want to protect these people."

Her tone, her posture, the language she used, made Beth sound like she wanted to accuse Jacob. This country's history of brutality against Black bodies. Year after year, one decade after the next, the centuries of uninterrupted violence, an avalanche of sanctioned savagery. Not just lynchings. Not just rapes. Not just some white person's unsupported accusations that led to a Black person's death. Medical experimentations. Entire families wiped out. Whole towns burned, flooded, bulldozed, erased. And that wasn't the sum of it. The economic antagonisms and political machinations that transformed places, displaced entire communities of people who struggled with the effort it took to simply live every day. The assault was a dangerous moment. But Jacob understood he was not being attacked so much as he was in the way.

"Nothing to say?"

"I have something to say," Thomas interjected. "While this is certainly an important project to the council member, ultimately, what's critical is the treatment of the people in this community."

"I'm not clear what you mean, Thomas." Beth spoke.

"I'm sure the more you think about it, the clearer it will become."

Silence.

"And while you think about what I just said, let's go ahead and have the detectives release those people. Then you, Daniel, and Jacob need to decide how you're going to engage Ms. Elsie Grace and PSGM to keep things moving forward."

At first, Jacob hadn't paid attention to Sherman. Not that he ignored the man, but Sherman was just another guest Rodney and Sean had invited to Thursday family night. Sherman was just another brother who showed up for free food, liquor, and conversation. Sean said they weren't trying to set up Jacob, just arranging introductions, but if something happened? Perfect. As he drove home that night, Jacob thought about his predicament at work. His refusal to press charges made everything more stressful. And the council member's protection didn't help—Beth treated him like a threat. He arrived to work early and stayed late, finished tasks efficiently, hustled hard to anticipate new assignments. The new-job glow had completely tarnished, and Jacob knew he'd be gone as soon as Beth received the project approval she needed from Cornelius. He even updated his résumé. For most of the week following their meeting at the precinct, Jacob and Daniel went back and forth with Thomas, pitched different ideas about community benefits for Cornelius to present when they met with PSGM. Beth wanted to keep it simple, sprinkle a few grand for new computers in one or two public schools; contribute a few thousand more to renovate a playground; purchase a projection television system for a senior citizen center. Thomas wanted a percentage of affordable housing. He proposed clear benchmarks for local hiring. Wanted Summerhill-based contractors to receive a majority of the building contracts, and identified suppliers in Cornelius's district where construction materials could be purchased. Beth didn't like any of that, said she felt like she was being held for ransom.

"What am I going to do?" Beth mused more to herself than to Jacob or Daniel, her voice teetering on the edge of cracking. She cleared her throat, one arm crossed over her chest, the other tucked a fist under her chin. They were downtown in her twelfth-floor office. Sunlight streamed through the floor-to-ceiling windows. Beth sat silhouetted against a backdrop of trees extending outward, an endless green field expanding to the horizon. What was supposed to be front-page headlines in the *Atlanta Journal-Constitution* trumpeting a transformative project in the neighborhood that would be ground zero for the Olympics had turned into an exposé about gentrification and economic displacement. They even quoted Cornelius: "I have every confidence that we'll be able to work with the developer to complete a beneficial project for the community. One from which the developer will also make an equitable profit." Beth shook her head, shuffled papers, recounted calls she'd been having with investors. When Jacob retold all of this during Thursday family night with Sherman, that started their argument.

Jacob drove with the music off, enjoyed the wind rushing through the windows, the feel of it against his face. Atlanta after dark offered less movement, less rushing, fewer people everywhere, as the city morphed, collecting itself for a night's rest. Trees stretched past the roofs of houses, their branches twisted around streetlamps, a strange, haunting glow emanating from green leaves cradling white light. The wind sliding between the lamps and the leaves made faint rustling noises. Shadows crawled against buildings, roamed across sidewalks, their black shapes moved against a blacker, tar-pitched street. The air was charged with action in quiet, hushed display.

Jacob thought about his decision to take the position with Beth's small, community-oriented neighborhood development company because he didn't want to sit behind a desk, crunch numbers, and make phone calls asking faceless voices if they wanted to sell their property. Those calls quickly got cut down to a few short words and a dial tone. He thought it was better to be in the field, to be part of the action. The ways in which new development impacted a neighborhood. Partner with city and state agencies to lower property taxes and make homeownership in neighborhoods like Summerhill a reality. Incentivize commercial landlords to use their properties to support local businesses—a fresh-food grocer, neighborhood restaurants, a coffee shop, even set aside space that functioned as a small-business incubator. That was how Beth said she intended to grow her company. Jacob thought hitting the ground immediately versus being trapped behind a desk was worth the ten-thousand-dollar reduction in salary he took working for Beth rather than a name-brand developer. But the work he was doing was different from what Beth had described during their interview. It was like discovering the boom box under the Christmas tree that came packaged as a Sony was actually from RadioShack.

Sherman was already there by the time Jacob got home that night. Sean and Rodney pulled down plates, got glasses, called in an order for pizza. Sherman fixed drinks at the counter.

"Oh hey." Rodney introduced them. "This my boy from grad school, Sherman. This our ride or die, Jacob." They shook hands.

"What you having?"

"Rum-and-Coke."

Sherman was an inch or two taller than Jacob. He looked serious and very bookish—wore glasses with thick black frames that reminded Jacob of a professor. Jacob noted the curve of Sherman's chest and biceps in his Tuskegee T-shirt, his thick thighs in stonewashed jeans. He had the tawny coloring of a lion, but his shading was closer to deep brown than high yellow. Where his low-cut Caesar tapered down the nape of his neck, Sherman's skin had a more reddish tint. Jacob took a swallow of the drink Sherman handed him.

"Wow." He coughed to clear his throat. "Good thing I'm already home."

Sherman smiled and the kitchen lit up; the pearly whites of his teeth absolutely sparkled. "Oh, my fault. You want me to add some more Coke?" He reached for Jacob's glass.

"Nah, it's okay." Now Jacob noticed Sherman was good-looking—the way his eyebrows rose and fell just above the rim of his glasses, the dimples in his cheeks when he smiled, his full, berry-colored lips topped off by a well-trimmed mustache. Jacob leaned in his direction.

The pizza arrived and they moved to the living room, settled in front of the television. Sean had taped the two episodes of *A Different World* involving Dwayne and Whitley's marriage. They wanted to watch the episodes back-to-back, which meant two weeks of avoiding friends to prevent any spoilers. The four of them had a good time watching and talking about the messy wedding, recapping Dwayne and Whitley's side dates and trip ups along their way to the altar. They debated if the two of them were always going to end up together. Jacob laughed, heard the sound of his voice and felt like he watched the four of them from a place outside himself. He forgot about the past few weeks of drama at work. Watched Sherman refresh their drinks. Thought about the few times he tried to date at Morehouse. Looked across to where Sean and Rodney sat on the couch across from him and Sherman. Rodney's left arm draped around Sean. Sean held on to it snugly, the entire right side of his body leaning comfortably into Rodney. A question occurred to Jacob: Was a life—*this life*—between two Black men possible? Two Black men in love and protecting each other against whatever was out there in the world, moving together toward an unknown future? Sean said something, glanced up, nodded at Jacob knowingly. *Just one brother.* Sherman returned with their drinks; they smiled at each other. He was a social worker. He told them about a visit with a family, started laughing. His leg brushed up against Jacob's and the question came again: Was this version of reality they attempted to create really a possibility? Could this version of himself—how and whom he loved—be the way he navigated the world? When would he tell his parents?

Sherman finished talking, asked what kind of work Jacob did. And because it was the end of an overwhelming day. Because of the intensity of the last few weeks. Because Jacob was full of food, filled with the moment and more than a little intoxicated with the newness of Sherman and the rum-and-Cokes he poured. Because Jacob wanted to impress upon him the importance of his work, wanted him to feel the ways in which his work altered the momentum of the future, gave gravity, formed dimension, assigned meaning and definition. Jacob described for Sherman— maybe for Rodney and Sean, too, maybe even for himself, so he could remember the excitement he first had for the position— how the company for which he worked was leading the redevelopment of Summerhill for the Olympics. He left out the ugliness, the displacement of people, the faces standing on the other side of the barricades, the stories he didn't want to remember about the families whose houses he'd walked through.

"You work for those people?"

The sound of that question coming out of Sherman's mouth was a chill of sobriety that swept through the room. The three roommates looked at one another before they looked at Sherman. The glare Sherman shot at Jacob through those professorial frames was intense. Jacob felt his head split open, his thoughts spilling out for the benefit of everyone.

"Some of my clients are families in that neighborhood. You think what your company is doing is worth it?"

Jacob didn't respond.

"Have you met with Council Member Jackson? Or PSGM? They've been trying to work with landlords in the area to provide people realistic, affordable living options. You people came in and fucked all that up."

Rodney sat up. "Yo, Sherman, chill. It's not like Jacob runs the company."

"You think I make these decisions? You think I like what's happening to those families?" Jacob hoped the conviction in his voice sounded stronger than the indecision he felt.

The two of them faced off with each other, the tension in the room a hard grip in the air.

"So what are you going to do about it?" Sherman finally relented.

"You here jumping at me like I'm the one throwing them out. You got some solutions?" Jacob heard the sound of his voice, still felt himself trying to force the strength of belief into his questions.

More silence as they studied each other. Sean and Rodney sat, frozen. Jacob heard the questions he had just asked Sherman. He had never felt so challenged—like Sherman had accused him of being a sellout. Was there something for him to do? Would quitting make any difference? Sherman had no response.

"Yeah, good to pop off at the mouth with no answers."

"You don't know me." Sherman got up, started toward the door for his sneakers.

"You don't know me either."

"You corporate types are all alike—nice packaging, but don't scratch below the surface."

Sherman's words reverberated in Jacob's head. The sound of them was just too much. The Olympics. The project. The protest. The riot. The police. Beth. He wasn't going to listen to this in his living room. He wasn't. "Yeah? And what type are you? Sitting on our couch, drinking our liquor, wolfing down our food.

Freeloading, broke-ass, goofy-looking social worker." Jacob stood up and followed Sherman. Maybe that much emotion between them that early said good things about their longevity. Rodney was on his feet in front of Sherman. Sean pulled Jacob into the kitchen.

"Jacob, you need to hold it together."

"I'm at home, Sean. This is where I *live*. I don't need to feel like this *here*." Sean blocked Jacob from getting back into the living room; they listened to Rodney and Sherman.

"What the fuck, Sherman? How you coming at my boy? We were just chilling."

"I know. I know. *I'm sorry*." He paused. "No, I'm not. You know what's happening? He tell you about this project?"

"This was just supposed to be an easy evening. A nice, low-key introduction."

"I know. Dammit, Rod. Fuck. Fuck, man, *fuck*. I can't believe this. Goddammit, man. *Fuck!*"

Jacob tried to decipher Sherman's cursing—if he cursed because things escalated so quickly out of control, or if the revelation of Jacob's involvement with this project was a disappointment. Maybe it was a little bit of both. Jacob tried to understand why he found Sherman's confrontation so challenging. Maybe because Sherman spoke a truth Jacob had tried to ignore. But quitting felt too easy. Plus, he needed the paycheck.

"Rod, I'm gonna go." He raised his voice higher. "Sean, I'm sorry." Then he paused. "Jacob . . . it was cool meeting you, until it wasn't."

"Fuck you too, Sherman."

SIX

DANIEL

Marty knocked at the door and Daniel answered it, stood wordlessly in the doorway. Marty's tall, gaunt frame contrasted with his brother's meatier build. Not sure what she'd do if they started fighting, Lilah watched from the couch, tense. Eventually, they mumbled a greeting, exchanged an awkwardly stiff hug before Daniel stepped aside. Marty greeted Lilah with a kiss, then went from room to room before he returned to the living room. This was the first time they'd been together in a year, the first time since Marty and Daniel fought at the cemetery. Marty had aged in the year since he'd been away—he'd lost weight, his face had gotten slimmer, and the deep brown of his hair had begun to whiten. He had something to tell them. He settled himself in a chair, took time to find the words with which to begin. When he spoke, he reminded his siblings how they always dreamed about being part of a traditional family: a doting mother, whose mood swings they understood; a dependable father, who made a productive living; disorderly but lovable siblings. The front yard of their two-level house would be the best evidence that the greenest thumb for miles around resided within, and their backyard would be the playground for every kid on the block. The cars parked in their two-car garage wouldn't be the fanciest or latest, but they would be nice, and their neighborhood wouldn't be described as better or worse than any other. It'd be what it was for them: families who watched out for each other, kids who enjoyed playing together, no neighbor a stranger. It'd be real life with all the usual squabbles over money and love and good neighborly competition—whose lawn was the best, whose kid biked the fastest, whose husband made the best barbecue sauce that had just the right balance between that tangy, sweet flavor and the bite of hot pepper. That was the dream they all had—even Mama. Marty told them to remember that, that Mama tried hard to make that dream a reality, but that there were circumstances she couldn't escape.

"Remember Grandma cleaned houses and kept kids for rich white folks who said they were too good to hire Blacks? Said they found them *distasteful*. Mama said the whole country was moving forward—Bill Cosby and Diahann Carroll on TV, the Civil Rights Movement—but these people didn't care. The evidence of poor white folks made these rich ones feel better. Said why hire Blacks when there was good, cheap, white labor available? That's who they hired—and kept themselves separate from the changes happening around them. Those were the kind of people Grandma worked for."

Marty coughed, shifted in his seat. Coming from the corner of the room where he sat, his voice sounded small at first. As if he spoke to himself. The intensity with which his siblings listened, helped. He gained confidence in the concentration etched on their faces and their reactions. His voice climbed in volume. His only movement came when he palmed a fist and squeezed, popped his knuckles, the noise of muscle against bone cracked through the quiet. As the story unfolded, Daniel and Lilah watched Marty's face, his eyes focused beyond the room in which they sat. A line defined a space, created a shape, told a story. Marty colored, he shaded, and the story grew at its own pace. But there were blank spaces, a hollowness that whistled through places where Marty hesitated, paused, revealing the missing pieces of the drawing. Listening to his brother, Daniel closed his eyes, imagined Mama talking. He wondered about the things Marty didn't say, the things for which the three of them didn't have the knowledge.

"Mama said they drove Grandma crazy. Remember how she was always running around here complaining about Ray? 'What is a poor white woman? Nothing. What is a poor white woman without a man? Nothing still.' Now imagine Grandma—a poor white woman with a daughter to feed, trying to get by without a man. She was at the mercy of the world. Mama said they drove her crazy—the Grants. Lived up on West Paces Ferry, a few blocks over from the governor's mansion. They made they money off shipping—railroads and trucks or something. Atlanta was the crossroads of the South. Atlanta and Birmingham. You wanted to move anything anywhere in the South—passengers, livestock, auto parts, whatever—you had to come through one of those two cities. The Grants had them sewn up. Wouldn't nothing get through either place without the Grants making something off the freight. And it was all legal. They wasn't stupid people, wouldn't bother wasting time concocting illegal schemes and fraud, just setting up to get busted by the law. I remember Grandma talking about how smart they were.

"They was old, old money. Money from back before the War for Southern Independence—Grandma said Old Man Grant used to snort whenever he heard the words 'Civil War' mentioned. *The War for Southern Independence!* he used to correct whoever was talking, and then start preaching about the meddlesome North. They money was old, back from when a piece of land was yours if you had enough gall to take it from whoever was on it and enough muscle to keep it. So, maybe in the beginning they money was illegal. You dig deep enough, look hard enough, go back far enough, it's all illegal or immoral or something. Grandma listened to Old Man Grant talk as she worked. Always talking history to his kids. How they beginnings were in the settling of Savannah and how they did alright until the crackers—they called the peanut farmers and people who worked agriculture 'crackers' back then—decided they needed to break away from England. Them Grants back then were merchant-type folk, and they got mixed up with them blue-collar people and eventually had to flee to north Georgia territory."

The room darkened as Marty talked. Daniel and Lilah closed the blinds and turned on the lights. If his sister had watched her younger brother closely, she would have seen the fascination in his eyes. How he greedily lapped up each word their older brother uttered, transfixed by the story.

"Those Grants almost lost everything. Damn near had to start over. They couldn't move back to England—rumors went ahead of them and word got back they weren't loyal. Had to scuffle around a few years, go into hiding. By the time the revolution was over, they settled into what eventually became Atlanta. Old Man Grant was always hollering that's how the family lost out way back then—missed out on investing in them gold rushes; by the time they had big money again they didn't think investment in the slave trade and the cotton industry was worth it. Grandma said that's how they ended up in trade routes. Shipping—'importing and exporting,' they called it. Old Man Grant preached about how the family lost time fooling around with no-count crackers. Reminded his kids, *Forecast and evolution. Figure out where things are going and get there first. That was the lesson of them crackers.* Taught the family an early lesson in survival and how to protect itself. Said his great-great-grandfather saw the downfall of slavery. It wasn't that them Grants harbored love for Blacks—I already told y'all how they didn't even see Black people. Slavery just didn't make sound long-term economic investment sense, according to him. Said, *Who the hell ever heard of property thinking for itself?* Property that could be deceitful, steal, lie, and cheat its owner? Property that could plot revolt, slit they owner's throat and be happy about it? Hell, that wasn't no property, that was a headache. So when the War for Southern Independence came, and while property ran off in bigger numbers, killed and plundered against its owners, joined up with Union forces, and slave owners began wondering and worrying about surviving and how they was going to make a living, that original Grant—with his trade routes and teams of white workers crisscrossing the South—sat back and laughed. Even before the war started, rumor was that they helped out the Underground Railroad. Not that he was an abolitionist, but that original Grant believed in making money and believed in protecting whatever he was shipping. Them crackers he employed was always armed to the teeth. Folks at one end knew they cargo would arrive at the other—trying to hijack Grant cargo could result in loss of life, and for anything that didn't arrive, the team would have to pay for themselves. For Blacks who could barter or pay, traveling that way was a guaranteed arrival. Them trade routes, importing and exporting, hell, even the Underground Railroad, all of it turned profits for them Grants. *Forecast and evolution.* They actually ended up ahead." Daniel was lost in Marty's story. The history Marty conjured in the space of the apartment cast a spell. They remembered a mother who kept them fed and clothed, kept a roof over their heads, made sure there was heat and hot water. They never knew the mystical forces that came to bear so those things were accomplished. Always hustling to keep half a step ahead of whatever was next; Mama was the evidence.

"That original Grant wasn't no fool either. He studied slavery, avoided putting his money in it, and denounced it as a flaw-filled foolhardy scheme. Meanwhile he put its merits to work for himself. Said what would eventually prove faulty between slave masters and Blacks with no pay, would work gloriously between employers and low-paid workers. Those workers he liked best and could control, they got ahead. The thinkers and uncontrollable factors, he kept near the bottom or fired. Passed that down too: *Don't pay a man to be an intellectual. Pay him to be smart about getting a job done. Keep the intellectuals in the family and make sure they inherit they worth.* Those philosophies survived. They changed when they had to— *forecast and evolution*—but the core stuff stayed the same.

"Grandma was always sweating, always working to make just enough. Around the holidays—Christmas, Thanksgiving, Easter—maybe the Grants would think about a bonus: a turkey or ham, treating her and Mama to dinner at a restaurant, maybe a day off. Never money, something that was actually useful. Never that. If Grant's wife remembered, maybe she'd give Grandma the clothes she and her children no longer wore. That made me understand Mama's loud boasting about the finds she made at those secondhand shops, why she did her best to make sure she was always among the first to arrive. They may not have been brand-new, but at least they weren't hand-me-downs. What Grandma must have felt like—to listen and know she was a walking example of lessons that old man was teaching. But what was she to do? Poor. In the 1950s, trying to take care of herself and a child. No man. No education."

Marty stopped talking, stretched, yawned. He felt lighter, like talking was relief itself. Daniel and Lilah watched their brother, thought of another reason Mama told these things to Marty: maturity. He had the confidence they hadn't yet cultivated. Maybe they were too young and inexperienced to understand the context in which she made decisions. And that inexperience would translate into misunderstanding.

"I used to see Mama getting out of this car. The first time I saw her was down in that park across from Eddie's. You know how Mama was always saying stay away from there. *Too many winos and whatnots, and what adults are there ain't fit company for children.* But I used to hang out there with some friends and shoot the shit—that's where I learned how to smoke. Used to pocket some of Ray's cigarettes and take them with me. Anyway, that was the first time I saw her getting out of this car. It pulled up on the far side of the block, and Mama hopped out the back and ducked into Eddie's. Maybe she didn't duck inside, maybe she just walked in. But she didn't come out until after the car left, and when she did, she was empty-handed. 'Course, I didn't know that was Mama until she came out of the store. A car like that in the kind of neighborhood we lived in, and we wasn't paying attention to somebody walking into Eddie's. Once I realized it was Mama coming out of the store, we moved to a different set of benches deeper in the park. My friends ain't wasted no time ribbing me.

"'Damn, Marty. Your mama riding around in cars? Y'all must got some money.'

"'Yeah, boy. Y'all must be about to move outta here.'

"'Why she get out way over here? I'd want people on the block to see me stepping out a car like that.'

"They were right. Mama riding around in cars instead of taking the bus was spending money we didn't have. And if she was already riding, being dropped off by Eddie's didn't make much sense. But what I knew was this: *my* mama looked damn fine stepping out that car. It was a spring day in May, late evening, and Mama was walking like the world was in a hurry. Me and my friends was somewhere none of us was supposed to be, and we had seen one of our mamas getting out of a fine car, looking like something. That was different. I was excited, sitting there. I remember thinking we finally getting out. No more watching Mama hustling for absolutely nothing. No more crossing our fingers that Ray would finally come through with a job or something. No more hopping from neighborhood to neighborhood, one shotgun house after another. I watched Mama tipping out that car and thought we were at a new beginning."

The size and the quiet of the room transformed Marty from the green grass, massive trees, and open spaces of the cemetery. There, he was slight of body, his presence overwhelmed by the dominance of nature. Here, he dominated the room—his height and angles, the wide severity of his shoulders, the length of his arms, even the way he sat cross-legged in the chair, all of it formidable, commanding his siblings' attention. The sound of a baseball against a bat cracked through the silence. Marty's voice came at them as though through the length of a tunnel. Daniel squinted to hear better, to help to focus the story. Marty dreamed, Daniel and Lilah dreamed with him, all of them remembered what it was like to yearn and hope and pray for something new and different and better.

"I wanted to get home but I had to wait for Mama to get there first, plus I couldn't let my boys think that I was actually pressed about whatever Mama was doing. So I stayed with them until it was dark. We'd be the hell out of there once it was dark because shit would just change in that park. As long as it was daylight and we could see what was around us, we didn't think there was much we couldn't handle. Especially since there was four of us. But shit just changed in the park once it was dark, and most of the lamps were busted. People would be doping up right there; they didn't care who was around. Men might start fighting or a pimp might rough up a trick or a drug deal might take a wrong turn. Plus, if we weren't within shouting distance of our mamas' voices once it was dark, that was an ass-whipping for sure. I was glad to be out of the park that night and on my way home. My boys wasn't having it.

"*Hold up, Marty. What you running for?*"

"*He's thinking his mama hit the jackpot or something.*"

"They laughed.

"'Jackpot nothing.'

"'Your mama probably just got lucky with some rich dude and he had his driver drop her off near the park so your daddy don't catch her.'

"More laughter, and my face got hot.

"'All you trash asses just pissed 'cause my mama was looking like something and we about to be the fuck up outta here and all y'all thinking about is the same ol' shit that's waiting with your mamas back at y'all's houses.'

"'Fuck you. Go run home to your mama, mama's boy.'

"'I ain't running nowhere. I ain't got to be home. Whatever's there is gonna be there when I get there. I just gotta go to the bathroom is all.'

"'Well, go pee up against that fence. Don't act like you ain't done it before.'

"'Nah. I gotta shit.'

"'Yeah, right.'

"'Go home, Marty-the-Mama's-Boy.'

"'Yeah, mama's boy, bye.'

"'Fuck y'all.'

"'Fuck you.'

"'I'm outta here.'

"'Bye, mama's boy.'

"I waited 'til I rounded the corner out of their sight to start running. I ran all the way home, and I was sweating by the time I got there. I didn't want to go inside like that and scare Mama, so I waited until I caught my breath. But Mama must've heard me, because she came to the screen door and opened it.

"'Honey, you okay?'

"'Yeah. Just running.'

"'Really? From who?'

"She stepped out, looked up the block.

"'*Nobody. Just running. I just felt like it.*'

"'*Oh. Okay. Well, come in and clean up for dinner.*'

"I stepped inside and looked at Mama. She didn't look no different—no sparkle in her eyes, no excitement in her voice; there was no hurry about her of making plans. I thought about my friends, how they were ribbing me in the park. I thought about what started me running in the first place, seeing Mama stepping out that car. I was hoping for something. The park, my friends, that car, Mama, the ghetto we was living in, our shotgun home, and me running home to it, hoping we were about to get away. I knew I shouldn't have hoped for nothing—I felt that— but I kept looking around for something, anything out of the ordinary. Maybe Mama was going to make the surprise something special—maybe the center of a big, fancy dinner. But Mama just stood there; nothing about her was changed or altered.

"Nothing had changed inside the house either. Lilah, you were screaming about something, and Ray was trying to shut you up. Things were as sloppy as ever, and somebody had set Grandma down in front of the TV. It didn't feel like anything was getting ready to change, and I couldn't sense the coming of nothing.

"'*Boy, what you gawking at?*'

"'*Nothing.*'

"'*You sure you okay?*'

"'*Yeah. Honest. What we having for dinner?*'

"'*Whatever I put on the table. Go wash up.*'

"I wanted to tell Mama to stop playing. I wanted to tell her that I saw her get out of that car and I knew she had a surprise waiting. I wanted to say that me and Lilah would do whatever she wanted, if she'd just let us in on the secret and tell us when to get started.

"'Marty. The bathroom. Now.'

"'Mama, don't you have something to tell us?'

"'Like what?'

"'Like a surprise? Ain't we moving or something?'

"'Boy, why would you think that? Take your little self to that bathroom so you can sit down here to this table.'

"In my mind, I started toward the bathroom, but not before me and Mama looked in each other's faces. I was feeling hope, disappointment, anger. And what I saw looking back at me was pain. I went to the bathroom, closed the door, sat down on the toilet and cried."

Marty uncrossed his legs, slid down to slouching, and tilted his head. He looked exhausted, like he could fall soundly asleep. Daniel still didn't have the answers to all his questions, but he felt like this conversation with his brother was the beginning of something.

Daniel thought about the protest. He thought about the police precinct, the conflict between Jacob and Beth. He thought about his grandmother and the Grants, the longing in Marty's voice as he had looked at Mama, the sorrow in the way she looked back. There was something about this project that Daniel must do, something he must make happen. Whatever it was, it was a chance to make sense of the blank spaces in Marty's story, a story that returned all three of them to the small, scared, trapped places of their childhood. Or maybe they were just bigger and had never left. Daniel felt this thing he must do was a way out, a lifeline for all three of them, and something they owed their mother.

SEVEN

JACOB

The meeting with PSGM and Cornelius was as disastrous as Jacob's introduction to Sherman. The only difference was that Beth was the focus of attention. For two weeks Beth and her team had negotiated with Thomas over the community-benefits agreement. She stopped suddenly, announced frustration with the lack of progress, and ordered the construction crew to start demolition. She wouldn't answer any of Thomas's calls. The construction crew worked one day before the buildings department shut them down. Beth was incensed, asked why demolition had been forced to stop. The buildings department rep told her to contact Cornelius's office.

Elsie Grace Boone was a slender woman, five foot ten, who sported a thick Afro with the poise and stature of Black Panther militancy. She wore a long-sleeved, black T-shirt and black denim jeans, coupled with solid wedge heels. She didn't wear makeup, but her colorful earrings looked like miniature dream catchers that dangled from her ears. Her entire presentation recalled pictures of Kathleen Cleaver and Angela Davis outfitted in black mock turtlenecks, Afros trimmed to razor-like precision. Elsie Grace was darker than both of those women, had the coloring and stature of Nina Simone. Regally defiant. She sat next to Cornelius at his conference table and nodded when Beth walked in with Jacob and Daniel. Next to Elsie, Cornelius looked shorter than Jacob remembered. And fatter. At the press conference, he towered over everything—his voice boomed; his smile charmed. He broadcasted confidence like a beacon, so smooth and charismatic, shaking hands, laughing, taking pictures, maneuvering questions with cleverly crafted one-liners. He had a certain beguiling ability and knew it, played just so to people who leaned in his direction, pounced on the way they said, "Mr. Council Member," like a lord bestowing benevolence on his subjects. Engaging, magnetic—ministerial, even. Sitting just a few feet away, Jacob noticed he had no neck and his head nested between his shoulders. Before, his suit jacket suggested the right angles of shoulders, a stiff back, and a waistline, however expanded. Without the jacket, his body looked a bloated mess— his belly bumped against the table and tits protruded against his shirt. Cornelius asked everyone to introduce themselves. Elsie Grace finished hers with, "We appreciate your taking the time to meet with us," and tipping her head toward Beth. She spoke with a thick southern accent and enunciated each word with a measured, steady cadence.

"Where are you from, Ms. Grace?"

"Gadsden, Alabama. Right outside of Birmingham. Atlanta is the big city for us. And my surname is Boone. Grace was my grandmother's first name, Ms. Washington. Keeps her close to my heart for me to use it."

"Oh, that's lovely. Beth-Ann is actually my whole given name." Beth sounded awkward. She smiled too much and for no reason, which made her seem off-balance. "I dropped the 'Ann,' though—'Beth-Ann' didn't sound quite right in business settings. But I'm a southerner too—from Richmond."

"How interesting."

"That I'm from Richmond?"

"How you use your name."

"Oh. Well, doing the work you do, I can see how using your first and middle names can be a benefit." A ripple went through the room. Elsie Grace had two staff members with her: one noticeably grimaced at the end of Beth's comment, the other coughed. Thomas sat next to Cornelius, and Cornelius's assistant had joined the meeting as well. Cornelius was about to speak when Elsie Grace made a little motion with her hand, turned slightly in his direction.

"Beg pardon before we get started, CJ." She turned back toward Beth. "How does using my first and middle names benefit the work I do?"

Jacob noticed that Elsie Grace addressed Cornelius as "CJ"

and that Thomas didn't correct her. However, he did sigh audibly, as though the meeting had just taken a turn for the worse and gotten longer.

Beth was startled by the question. "I meant no offense. It's just establishing that kind of familiarity—that sort of connection—with people by using your first and middle names must be helpful in doing community work."

"What do you mean by community work, Ms. Washington?"

Beth stuttered to respond then stopped. She should have apologized, started over. Elsie Grace's control of the room was evident to everyone but her. It became clear Beth hadn't been invited to a meeting so much as a public rebuke. Jacob wondered if continuing the negotiations with Thomas would have mattered. Beth was going to lose the project; the machinations of Cornelius and Elsie Grace were apparent. The fact that Beth didn't think she could was why she didn't see it—in her reality, that possibility simply didn't exist. Just like at the precinct, her posture became defiant: arms crossed against her chest, head back, nose higher, legs planted firmly on the floor, her entire body leaning into the table, like she was about to spring forward.

"Ms. Boone, I imagine you already know the work you do and that you know the work I do as well. Why don't we focus our attention on figuring out how we can get this project moving forward?"

"It's my understanding that was exactly what Thomas was trying to do. Then you stopped responding."

Listening to Elsie Grace spar with Beth, Sherman's indictment echoed in Jacob's head. *You work for those people?* A group of Black people and one sole white woman. Tensions stirred the room, historical plot points reorganized into a contemporary, modern configuration.

"Ms. Boone, this is economic development. This is local job creation. This is community progress. That's the work I'm doing. What are you doing?" Both Cornelius and Thomas started to respond, but Elsie Grace held up her hand again.

"Ms. Washington, we have radically different ideas about what's happening here."

"I wonder how the Georgia Dome people feel?"

Elsie Grace smiled. "A wonderful new sports venue for the people of metro Atlanta. We established an equitable agreement with them. It's good that you're familiar with that project."

Beth didn't respond.

Elsie Grace held up a folder, waved it. "I'm going to leave this with Council Member Jackson. This fully outlines what a productive relationship looks like between you as the developer and us as the community. The Olympic clock is counting down, and if we're not going to arrive at an equitable agreement with you, we'll need to allow for enough time to explore other options. I don't need to be a part of the rest of this meeting, but I do look forward to continuing our conversation."

Once Elsie Grace left, Beth's shoulders relaxed and she sat back in her chair. Thomas rubbed the bridge of his nose. Even Cornelius seemed to breathe a little easier. Other than to introduce the meeting, he hadn't spoken, and Cornelius didn't seem like the kind of person who liked to keep quiet. Cornelius and Elsie Grace understood Beth's objectives versus the outcome they wanted, the necessary leverage that needed to be applied. Beth's desires were as indelicate as bare knuckles knocking on a table. Elsie Grace and Cornelius were a more nuanced pair. How far did Elsie Grace's "community" extend? Did Cornelius have political ambitions for higher office?

Cornelius read the benefits PSGM wanted:

- 25% of all new rental and homeownership units to be built affordable;
- 25% of all construction jobs to be allocated to people who've lived in Summerhill, Peoplestown, Mechanicsville, or Grant Park for at least the last ten years;
- For the developer to build a job training center in one of those four neighborhoods and provide it with two years of operational funding;
- 15% of all parking and sales tax revenue generated to be allocated to Atlanta public schools located in Council Member Jackson's district;
- Construction of at least two regionally—or nationally—recognized grocery stores within the boundaries of the neighborhoods previously noted.

Cornelius added that he wanted weekly progress reports—from the moment foundations were poured to the number of trees that were planted. He wanted information about the demolition crew that cleared the site. About the architects, about the public relations company to be used, and about strategies for attracting small-business tenants. He said he needed this information so he could answer questions and anticipate problems.

Especially since after that fiasco of a groundbreaking event, people were asking questions about Beth, her background, and her connection to Summerhill.

Beth bristled. "That is an unreasonable amount of information. This is a private project, Cornelius. My investors aren't going to like all the nosing around in their business."

"Beth, you only have control of seven houses. You need the land held by the other owners as well as that controlled by the city of Atlanta. Otherwise, you *don't have* a project. This project has the attention of this entire city and the national and international communities. Anything that's going to be built in that neighborhood is going to need my vote—mine and the city council and the support of the mayor. I'm sure your investors are aware of that."

Cars sped by on the two-way street three stories below them. Their sounds were of something constantly coming and going: the squeal of brakes indicating a momentary stop, then engines revved as a vehicle moved onward toward the driver's destination. Occasionally a horn blew and there were shouts—angry voices cursed; another honk followed by rubber screeching against tar. The sounds bounced off the buildings bordering either side of the street, a short concrete valley that made noise echo. The tension that came with Elsie Grace rematerialized. Cornelius and Beth studied each other, and Jacob thought about the history they were witnessing: A little Black boy and a little white girl are in the summertime of childhood. There is sunshine and water and lots of laughter. There are the tallest green trees, flowers blossoming, and birds making the noises of spring. Their parents tell them they can do anything. Change the world. Walk the moon. Swim the widest ocean. And so little Black boy goes to school, where he always pays attention. His eyes are bright; he walks with his head held high, his chest poked out, his nose up in the air. When he talks, it's in a strong, clear voice without stuttering or hesitation. But he does not know the contradictions he presents—the meaning of little Black boys who walk with their noses held high and look people dead in the eye. He does not know and he cannot see the fall coming and after that, winter.

Little white girl grows up in a world of frills and ruffles. It is pink and pure and as perfectly preserved as ice covering freshly fallen snow. She has a head full of the blondest Shirley Temple curls, the bluest eyes, and the pinkest lips, all resting within the softest, palest, alabaster-colored skin. Beyond beautiful, she is the unattainable possession. She will not evolve into womanhood so much as expand into a new realm of unblemished being. She does not understand the paralyzing effect of discouragement. How dreams can devolve into guesses, and guesses collapse into the rote functioning of getting from one day to the next.

So the one encounters the other—little Black boy, now an experienced man. His baby fat gone, replaced by the imperious, protruding roundness of his gut. There are hidden places where he remains soft, where the world can poke and prod at the vulnerability of his sanity. What once was unassailable, he's begun to question. His summertime of rose-colored dreams filled with bright sunlight have become sepia-toned and muted. It has transformed the little Black boy into a cunning, calculating, predatory man.

Cornelius saw Beth, and what used to be a set of gilded, untouchable, sky-high tits were now just two sacks of sagging flesh, pointing toward earth. What used to be the mystery of irreproachable, alabaster skin, milk white and damning to the touch, was just a pale, thin covering, freckled and developing liver spots. Her beaming blond helmet of hair was graying. Cornelius saw straight through Beth, saw deep into her flesh to the blood and bone and sinew, to the pattern of her breathing, the pulse that fired her heart, the very thing that set her in motion. Cornelius looked at Beth, and Jacob saw the history of what little Black boys and little white girls have always been told about each other. And Beth, that precious little white girl in her blond and perfect curls, who had become a frozen, stiff woman, looked down the porcelain, sloped femininity of her nose and believed what she'd always heard—that Cornelius was Black. Arrogant. And fat. She was buoyed by a life spent floating on a truth given to her by other people: that her Southern White Womanhood was a righteous sanctuary beyond reproach. Propped on a pedestal of perfection and paraded about for the world's admiration, she had curdled and soured, was disfigured with adulation. Her expansion from girlhood into the realm of unblemished being made her comfortable knowing any challenger—much less the bloated, pudgy fucker who sat right in front of her—simply didn't exist. She almost said the words out loud: *Look, nigger.*

Cornelius watched Beth, recalled she had no sense of the rise and buck of his life, how conflict and confrontation and transformation had shaped his will. However hard she believed herself to be, she was soft from a world obsessed with its own definition of itself and blind to an evolving future. And now she sat in front of him trying to dictate the terms of his existence. Well. The room flickered, shifted, tilted off the axis of gravity anchoring it. Cornelius grunted a low sound that came from deep in his throat. Daniel, Thomas, and Jacob sat still; their breathing barely disturbed the air. Phones rang beyond the closed door. Someone typed on a computer. The laughter and chatter of people echoed in the silence. Cornelius cleared his throat, a harsh sound that cut through the quiet. He shifted again, rearranged himself in his chair and again resembled the person at the groundbreaking: A massively charming, big, bald, Black man possessed of an unstoppable ego; a shaman endowed with determination enough to raise the dead. He was the sorcerer back on the podium, casting a spell. He smirked, leaned to one side, rested on the arm of his chair, his vision cleared, and he remembered what he must never forget. His attention focused, sharpened on Beth: *pompous cunt.* He would make this a hard, important lesson for her.

EIGHT

DANIEL

The meeting with Cornelius and PSGM made things worse between Jacob and Beth. She wanted him to help convince Cornelius and Elsie Grace that a formal community-benefits agreement wasn't needed. Just like at the precinct where she expected Jacob to press charges against those suspects. As though Jacob had some special power to make both Cornelius and Elsie Grace endorse the future Beth wanted. But Beth's desire went unfulfilled, just like at the precinct. Now she paced, a caged animal trapped in her office. She seethed, a hand cocked under her chin, the look in her eyes distant, watched the changing landscape of her future. She began to suspect that Jacob worked with Cornelius to sabotage her project.

"So what are we going to do about this?" she said to Jacob, her tone hard, sharp.

Jacob hesitated. "What are we going to do about what, Beth?"

Beth stared at him, started to speak, then went back to pacing instead. "This goddam motherfucking community-benefits bullshit. I cannot believe how this happened. What do you think, Daniel?"

This was their weekly staff meeting. On the conference table in front of them was an artist's rendering of the finished project. It showed neat, two-story Craftsman-style houses with trimmed lawns and driveways in front of two-car garages. There were sidewalks and trees and adults on porches watching children. There were girls jumping rope, boys playing softball, and dogs running across lawns. A car drove by, the passenger waving at her neighbors. The sporty red convertible shined, looked new and sleek and foreign rolling along the tarmac of the pitch-black street. It was easy to imagine the driver turning at the corner, driving to a similar block with similar houses and similar children playing with similar dogs running, all being watched by similar neighbors on similar porches, all of whom waved back, locks of hair dancing in the wind before the driver turned into a similar driveway of her own. Nowhere was there evidence of the seven houses and the people and the neighborhood that used to exist. Even the hovering bulk of the Atlanta–Fulton County Stadium had vanished. In its place was a rendering of a park with a digital billboard that simply read OLYMPICS. Pretty and perfectly presented. In this new world with the new people Beth envisioned, there was no space to accommodate the far-flung dreams of Cornelius and Elsie Grace. There was only the hard fact of reality—the operational function of Darwin's natural selection supposedly at work, that the neighborhood laid out before them was different and better and of higher order than what previously existed. Surely

Daniel understood that—the evolution of this southern town, birthplace of his childhood, into the burgeoning metropolis teeming with opportunity for him as an adult? Beth explained all this to Daniel on their ride back to the office after she blocked him from riding back with Jacob. She was so desperate to secure an ally in this fight with Cornelius and Elsie Grace that her sudden attention on him surprised Daniel. When he wasn't assisting Jacob with his various tasks of project management and community outreach or keeping Beth up-to-date on their progress from one week to the next, most days Beth treated Daniel as little more than her office lackey.

As he rode next to her, cocooned in the plush leather seats of the big gunmetal-gray Mercedes she navigated, his surprise slowly morphed into suspicion. The car slid through traffic, the cabin so quiet and isolated from the world outside. The automobile was fantastic—the instrument panel twinkled, the wood finish shined, the climate-controlled interior sheltered them from the heat outside. Her slightest move—a tap on the gas pedal, a turn of the steering wheel, a flick of her finger—and the car leaped ahead of a slower driver, hugged a curve in the road, played crisp, clear music that sparkled. Daniel felt Beth's tension mounting. He looked at her: manicured nails on soft-looking hands gripped the leather-wrapped steering wheel; a diamond engagement ring rested on top of a diamond-studded wedding band; a diamond-and-pearl tennis bracelet dangled from her wrist. Clad in a white silk blouse, a pale pink linen summer suit, and expensive-looking shoes. Pitch-black sunglasses rode her nose and her hair was swept back, curled behind each ear. Diamond studded earrings winked from each lobe. Daniel watched Beth, cradled in the driver's seat of a car that probably cost at least ten times what Mama made in her best year. It certainly cost more than his and Jacob's salaries combined. Beth from Richmond, Virginia, the seat of the Confederacy. Daniel wondered if she willed herself not to remember a history of lynchings and the Freedom Summer and nonviolent protests. If she ignored stories about a South of sit-ins and blood-spattered headlines, where the police force was a death squad ruled by a mob. Did she even care? What would she do if her son suddenly disappeared? Could Beth live Mama's life? Or Cornelius's? Or that of Elsie Grace? Or any of the lives of the people who had lived in those houses?

"Did you hear me?"

Beth and Jacob were looking at him. She stood next to a bookcase loaded with decorative books designed only to be displayed. Smaller books on upper shelves, larger ones near the bottom, all arranged alphabetically by author. A paperweight anchored a stack of files on a credenza that displayed pictures of her family: Beth with her husband and their son dressed up, posed against a marble gray backdrop. Another in street clothes and seated on a couch. Her son on a tricycle sitting in the driveway to their house.

"Daniel?"

Daniel studied Beth as she stood in front of him, a woman who didn't know the reality of a life spiraling down. Never scrambled to feed her kids. Never doubted the safety and security of her children. Never worried about shelter over her head. A fool white woman who sat on what she thought was her throne.

"I heard you." Daniel spat the words, tried to rid himself of the distaste in his mouth. Beth looked startled and Jacob stiffened, focused on Daniel like he saw someone different. In Daniel's mind, they were back to standing in front of the houses, moments before their walk-through.

"'I heard you'—that's your response?" Beth returned to pacing, head down, hand under chin, her brilliant redevelopment scheme to rescue a blighted part of Atlanta gone completely off course. Daniel thought about the price of human experimentation, how people like Beth and the Grants lived their lives protected from the results of their actions. Perfected the alchemy of their success at the expense of others.

Daniel pondered how to answer Beth. Thought about what it meant to live in this world among living, breathing, feeling people, who love and cry and shout and scream, who feel pain and can bleed and get high when they laugh. Who do not live in the fantasies of future things yet to be, because they are frightened of a chaotic present. Who live with passion and intensity and know what it means when fear rests in the pit of the belly—but who must go and do the very things they fear anyway.

"Did you hear me? What are you looking at?" Beth's voice was high and thin, treaded between irritation and hysteria. Jacob shifted in his seat, a smile tugged at the corners of his mouth. The flash of his tongue over his lips sent a jolt through Daniel. He did it again—slowly—scattered Daniel's thoughts in a new and heightened direction.

Daniel didn't respond to Beth. Outside her window, twelve stories below, the small-town scene of Summerhill gave way to downtown Atlanta's office towers. Sleek and modern images, purposefully organized: streets divided into equal lanes, cars motored in neat packs; outdoor gardens and plazas of office buildings adorned and resplendent; people gathered at corners. Atlanta in transformation. But what would happen to those parts still early in gestation, those neighborhoods in the throes of metamorphoses? What would emerge from the chrysalides? Butterflies or moths? Beth shouted her question a third time.

"Why are you shouting, Beth? It's just the three of us." Daniel now recognized Beth for what she was: a coward. The evidence so obvious he was embarrassed his realization took so long. Wrapped so smugly in her trappings of nothing, if Beth lost all of what she had right now, she'd be dead tomorrow. If Mama had been born Beth, she'd be queen of the world right now.

Beth turned red-faced. "I think you need to remember who I am. I *can* fire you—I can fire both of you."

Jacob was smiling now, full and wide, his teeth flashes of glittering white. "That's true, Beth, you could, but then would *you* have a project?" Daniel was thrilled by the confirmation of their unspoken alliance, the proof of his excitement difficult to contain.

Beth cleared her throat, smoothed her hands along her pants, stepped from behind her desk. The late-afternoon sun was not kind—the lines at the corners of her eyes, the wrinkles at the edges of her mouth, the skin under her chin that gathered, sagged, began to pouch. She glanced at the artist's rendering. Sighed. Could she remember the first time—recall what led her here? Or did it no longer matter? When did she realize it was too late to go back? That the tumor of her cowardice had metastasized? Each spineless decision mounted a rationale for the next one and the one after that until . . . in the early morning, still in bed, while she contemplated another day to come, a revelation: she was disfigured. It wasn't one moment or one specific action that led to her discovery; it was the accumulation of them all, the mutation of where she started into what she had become, the history of it lying there in the morning cushioned under the sheets next to the mass of her husband, nestled in the comfort of a home built to exacting specifications to shelter the children and the life and the dreams she had set out so earnestly so many years ago to accomplish. Her disfigurement was a grotesque horror. Surely, she knew the small bubble of the world in which she lived was equally as disfigured, its existence based on the most fragile and crudest ignorance. They all knew at least that, the three of them in her office. And Mama. And Cornelius. And Elsie Grace.

Beth exhaled, swallowed, took a deep breath. "Why don't we focus on what's important here? Collectively think of an alternative to this community-benefits agreement?"

"I have to go to the bathroom."

"Excuse me—"

Daniel headed for the door, his back to Beth, the thrill of his excitement swelling toward Jacob. Hoping he would follow, Daniel paused just long enough to make sure Jacob noticed. Then he was out the door, down the hall, and headed to the bathroom.

|| NINE ||

JACOB

For two weeks Sherman called Jacob, tried to apologize. Jacob picked up the first time before he looked at the caller ID. As soon as Sherman announced himself Jacob hung up, told Rodney he should have asked before giving Sherman his number. Rodney laughed, shook his head, told Jacob to ease up, that Sherman was a good brother. Who was relentless. Undeterred, he had to leave a voicemail; he called a few more times. Jacob even blocked his number. Sherman responded by sending flowers—yellow roses. It was the first time anyone had ever sent Jacob flowers. The card read: *For friendship. Let's meet again for the first time. I swear it'll be better.* Followed by another phone call, this time from a number that read *Unknown Caller*.

"Drove by the site a few times, but I mostly see that other guy. I guess he has more worker-bee status, while you're busy up in the hive." Sherman chuckled a low, friendly rumble. "An apology usually works better in person." Both Sean and Rodney stood at Jacob's bedroom door, listening.

"Thank you for the flowers."

"You're welcome. There is a catch, though."

"I already got the flowers."

"C'mon, be nice, Jay."

"I'm listening."

"Come meet me at my office." Jacob heard him smiling. "Let's talk about those houses you're tearing down."

"I'm not tearing down nothing."

"Okay. Those people you work for, then."

Jacob thought about it. "I can meet you tomorrow morning."

"I look forward to seeing you then." He hung up and Jacob was smiling.

Sherman worked at a one-story, pleasant-looking dark-blue building set back on a corner lot on Boulevard, across the street from Grant Park. Pink, red, and white rosebushes made a colorful barrier separating the lawn from the parking spaces in front. Sherman said the house used to belong to the woman who founded the agency. She left the house to the agency when she passed. It had a shingled pitched roof, a waist-high wooden fence, and lots of windows. A slate stone path circled the house, ending at three steps that led up to a spacious veranda, where two wicker chairs and two wicker love seats were set around a table. Jacob was enchanted; the cozy house nestled amid so much green, and a sitting area that conjured up conversation.

Screams came from behind the house. He followed the path to where a few children played on a swing set in the backyard. Their legs tucked tightly beneath their seats as they hurdled backward toward the ground, they shrieked with glee. They swept past the bottom before rising to the opposite summit of their arc, mouths open, eyes squinting, joyful sounds gurgling from their throats. Then their legs shot straight out and little brown bodies became hard, rigid lines slicing through the air. Over and over, again and again, each scream more breathless, more exhilarating than the last. Two more children played on a slide next to the swings, and Jacob watched as they climbed to the top. All teeth and tongue and tonsils, they screeched on the way down. They did this a few more times until one of them suggested they go at the same time, then one sat behind the other. The pure simplicity of their enjoyment made Jacob smile. This was his introduction to the Fund for Atlanta.

"I was wondering where you went." Jacob startled, turning to see Sherman standing next to him, watching the children.

"Hey. I didn't hear you walk up."

"I know. You were somewhere else." He nodded toward the children. "Thanks for coming. I know this is awkward."

They looked at each other—Sherman's brilliant smile still dazzled, mesmerized Jacob. Sherman looked down at his feet, pushed his glasses back up his nose. Looked at Jacob. Jacob's smile in response was natural. He thought about his parents, searched for the language that would explain this part of himself to them. He wanted to move past one-night stands that started in a club and found him waking up in a strange bed the next morning. He wanted acknowledgment from his parents. He was back in the living room confronting Sherman, felt the shadow of strangeness again—his presence a challenge, a challenge that was hard to ignore.

"Take a ride with me. I want to show you around."

They drove south on Boulevard, turned west at Atlanta Avenue, continued along Grant Park's southern perimeter before they turned north on Cherokee and rode along its western edge. Mammoth Victorians lined the streets, their generous porches lorded over the park like it was their lawn. The houses were as picturesque as a postcard. Fences crafted to complement the style of the houses—sturdy wooden fences with gated arbor entrances; iron fences with intricate historic details, some with posts that soared dramatically upward like spires. Trees wove a verdant canopy over their heads. While moms jogged behind three-wheeled baby carriages, cyclists biked in designated lanes.

Sherman continued north to Georgia Avenue, then turned left and headed west toward Summerhill. Gradually, block by block, the houses, the feel of the streets began to change, and by the time they crossed Grant Terrace, the border between Summerhill and Grant Park, the neighborhood was clearly different. Victorian grandeur regressed into matchbox houses. A few houses were renovated, but it was mostly the original frame houses still standing. Nissans or Toyotas, occasionally a 3 series BMW, sat on the startling white concrete parking pads of the renovated houses, their lawns a brilliant deep green. Elderly Black folks puttered about the yards of those original houses, tended to thick, dense gardens, or talked on weathered porches. Sherman navigated the blocks south of Georgia Avenue, down Martin to Ormond Street, the neighborhood division between Summerhill and Peoplestown, then went west on Ormond toward Capitol Avenue, a feeder street into the capital district that led to downtown Atlanta. On the artist's rendering in Beth's office, Capitol became Hank Aaron Drive, a proper legendary name to go along with the new Olympic stadium. Unlike the distinction between Summerhill and Grant Park, the transition between Summerhill and Peoplestown was unremarkable. They passed through blocks with trees more crooked than straight, their thin, skeletal branches bare limbs etched against the sky. The houses looked as though they needed relief and were in various states of disrepair—not exactly the condemnation of the seven houses slated to be demolished, but definitely on their way.

Once upon a time, before the Atlanta–Fulton County Stadium destroyed the neighborhood, Capitol Avenue was a dignified, august boulevard—stately homes and sturdy, husky trees lined the street, and there were benches for pedestrians. Years of disinvestment and neglect cast the neighborhood into decline, during which Capitol had devolved into a four-lane, two-way street buttressed by worn apartment buildings and single-family houses teetering on the edge of abandonment. The entire area was a whisper of its former beauty—a great Black community that birthed a generation of dynamic leaders who moved heaven and earth, shepherded Atlanta through its most turbulent times. Leaders who dreamed for Atlanta a future of fairness and equity, who toiled under that weighty aspirational burden, the immensity of which Atlanta still carried.

Sherman drove, glanced at Jacob every so often—to gauge his reaction to the scenery. Gripping the steering with his left hand, his arm was an unbroken line to his shoulder. That was new for

Jacob, to be sitting next to a man to whom he was attracted and who was attracted to him and be focused on something other than the immediate mechanics of who was about to do what to whom. There was sturdiness in that, a solid place from which he could talk to his parents about how his life would be different from what they expected. Sherman retraced the route back to Summerhill, pointed out a food pantry that was operated by a local food cooperative in Little Five Points.

"That's where I live," Jacob mentioned.

"I know—remember?"

Embarrassed, Jacob smiled. The pantry held lunch for Summerhill's seniors on Tuesdays and Fridays. When Jacob asked the significance of those days, Sherman explained that a local senior citizen center had Mondays and Thursdays covered. Summerhill First Baptist invited the community to dine with its congregation after Sunday service and fed folks after midweek prayer service on Wednesdays. The cooperative wanted to provide access to at least one meal a day from Sunday to Friday. And on Fridays the cooperative tried to give folks enough food to last through Saturday, then the cycle repeated.

"How many people are fed?"

"It's not earth-shattering—probably fifty altogether. But it's a net to catch people from falling. And mostly because of volunteers and us underfunded not-for-profits working with staff at government officials' offices, a few local foundations, and a lot of big hearts with deep pockets to get something done." Sherman cruised past people sitting on folding chairs haphazardly set up on lawns in front of houses, standing against walls on the shady side of corner stores, occupying patches of dirt under more skinny trees. He honked, waved. Everyone waved back. "This is special." He turned onto a block that Jacob recognized was close to the construction site. A row of newly built, four-story, mixed-use brick buildings appeared. Commercial spaces for neighborhood businesses occupied the ground levels. Restaurants, coffee shops, cafés, or other needs Summerhill residents might have. The upper floors were a mix of live-work spaces for artists and subsidized shared office spaces for entrepreneurs. Jacob and Daniel told Beth this location was a better option for their office instead of twenty minutes away in a downtown office tower. They emphasized that the proximity of Council Member Jackson's district office would help cultivate a more productive relationship. Beth disagreed, said the neighborhood location was the wrong image to present.

Plans for the brick buildings included a job placement office for local residents. A skills-assessment-and-training center. Morehouse Medical School, Georgia State, and Emory partnered on a community health center. The Center for a Progressive Atlanta had agreements from national and local banks to fund a small-business-development center dedicated to assisting entrepreneurs opening businesses in Summerhill or Peoplestown. The center would also have homeownership and financial literacy programs to educate residents.

"It's hard work, Jacob. A lot of slogging through bureaucratic bullshit, and you wouldn't believe how many egomaniacs are attracted to this stuff—lots of folks who want to meet and make decisions but are ghosts when it's time to get dirt under their fingernails. It's a good hustle, though. You put your head down, apply your shoulders, and after a while you peek up and good stuff is happening. I love it. There's about seven of us from these local offices around here who come together to help plot and plan, figure out how to execute. Elsie Grace is a part of it." Sherman paused, waiting for a reaction. "We're supposed to be working under the leadership of the council member's office, but he doesn't always pay attention. That's how your boss got her hands on those houses. Cornelius was supposed to introduce legislation for incentives that encouraged landlords to transfer properties like that to the city in exchange for development breaks in higher-cost areas of Atlanta. Beth made that landlord an offer that caught Cornelius flat on his heels, got him spinning, trying to catch up."

"Will he?"

"Good question. He might need a little inside help. We all might need a little inside help." Sherman hesitated again, glanced over at Jacob once more. "So what does your future look like?"

Jacob listened, turned the question over in his head. He was heartened by everything he saw. The history. All the work being done by all the different partners. He was even flattered by Sherman's attention: The calls. The flowers. The glances. But riding around for what felt like hours made Jacob feel like Sherman wanted to sell him something, or was taking him on an extended guilt trip. He kept hearing his accusation: *You work for those people?* He felt the temperature rising as midday approached. The air conditioner was cranked as high as it could go. The warmth in the car wasn't uncomfortable yet, had only begun to nibble at the edges of patience. The volume of the radio was turned low—Jacob heard snippets of P.M. Dawn's "I'd Die Without You." When they were both quiet, they heard muffled sounds from outside the car, like hearing noises from the other side of a wall. Sherman came to a stop sign, checked both directions before he continued. Jacob thought about the circumstances of their meeting. In junior and senior years of high school he had girlfriends. Tried dating women his freshman year at Morehouse. He did what was expected—went to movies, grabbed a bite, spent hours on the phone talking. And that had led to this.

"All I mean is, you work for these people. You share an apartment with Rodney and Sean. You're single. How long you going to keep all that going?" Sherman turned from driving long enough for his eyes to find Jacob's. They held each other like that for a moment before Sherman turned back to the road. He gripped the top of the steering wheel with his fist, leaned to the right. His right elbow perched on the armrest; his legs gapped wide open, right foot worked the pedals while his left leg rested against the door. His bent knee was just shy of Jacob's view of the driver's-side mirror. There was the indictment again in Sherman's question, like Jacob had either failed to do something or was about to. Jacob wished he'd driven. It would have been much easier to turn around and drop Sherman off. Or tell him to get out. *Now* it was hot and he didn't feel like walking all the way back to Sherman's office. The heat gnawed its way through Jacob's patience.

"Why is my future so important to you?"

"I didn't mean to offend."

"Yes you did. That was exactly your point when we met."

"No, that wasn't my point." More silent stops and starts through a few more blocks. More muffled noises floating through the car.

"Well?"

Sherman started to speak, stopped, then, "I said that to make you think."

Goddammit. Shit. Motherfucker. And out in that heat. "Stop right here." Jacob reached for the door handle.

"What—wait. Jacob? Oh, come on."

Jacob tried to be cool about it, waited for the car to stop before opening the door, moved methodically and placed one foot on the ground. The other foot followed. He checked his breathing, did his best to keep it shallow. Stood up. Squared his shoulders.

"Jacob."

Easily, gently, Jacob closed the door. Walked in the direction of Sherman's office. Sherman was out after him, left the car engine running. Jacob was sweating. He pictured how this might look to anyone watching, him having an argument with a man on a street corner, and they weren't even fucking. Jacob never imagined himself to be that person. Sherman caught up to him, matching him stride for stride.

"I didn't mean that—not the way it sounded."

Sherman grabbed Jacob's hand, pulled him to a stop. As they stood on the sidewalk, facing each other, Jacob had to admit that professorial, goofy-looking brother was handsome: his skin soaked in light and his eyes were twin marbles of onyx. Sherman stared at him, concentrating, sweating. Jacob imagined his fingertips tracing the lines of Sherman's cheekbones, his thumb smoothing each eyebrow. Jacob marveled at what Sherman's face would feel like in the palm of his hand, Sherman's nose rubbing, lips kissing each finger. He remembered them on the couch in his living room. Envisioned a conversation with his parents.

"Jacob. I'm sorry."

"That's your second apology."

They stood there, the sun furiously beaming down. Sherman rolled up his sleeves; he started at the cuffs, folded the material backward in neat little squares, smoothed out the wrinkles as he went, finished each one with a tuck just beneath his elbows. Against the contrast of his light-colored shirt, his forearms were dark, sculpted elegance.

"Why did you call me?"

"Why did you come?"

"Friend of Sean and Rodney. You're cute. I'm curious about what might happen."

"Me too."

Each of them still staring, they stood quietly, still sweating. Sherman's car sat at the curb a few feet away, engine still running.

"Let's go back to my office."

Jacob watched Sherman, still wondered how he arrived at this moment. He shook his arms and legs, like loosening up for a swim meet. Important to get the kinks out, stretch and loosen the muscles, tight and hard not good for competition. The more vigorously he moved, the more profusely he sweated, and Sherman watched him, concerned, asked if he was okay. Jacob hunched his shoulders up and down, wobbled his head from side to side, then front to back, hunched his shoulders again, faster, before he wiggled his arms from his shoulders to his wrists like they were rubber bands. In the heat, Jacob's face became a liquid mask, and Sherman looked more concerned. He asked again if Jacob was okay, said he shouldn't move so much in the heat without water. He stepped closer, grabbed Jacob by the shoulders to keep him from moving, but Jacob was focused on loosening his hips: wiggling from side to side, then the right leg from hip to toe, one long rubber band, flexing his ankle. Then he did the left side. Then he repeated both sides again. When he was finished, he stood there, breathing hard and sweating. But he felt ready. He hoped Sherman had paper towels in his car.

"Okay. Let's go."

TEN

DANIEL

Marty laughed: head back, hands up; his legs shook, voice bounced off the ceiling. The sound was rude, dismissive even, and Daniel and Lilah stared, waited for him to finish. He laughed at what Daniel suggested: that he was Mama's favorite. All the time they spent together, their walks to nowhere, their long talks, *Marty, my-best-boy-Marty*, meant to remind the younger siblings of the firstborn's position. When Lilah agreed, Marty doubled over at the image they presented of Mama and Marty against them. Marty's laughter reminded Daniel of his school years. His schoolmates were openly inquisitive about the differences between him, Lilah, and Marty. News the three of them were siblings prompted curiosity—Lilah and Marty's relationship was obvious, but Daniel's biological connection to them wasn't so evident. He was darker. Not the difference between night and day, more like the variation between vanilla ice cream and butter pecan—similar overall, but the subtleties were distinct enough. Marty's and Lilah's straight, flowing locks versus Daniel's thick, bouncy curls. The deep blue of their eyes compared with his steel-toned light gray. In eighth grade a girl told Daniel he'd make the prettiest babies. A basketball teammate smirked after flashing him in the locker room after practice. Told Daniel to do it back. Wanted to see if Daniel was as curly on the bottom as he was on top, but upon close inspection discovered they were both just nappy.

The summer before his sophomore year of high school, he lost his virginity to a neighbor. She was a junior. Had the prettiest, whitest teeth he'd ever seen, and her skin was reddish brown, especially around the eyes. Like she wore permanent auburn eye shadow. What started out as a summer day with a bunch of kids hanging around shooting the shit, ended up with just him and her late at night behind her house. It was dark and hot and quick. She laughed after they finished—Daniel was leaning over, holding his knees, breathless. He nodded when she asked if it was his first time. She was squatting, taking a piss, said she was too young to get stuck in some nowhere Decatur ghetto, making babies with a pretty-ass, light-skinned nigga. She asked if Marty and Lilah were his cousins, grunted like he made a revelation when he answered that they were his siblings. It was those unvoiced observations that bothered Daniel most, the differences in looks between him and his siblings that people always noticed. At home, those differences were met with silence, or Mama snapped at whoever spoke, delivered with a quick pop to the mouth. "Mind your business." The only one who ever dared talk openly about it was Ray. Some days he looked at Daniel, then muttered to himself. The more he drank the louder he muttered, until he started bad-mouthing Mama.

"You made a fool out of me, Sue." Ray sat in a chair in the living room in front of the TV, talked over his shoulder.

Mama let loose a long, heavy sigh. "Not now, Ray, the kids are here."

"So what?"

Mama heard the slur in Ray's voice and decided to stay quiet. She was in the kitchen, cleaning up after cooking, trying to get ahead of the next day to come.

"How I look with my embarrassment walking around?" Ray turned in the chair so he could talk directly to her. Marty, Lilah, and Daniel were huddled in their back room, doing their best to keep quiet.

"Shut up, Ray."

"You not even shamed about it. Rutting around like you lost good sense."

"Okay—how 'bout you, Ray? Look at me, taking care of a goddammed grown-ass man. You should be the one embarrassed. And I should know better. You goddam right—I lost all the good sense I got." That got Ray to going on about trust and violation of marriage and nature and the ways he should teach Mama and that uppity landlord a lesson. They might live in Atlanta, but it was still the South.

"You a big man, Ray? C'mon with it, then. Get your fat ass out that chair and come teach me a lesson." The siblings held one another as something clattered in the kitchen. The twinkling sound of metal floated through, then came Mama's quick, urgent footsteps.

Ray's grunt of surprise startled them, then he cursed. His chair made a creaking noise as he got up, his heavy footsteps going toward the front door. The door opened; the screen door unlatched, made a whisking sound, then slapped closed. The floorboards groaned as Ray made his way across the tiny porch and down the three steps. Marty, Lilah, and Daniel didn't move until Mama called them for dinner, and it was a few days before Ray came back home.

"If anything, it was Mama against the three of us." Hopscotching her family from one neighborhood to the next, Mama still managed to have her children attend the same schools. Marty was the trailblazer, making his way through Houghton Elementary, then East Atlanta Intermediate, before finally landing at Southside Terminus High. Lilah followed four years later, and by the time Daniel set foot in first grade five years after her, "Milton" was a well-known name. It was a lesson Mama taught the three of them: protect one another. An innocent moment prompted the education, a mother sitting with her children, listening to the happenings of a day at school.

"Ms. Andersen. She's weird." Daniel was talking about his first-grade homeroom teacher. She had first been Marty's fifth-grade social studies teacher, then Lilah's English teacher, four years afterward. Black woman. A year or two younger than Mama. Graduated from Howard or Hampton, Mama could never remember which, but Ms. Andersen was always making noise about it. Mama thought she was full of herself. Their parent-teacher conferences pushed the limits of Mama's patience, the way Ms. Andersen spoke, she always sounded so haughty.

"Marty was so independent. Decent student but a bit willful and high-spirited. Had she ever thought about putting him in sports?" She said that would help him build his maturity, teach him to collaborate with others. *"Col-lab-o-rate—teamwork, you know?"* She recommended two after-school programs; said they had strong role models, good coaches from whatever-that-school-was, great examples to get boys started on the road to life, backup for the kinds of lessons he was certainly getting at home from his father. Always sounded like Ms. Andersen was trying to ask a question, but Mama just nodded, ignoring the inference. All the times they spoke, and she'd never once looked directly at Mama, full in the face, eye to eye, one woman to another.

"What'd she do?" A note in Daniel's voice caught Mama's attention.

Lilah interrupted, flashed her brother a warning. "She didn't do nothing, Mama."

Lilah's interruption meant something had happened that probably required her attention. "Be quiet and let him finish."

Heeding his sister, Daniel tried to backpedal, shrugged with indifference. "She just said something. Probably nothing."

Staring grim-faced at Daniel, Marty joined them in the kitchen, echoing their sister's warning.

"Somebody had better tell me what fucking happened."

Both Daniel and Lilah looked helplessly at Marty.

"I met them at school like we usually do to walk home."

"Yeah?"

"Ms. Andersen had just walked the class out and Daniel walked over to meet us." Marty looked uncomfortable but kept talking. "She noticed the three of us standing together."

Mama waited.

"She walked over to us, asked how we were related. I told her we were siblings."

"And what did she say?"

"She laughed, nodded her head, and said, 'Now it all makes sense.' Then she walked away."

"In front of all those people?"

Marty nodded. "Danny's whole class, some other kids, and a few teachers."

"And what did y'all do?"

"We came home, Mama." Marty's voice sounded heavy, like he was trying to avoid exactly this moment.

"You didn't ask her what she was talking about or laughing at or what suddenly made sense?"

Daniel and Lilah were sitting at the kitchen table, homework finished. Marty was doing his best to stand still, but he fidgeted, withering under the silent rage emanating from Mama. He braced himself as she stepped closer.

"I'm talking to myself now?"

"Mama, what should we have done? What would you have us do?"

Mama thought about it, decided not to slap Marty; he was right, what Ms. Andersen did required her direct involvement. She looked at her children gathered around the kitchen table and nodded; she was sitting in front of the principal later that week.

"Ms. Andersen has been around for a while. She's taught both Marty and Lilah. And now Daniel. That's nine years, Principal Hughes. She was here already when you started?"

Principal Hughes listened to Sue Ellen Milton. He heard

that Ms. Andersen made a scene after school and confronted the three children about their familial relations, then laughed and made an offhanded remark. Apparently, from the looks of things, the youngest had a different father from his siblings. Principal Hughes shook his head—whatever had possessed Ms. Andersen that was any of her business? Probably all that civil rights activism and Black college stuff gone straight to her head—but a good, solid teacher, if at times a bit uppity and unruly.

"She's one of our best, Ms. Milton—"

"*Mrs.* Milton. I'm a married woman."

"Mrs. Milton, yes, excuse me. Ms. Andersen is one of our best teachers. She's been in the classroom for ten years. Yes, she was here when I became principal."

"Seems like she's gotten quite comfortable. I'm concerned she doesn't understand the limits of her position or the times in which we're living."

"I don't understand what you mean."

Sue Ellen had prepared carefully for their meeting. She wore one of her pant suits—deep blue with a cropped jacket that stopped right at her waist. She decided on a prim white-collared shirt that she had starched at the cleaners, just for this meeting. She put on makeup: not heavy, just a light, sure, certain touch, a pleasant professional woman going to check on her children at school. She combed her hair back and away from her face, the shock black of it against her white skin hung loose, flowed down her shoulders. That she was beautiful helped. Looking at herself in the mirror before she left home, Sue Ellen decided she looked like someone she was not used to being. She justified it, in defense of her children.

"That Ms. Andersen always got a nose for other people's business. She says things out of place and out of step for who she is and the times we're living in. I came to you first, hoping not to make a big fuss. An apology should work. And an understanding that something like what she did won't ever happen again."

Sue Ellen thought about the decision she made a lifetime ago. She thought about the things that had brought her to that moment. The simplicity of age-old chemistry between a man and woman set in a modern southern context riddled with taboo. Ralph Reid and Sue Milton impressed each other. He with the confidence she wielded like a weapon, carving out a niche in this life for her and her children, convention be damned. She with his industriousness, taking advantage of a time and place to create even more possibilities for his future. But it was 1970s Atlanta, and neither of them had the constitution or courage to disrupt the social order. They shared a few moments. A mistake happened. She didn't even know where Ralph lived. And Ray forced them to move as soon as he realized she was pregnant. She wasn't going to apologize for the rest of her life. And she wasn't going to allow some grade-school teacher to humiliate her by way of her children. Not when she had the power to remind everyone about the reality in which they all lived.

Principal Hughes wondered just how much of a fuss Sue Ellen was willing to make. Was it embarrassing? Sure, but weren't times changing? A few more years and no one would bat an eye. But if he didn't do a thing and she decided to cause problems . . . Or if Ms. Andersen made another comment that made things worse? And if Sue Ellen decided to kick up a fuss, other parents might ask questions. Then the neighborhood would get involved, and that might bring the superintendent to his office. No. Sue Ellen was right. An apology was in order. Best way to keep things quiet. But maybe he could delay doing anything and the situation would simply go away. He'd have a quick, discreet word with Ms. Andersen, anyway—to keep any future incidents from happening, remind her times haven't changed as much as she thought.

"Okay. I'll schedule a meeting with Ms. Andersen for early next week."

"What's wrong with right now?"

"Right now?"

Sue Ellen nodded. "No time like the present."

"Well, let's see if she's around."

Principal Hughes excused himself. Scratched at the bald spot on his head, then tugged at his comb-over. He relieved himself in the bathroom on the way to Ms. Andersen's classroom. He hoped she wouldn't be trouble.

Ms. Andersen was as surprised to see Sue Ellen Milton sitting in the principal's office as she had been with Principal Hughes showing up at her classroom, right as she'd started to organize herself for the next day. She passed by Daniel and his siblings in the reception area outside Principal Hughes's office, but didn't give them much thought. Principal Hughes waved for her to sit down.

"Ms. Andersen. Thank you for coming."

She wore dark tailored slacks that flared at the bottom, cuffs hovered just above tan-colored loafers. A red, fitted, short-sleeved mock turtleneck, gold hoop earrings, her Afro tied back with a deep-green scarf, the ends trailing down her back—the silhouette Ms. Andersen presented was of a sophisticated, modern woman of the time. Her look contrasted distinctly with Sue Ellen's regal, rigid, conservative dispatchment.

"Not a problem." She took a seat, nodded to Sue Ellen. "Ms. Milton."

"*Mrs.*"

"Excuse me?"

"Indeed. *Mrs.* Milton. I'm married."

"Okay." Ms. Andersen looked at Principal Hughes. "Principal Hughes, what's this about?"

"This is what I'm talking about, Principal Hughes. So disrespectful. She won't even address me correctly."

Ms. Andersen started to respond, but Principal Hughes stopped her by holding up his hand. "There's a question about something that happened between you and the Milton children, Ms. Andersen."

Sue Ellen waited for Ms. Andersen to understand she'd been summoned to a reckoning. Sue Ellen was tired of losing the fights she'd waged for the little space she occupied in the world. It was time for someone else to feel trapped.

"I don't understand what's happening here." The woman Ms. Andersen was used to, who came only to parent-teacher conferences, if she came to the school at all, was different from this Sue Ellen Milton. She would arrive after work, usually looking exhausted, and fidget, anxious for the meeting to be over. The woman seated next to her now was different. She wasn't there to hear the latest updates about the progress of her children in social studies or English. The woman next to Ms. Andersen sat with the air of a different, loftier composition. She hadn't even bothered to return the greeting Ms. Andersen offered.

"You have questions about my family?"

"Not really."

Sue Ellen raised her voice: "Daniel!"

He came to the door. "Yes?"

"Come in here and tell us what happened between all of you and Ms. Andersen."

They listened as Daniel spoke, his small voice cracking at times, causing him to clear his throat. He recounted Ms. Andersen's approach, a finger leveled at him and his siblings as though they'd done something wrong instead of just getting ready to walk home. And it wasn't just her laughter after Marty answered her question; it was the way she waved her hand and shook her head. Like the three of them had made some kind of mistake.

"Made me feel weird," Daniel finished.

"You have anything to add, Ms. Andersen?" Principal Hughes nodded.

She stared incredulously from Daniel, then to Sue Ellen, and finally to Principal Hughes. "Yes, Principal Hughes. I can't believe you have me in here like this."

Principal Hughes started to talk, but Sue Ellen cut him off. "He didn't have a choice." This was the third time Sue Ellen had been in the principal's office. The other two times were when Marty and Lilah started school. She never paid it much attention before—the way it was decorated, the desk that dominated the room, the height of the chairs in front of it as compared with the principal's desk, how the chairs were so low and the principal sat so much higher. The sofa along the wall was the same height as the chairs. She stood up, walked behind the principal's desk, and stood next to his chair. The ceiling was low and the light fixture was large, occupied most of the headspace over the chairs and sofa. From her vantage point behind the desk, Sue Ellen realized a person had an instinctive impulse to shrink a bit when entering the office to avoid hitting the light fixture. But from where Sue Ellen stood, she saw there was more than enough room to stand up straight anywhere in the office. Principal Hughes and Ms. Andersen watched Sue Ellen as she observed the office. Facing the school grounds and parking lot outside the window, she turned her back to them. Life roamed beyond them in that office—wild, reckless, unpredictably wonderful, and unexpected. Life, large and sweeping, filled with gasps of intensity and excitement. It wasn't the doldrums trapped where she was—the pettiness, the small minds occupied with little thoughts, obsessed with the infinitesimally unimportant nuances of existence. Sue Ellen knew she didn't look her usual self—the pants suit, her hair out, the formality so different, so commanding. She didn't return to her seat; standing, she felt larger than what the room allowed.

"Mrs. Milton, are you okay?"

"I'm fine, Principal Hughes. Just waiting for my apology— me and my children." Turning back toward the room, she called for Marty and Lilah to join Daniel.

Ms. Andersen was on her feet. *"What?"*

Principal Hughes was on his feet too. "It's okay, Ms. Andersen, let's just think this through. An apology will avoid unnecessary headaches with the PTA and the neighborhood and the district office. Also best way to avoid any ultimate actions I might be forced to take. It really is just a small thing, considering."

"Considering what?"

"Considering what you started." Sue Ellen shot back.

"What I started?"

"Yes." It was savage, the iciness with which Sue Ellen considered Ms. Andersen. She thought, *This is the pecking order of a barbaric world and Ms. Andersen is at the lowest rung on the ladder.* Nothing could save her from the brutality Sue Ellen wielded like a cudgel. Ms. Andersen was surrounded—by the room, by the principal, by Sue Ellen and her children, by the time and place in which they lived. If Sue Ellen was going to be reminded about Ralph Reid, she'd remind all of them what it meant that they still lived in the South. She smoothed her hair behind each ear, straightened her jacket, made sure her pants fell flat. She tidied each one of her children, arranged them in order standing next to her—Marty, Lilah, then Daniel. Principal Hughes sat down, and everyone watched Ms. Andersen. Waited.

ELEVEN

JACOB

Their tour around Summerhill was the spark that ignited Jacob and Sherman to start over. They decided on a proper first date, settled on meeting at a soul food place in East Point called the Family Table. Jacob was anxious about their appearance, wondered if they looked like two men out on a date or just two friends catching up. And there was also their interaction once they returned to Sherman's office, the way his silent confidence challenged Jacob.

"Where you at?"

Sherman's voice brought him back to the restaurant.

"Figuring out how heavy your wallet is." Jacob looked over the menu.

"Oh, I'm paying?" He reached across the table for Jacob's hand. "So you putting out?"

A couple sat at a table to their left. The guy's limbs stretched everywhere—legs extended across the floor between his chair and hers, his elbows and forearms rested on the table, hands grabbed the salt and pepper shakers before he rearranged the little packets of sweeteners into neat bundles of pinks and blues and whites. She was his opposite, told him to put his feet under his own chair, to remove his elbows and forearms from the table, brushed his hands away from the salt and pepper shakers and the packets of sweeteners. She noticed Sherman reach for Jacob's hand, which reminded Jacob they were in public. Jacob withdrew from his touch, burrowed down in the menu as Sherman looked from him to her.

Back at Sherman's office, the little blue house was just as picturesque as when they'd left. But the swings and slides were empty, the missing children a noticeable absence. Jacob asked about the missing children.

"You like kids?"

Before Jacob could answer, one of the little boys from the slide appeared, screamed Sherman's name as he ran full throttle through the gate. Sherman bent and the little boy hurtled into his arms. He was a blur of movement, wiggled and laughed and held on as Sherman scooped him up.

"Auggie, where did you come from? You know you're not supposed to come out the gate."

The little boy's smile immediately became a frown. He pointed to where he and the other children were having lunch on the covered back porch. "But I saw you and I wanted to say hi."

"Hello." Sherman smiled back, and Auggie's face brightened. "Where is Miss Toni?"

"Over there." He pointed again. A woman hurried in their direction, held out her hand toward the little boy.

"He moves so quickly. And he's figured out the latch on the gate."

Sherman nodded, lowered Auggie back to the ground. The sight of them together was intoxicating, smiling brown man and smiling brown boy, each of them so obviously in love. Jacob wondered what he'd look like in that picture.

"Bye-bye, Auggie. Now be a good boy and stay inside the gate." To Miss Toni, "I'll see about a more complicated latch." Back to Jacob. "So—kids?"

He squinted, looked at Sherman. "I like them fine."

"You want some one day?"

———

Jacob hadn't known how to answer that question, just like he didn't know how to react when Sherman reached for his hand. He pulled away instinctively. Wondered what Sherman knew that he didn't. The shame of withdrawing his hand hot on his face, he read the menu, his focus not in the restaurant at that table. He heard a mantra from his parents:

Here is Love.
This is Family.
There is Education.
That is what Responsibility looks like.

Here is Manhood.
This is Blackness.
There is Community.
That is where You get your start.

Here is Woman.
This is Marriage.
There are Children.
That is our Expectation.

———————

Standing in front of the little blue house, Jacob fantasized over the image of him and Sherman together. Should they walk up the steps holding hands? Should they stand on the veranda, turn to wave to their neighbors and the world? Which one of them would carry the other across the threshold? Would that be the beginning of their future? And for how long and what would that look like—a Black male couple in the future together? Jacob had no idea how that happened. He had no idea how to get to where Sherman was. He saw his mother. He saw his father. He saw Rodney. He saw Sean. And there he was. They walked past the receptionist and into the calm beige color of Sherman's office, their feet firmly planted on the ground.

"It was just a question, about kids. Only trying to make a little conversation."

"Is that true? About just making conversation?"

"Sure." Sherman shrugged but his eyes didn't meet Jacob's and his voice went up slightly, and it occurred to Jacob that— controversial project aside—Sherman might also be anxious with the newness of their meeting. He recognized it in those moments they looked away from each other instead of staring one another full in the face, deadly serious: *this* was about the future. It was the youthfulness they were robbed of, the silly crushes and daydreams and the ache of puppy love, cheated as they were, learning too early, *this* was wrong. The grade-school kisses stolen. The passage of secret notes, the trading of shy whispers that were supposed to happen years ago, dismissed. The excitement of liking someone—the butterflies in the stomach, the heady lightness, the wonder of being liked in return—murdered. It was a revelation that *him liking him* wasn't supposed to happen, the thrill and innocence slowly subsumed by fear. The giddiness and delight of new love contorted into horror and shame at the mere thought. And then they arrived as adults. They *should* be equipped with all manner of innocent tinkering, experiences, mistakes large and small. They *should* be prepared to engage in the work of relationships. But they were caught in the rush of trying to learn so much in such a hurry.

"Jacob."

He heard his name through the fog of his thoughts. Their waiter had arrived with glasses of water, asked if they were ready to order.

"So, what's good here?"

"Everything is terrific."

"I can come back in a few minutes."

"No, no, I'm ready. Pancakes and bacon."

Through the huge picture window that fronted their table,

they watched cars pass by. The neighborhood's East Point location was like Grant Park, just a little less showy. Instead of grand Victorians sitting on obsessively manicured lawns, mature trees lined streets with modest ranch houses. Gardens featured trimmed, tidy hedges, grass so green it made feet ache with the invitation to walk on it. Explosions of roses the size of fists and begonias in the most brilliant colors. When they decided on the Family Table, Jacob thought about the Black gay couples he knew lived in the area. Seeing Sean and Rodney every day, he understood the theory of relationships, but sitting with Sherman in the restaurant, he was uncertain of how to actually get one started.

"How this works is I think we're supposed to talk to each other." Sherman *was* nervous. His anxiety made him more attractive; his insecurity more tangible to Jacob, who wondered if Sherman had really uncoupled himself from the expectations of the world. He behaved as though stares and whispers didn't matter. Jacob wanted to know what kinds of conversations Sherman had with his parents. It was hard, the process of molding, building, creating a new self with no idea of how or where or with whom to begin, or the kind of result to expect.

Jacob picked up his water, took a long swallow. "How many relationships have you had?" He hoped Sherman heard him stretching, reaching for a certain direction.

"One. Started senior year. He followed me here after we graduated. Stayed together two years and then that was it. That was a year ago." Again, he avoided eye contact, stared at the table instead, played with his fork as he talked. Once finished, he shrugged, then looked away, and his eyes darted around the restaurant—paused to study the people closest to them; in a glance he surveyed the people waiting for tables, then his eyes were moving again: the ceiling; the floor; the clock on the wall. Finally, back to his fingers and the fork and the table. He'd gone back to being a little boy— just like Auggie—running, screaming, reaching, searching, grasping. Jacob considered that: as grown as they thought they were, as independent, as confident, as smart, and as focused on the future, each of them—Sherman, Jacob, maybe even Daniel—was Auggie.

There is this boy.
Small.
Dark.
Floating. . .

That's when Jacob acknowledged he was infatuated with Sherman. That fact was as certain as the folder Sherman had handed him in his office. It told the story of a coffee-colored woman and her children, one a little girl, the other a little boy. There were pictures: See the mother. See the daughter. See the son. A family. See the mother in a neat black dress sprinkled with tiny white polka dots, a matching jacket, white blouse underneath, a bow smartly tied at her neck. See the daughter with two pigtails in her hair, each one resting on a shoulder. Dressed in a butter-colored dress with small lace ticking around the openings for her arms and legs. A pink belt curled around her waist, and on her feet patent-leather Mary Janes over white ankle socks. She looked to be about nine. See the son in a white, short-sleeved collared shirt, dark jeans, and a pair of white sneakers. His hair freshly cut and shaped into a short Afro. His smile still the same as when Jacob had seen him wiggling and laughing in Sherman's arms. Sherman told him this was Auggie and his family standing outside what they thought was going to be their new home. A tiny house with a front porch and a backyard standing in a row with six others. The Fund for Atlanta negotiated to lease the property. It cost the owner nothing—the Fund partnered with the city and private funders to finance the cost of renovations. The owner retained ownership of the property, but the Fund held a ten-year lease. The Fund even arranged for the owner to receive market-rate rent.

And while the Fund finalized details, Auggie's family waited. They dreamed dreams of a new house in which they were safe and protected. Instead of a chair propped under the doorknob, they imagined a door locked with a dead bolt. They made themselves silly thinking about rooms painted different colors. They thought about having hot water every morning and heat in the winter. But tiny shotgun dreams couldn't compete with Atlanta's Olympic aspirations.

The day the dumpsters had arrived, Jacob supervised the clean out of the houses. He took notice of the things left behind from someone else's life: a couch (maybe too big to take to the next place?); a ball that rolled out from under it (did it belong to a child?); markings on a wall that tracked a child's growth (how old?). Beth was triumphant the day she acquired those houses: *Here is where this neighborhood starts, a new and better beginning.*

Sherman's office spun as Jacob closed that folder. It was the same dizzying effect Jacob now experienced listening to Sherman talk about his relationship. Silence settled at the table. Noises of the restaurant intruded on their quiet.

"Tough subject, huh?"

"Here I am." Sherman shrugged. "What about you?"

Jacob shook his head. "Never had a relationship."

"Who's that cute yellow dude you work with?"

"Who—Daniel?"

"I guess. I see you standing out there with him when I drive by the site sometimes."

Jacob tried to hold his face still so he didn't reveal too much by smiling. "You stalking me, Sherman?"

"Maybe." Now he looked directly at Jacob. "Just kidding. But the way y'all check each other out has me wondering."

Jacob shrugged. He and Daniel were still getting to know each other. At most, Daniel was a pretty-boy distraction at work. "Daniel and I just work together. It's intense—all this redevelopment stuff. Lots of anxiety and lots of emotions in addition to all the work. That's probably what you're seeing watching us. I don't even know if he gets down like that." That was a lie. Jacob saw very clearly what Daniel showed him while they were in Beth's office.

Another moment, then, "You interested in having one—a relationship?"

"Isn't everyone?"

"Are they?" Sherman shifted in his chair. "The evidence suggests something different." Just beneath their conversation, Jacob felt another one lurking. It murmured that Black men were never supposed to reveal themselves. Their hurt places always unclaimed, always undiscovered. Their passions always to be deafeningly boisterous. It was an unvoiced masculinity code. Jacob heard it from his father all the time. He heard it when he talked to his brother. It roamed the streets that he walked. It haunted his friendships. It ran rampant in places most familiar—at barbershops and on playgrounds and in locker rooms. Things between Black men that were known but not spoken—a collective resistance to translate into audible language the things they felt or loved or what scared them. Jacob felt it between him and Sherman, was certain Sherman felt it too. But they lacked either the experience or courage to interrupt it.

Their food arrived, and eating was a welcome diversion. Finished, the couple to the left prepared to leave. He pulled out her chair, scooped up her scarf when it fell. She smiled thank-you, blew him a kiss. It was quick, the way they held each other, his chest to her back; she cradled his hands to her breast, his chin rested on the crown of her head. For just a second, their eyes closed, and when they opened them, Jacob's eyes met theirs. They gave a nod, smiled, then quickly left.

"Have you told your parents?"

Jacob shook his head. "And you?"

"They figured it out. The breakup with my ex was kind of a mess, and I was a mess afterward."

"What did they say?"

"We have our moments."

"What does that mean?"

"My family being in the mortuary business in a place like Birmingham, my parents get to see a lot. We saw families who lived in silence with their secrets. Kids grown and moved away—maybe they ran away—and lost touch with the family. Eventually the kids came back—with broken spirits, wounded bodies, and their parents didn't recognize their own children. And the kids didn't talk to them about the lives they'd lived. Quick trip from there to the grave.

"Or their kids would simply disappear after they left home. Never to be heard from or seen by their parents again. The parents would end up in a hospital room or some nursing home, waiting to die. Alone. They'd get so angry, trying to figure out what happened. Trying to figure out how a child could just abandon a parent—how their child could just abandon them. Everyone would call the child ungrateful, selfish, arrogant. After all the sacrifices their parents made—to just walk away and disappear. Then once their parents were dead and cold, here comes the kid at the funeral with some lover in tow. All hell would really break loose. *How disrespectful. Disgusting sinner. Good thing so-and-so is already dead because this would've certainly killed them.* So when my parents finally forced me to tell them, they weren't thrilled with the news, but they said they'd rather know instead of having to bury me or risk never seeing me again. And they'd rather I'd not waste time trying to live a lie. Whether it gets talked about or not, eventually everyone finds out, one way or another."

His pancakes finished, Jacob stared at Sherman, imagined how that conversation might go with his parents:

Dad, I like men.

What's that? Speak up—I can't understand what you're saying.

He'd try a second time, a little louder, his voice deeper, staring steadily at his father without blinking. *I like men, Dad. I'm gay. Can you understand what I'm saying?*

His father would look at Jacob like he spoke a different language. *Speak to your mother—I have no idea what you're saying.*

But when Jacob would say the same thing to his mother, she

would give him a look that translated as, *Oh.* Then she would go back to whatever she was doing—reading a book, flipping through a magazine, or she'd disappear into the kitchen.

"You realize you do that a lot?"

"Do what?" Jacob held Sherman's stare, then looked away.

"Withdraw."

It wasn't a complaint, just a statement of fact. Sherman was reaching for a future, asking Jacob—pleading with him, really—to reach with him, was trying to show Jacob they could be the beginning of something.

"You make me think, Jacob." Jacob heard Sherman searching for the language to make the unvoiced masculinity code audible. Trying to break through to the conversation that lurked just beneath their discussion. Break through those loud, boisterous places, the barbershops and playgrounds and locker rooms. Break through to the soft protected places that were quiet, to the places where Black men heard each other in their silence and knew that, despite everything they'd been told, they were worth fighting for their survival.

"Oh really—about what?"

"Come on, man, I'm trying. At least you can help me out. There's two of us sitting here, and I know I can't be the only one shaking in his shoes."

The world moved around them—a new couple sat at the table to their left, but Jacob didn't pay them any attention. Jacob wondered what would happen if Sherman reached for his hand again. Or if he dared reach for Sherman's. Made him think about the seconds, minutes, and hours, the days and weeks and months; the years—at the end of the long decades of them—when he'd look around and ask what this was all for. And with whom did he share it?

Sherman said something again, was waiting for Jacob to answer. He just shook his head and sighed when Jacob asked him to repeat himself. Jacob didn't know why it was so difficult for him to say, *Sherman, I think we want the same things. I just don't know how it works. I don't know how to get started. Can we show each other?* Those words were trapped, stuck under layers of who he thought he was supposed to be. He hadn't figured out the right code or sequences of experiences to release himself to new possibilities. The check arrived, and they paid separately.

They were standing next to Jacob's car when Sherman asked about Auggie. He stiffened up, faced forward, became suddenly distant. Maybe their date wasn't what he expected, so he'd better check to make sure they were clear about the main objective. Maybe his primary goal all along had been to make sure Jacob helped him with Auggie. After the last few hours that they'd spent together, Sherman waiting to ask Jacob about Auggie at the end of their date felt like he was trying to get something done in a hurry. Jacob remembered the hard places that were the history of their experiences—the barbershops and playgrounds and locker rooms. Much easier to remember those places than recall all the emotions he just experienced at brunch. He felt tricked. His groin tightened. The pit of his stomach hardened as he sized Sherman up. Sherman was two inches taller, heavier, and had spent more time in the gym. Maybe Jacob could get in a few good blows before Sherman pummeled him to the ground.

"We didn't have to go through all this for you to get an answer to that question."

They stood in the narrow space between two cars. There was barely enough room to open a car door, much less for two people to fight. His back pressed against his car, Jacob was already at a disadvantage.

"Is that what you think of me?" Sherman spoke each word in a measured, even tone, their noses almost touching. "Is that really what you think of yourself?" Sherman's voice was a slow, hot knife cutting in places Jacob hadn't felt. He looked down, fought hard to keep his breathing even, tried to control the rapid-fire pace of his blinking. Sherman pinned him against the car with a kiss. He didn't hesitate, was steady and focused, as his hands tilted Jacob's head at an angle. Jacob was tense at first; he'd never been kissed like that before—a blooming, opening invitation—and the thickness of Sherman's erection against his leg was exciting. As their kiss lingered, Jacob's responding hardness was Sherman's encouragement. And at that moment, if anyone in the world— Jacob's mother or father or any random stranger—said anything at all about the two of them coupled together in the open air of a parking lot under the brightness of the sun and the startlingly blue sky, Jacob didn't hear them for the thundering sound of his heartbeat.

HOPE

TWELVE

JACOB

Jacob and Daniel went driving. Daniel wanted to show Jacob a different Atlanta. Said there were entire universes beyond southwest Atlanta and Buckhead and the neighborhoods Sherman showed him. That there were places in Atlanta just as plain and undiscovered as anywhere else in America. They headed south, past East Point, past College Park and beyond Fulton County into Riverdale, then into Jonesboro and the outer edges of Clayton County. They started out with the windows up and the air conditioner blasting. In blurs of tree-green and white concrete and the dashed line dividing lane from lane endlessly stretching behind them, the highway whizzed by. Kris Kross's "Jump" pumped on the radio. Jacob held the steering wheel so tightly he could feel the road underneath the tires. He pressed hard on the gas and the engine revved, sent cooler air through the vents. Daniel said he could tell Jacob liked driving. Jacob smiled. Seventy. Seventy-five. Eighty. Daniel slid down in his seat, leaned back, and closed his eyes. Thick black lashes against buttery-yellow smoothness. Loose-fitting T-shirt, denim stretched around his thighs, curved against his crotch, his knees propped up against the glove compartment. He looked easy, less like a conflicted person searching for something he'd lost. Pretty and riding and making Jacob think too much about what he had seen in Beth's office. Jacob hadn't had sex in three months. Daniel opened his eyes, saw Jacob watching him, smiled, nodded, leaned back, and closed his eyes again. Jacob's groin pulsed.

"Jump" changed to En Vogue's "Hold On," bass beats pounding, trumpets blaring, their lyricism weaving through the air. Jacob cranked the volume higher, pressed even harder on the gas. They surged forward. The little starter car was a graduation gift from his parents: a Chevy Cavalier Coupe, white, four-cylinder automatic with crank windows. The air conditioner and a cassette stereo system were the only extras his father had agreed to. Jacob said that, not intending to start a conversation, was really thinking out loud, comparing his awkward date with Sherman to how comfortable he felt with Daniel. But when Daniel responded, it sounded like the man wanted to talk, so Jacob turned down the volume of the radio. Daniel said he didn't know his father, that his mother was basically a single parent. He finished a few semesters at Atlanta Metropolitan Community College; maybe one day he'd think about going back. He opened his eyes, watched quietly as Jacob drove. After a few seconds Daniel closed his eyes again, tilted his head back and swallowed. His Adam's apple moved up and down. Jacob's dick stopped pulsing and started to swell.

They rode like that for a while, the engine humming, the music a murmuring undercurrent, the wind rushing past the windows. Jacob thought about summer vacations at his grandmother's. When he explored the remains of abandoned houses with his cousins as they trekked to the community pool. Where the landscape was startling to his city-raised, concrete-bound vision: pinkish-white dogwood blossoms were dramatic flashes against a backdrop of green; clusters of purple flowers with yellow bursting at their centers; the haze of heat so thick, pine trees towering so high, urban Atlanta could've been a thousand miles away.

South of Stockbridge, they turned off the highway, drove past ordinary, split-level and ranch-style houses that sat on huge, grassy, unmanicured lawns. They continued east, hit Covington, then traveled northwest to Conyers. Cars and station wagons and minivans sat on concrete parking pads. More trees and grass and even brighter flowers. Children rode bikes and adults sat on porches. Daniel sat up and started talking, said he and his sister drove around there all the time. "To escape from the city. To look at how we should be living." The landscape became even lovelier in the language lilting over Daniel's tongue. He spoke in pure love. His tone reminded Jacob of Sherman and Auggie—a love that you could see, imagine the comfort of its touch. Daniel's voice became a song, trilled high as they rode through the neighborhoods where he and his sister dreamed of living. He pointed out the details of his favorite houses: an oversized bay window fronting a sloping lawn; another house set far back on a fenced-in corner lot; a third with so much land between it and its neighbor, Daniel mused what it would be like to have so much privacy, "... a sanctuary in which to escape and not be crammed one person on top of the next, bunches of lives all jammed together, experiences indistinct from one another. Must be nice not to hear people fight and fuck." Jacob interrupted TLC's proud begging mid-lyric, turned the music off completely, and listened to Daniel's narration; imagined the resonance of his southern accent mimicked in the voices of the people they saw. The way Daniel spoke made Jacob listen more closely. It was the artist's rendering in Beth's office come to life, except the real-life version was better. The different people, different rhythms. Daniel showed him the cadence of their living, the sounds and tempo of their movements. Jacob wanted to pull over, close his eyes so he could absorb every word Daniel said. He was becoming less the stranger Jacob worked with and more like someone he wouldn't mind knowing. Listening to Daniel, Jacob felt like he was in a hallucination. What Daniel showed Jacob wasn't so different from how Jacob grew up in Brooklyn. Different skin tones, maybe, a different region of the country, warmer even, with a few different customs. But similar motivations, similar dreams, people living similar situations. Listening to Daniel made Jacob think of Sherman. Made him think about the different possibilities of living.

As the sun moved west, they made their way back toward the city. There was more Daniel wanted to show Jacob. Yes, places different from Summerhill and southwest Atlanta and Buckhead, but different still from where they had just been. Places that fell under the shadow of Atlanta with her skyscrapers and dreams of equality for everyone everywhere. *The City Too Busy to Hate.* Daniel showed Jacob the fallacy of that motto, showed him what the lure and beauty of the South—the pace and poetry of it—beat down, rolled over, and suppressed: the trash, the grit, the abandoned buildings, the homelessness, the way the outer beauty distracted the eye, covered up, and made that kind of ugliness disappear. Daniel was familiar with it, knew how it had been moved away from downtown aspirations for the Olympics and pushed to the outer edges of the city's limits and beyond. Where skyscrapers and the gloss of glass and the hardness of concrete of the new South became barren open spaces, roads with no sidewalks, just fields of grass, up-stretched trees, and things of the old South that weren't hard to imagine. Like rednecks with rifles hung upside down in the back windows of pickup trucks and Confederate-flag stickers stuck to their bumpers. Where a northerner didn't have to witness a trailer park on television, didn't have to wonder about the circumstances of people who lived with wheels attached to their houses, because it was there: barefoot, pale-skinned, straight-haired children wearing diapers or once-white T-shirts and cut-offs darted from trailer to trailer or played around disabled cars perched up on blocks. Adults—women, mostly—sat on rickety lawn chairs, smoked, and talked, their language not the laughter of sunshine and flowers and wide-open green spaces, but the gutturals of vulgarities, flipping the bird at Daniel and Jacob as they rode by in Jacob's little white car, staring at them like spectators on a safari.

Jacob never noticed when Daniel stopped talking. They continued riding and it just seemed like his voice was a constant sound until Jacob realized somewhere between the open spaces of suburbia and the no-man's-land populated by trailer after trailer, Daniel's voice had stopped. But the scenery rushed in to fill the silence: the trailers had turned into shotgun houses, and the cars perched on blocks had become abandoned rusted bulks, and instead of being white, the dirty children playing, the women sitting and talking and smoking and flipping the bird at them were mostly Black. When Jacob said he was lost, Daniel responded that they were in an obscure southeast corner of DeKalb County, about an hour away from downtown Atlanta. He directed Jacob through a few more turns, then told him to park on a block that was empty save for towering weeds in tree-filled lots and the husks of decaying houses.

"So. Auggie?"

Jacob had given Daniel Sherman's folder. Daniel studied it, asked how the two met and what prompted Sherman to ask for Jacob's help. Jacob was unprepared for Daniel's questions, stumbled through an explanation connecting Sherman to Cornelius to Elsie Grace. He explained this was something different from the community-benefits agreement. Something better. Daniel asked why Jacob hadn't mentioned Sherman earlier. He heard Daniel thinking through the gaps in his story.

"This is a maybe. Of course we can't show this to Beth."

Jacob nodded agreement. "This is for Cornelius. Cornelius saves the day from the big bad developer. Gets a new house for Auggie and his family." What Jacob didn't say was that helping Auggie might save them, too, that this was part of his life reorganization plan. It could save them from all those faces that had stared from behind those barricades the morning of the riot. From the artist's rendering of that faux neighborhood sitting on Beth's desk. From the plaguing, bothersome, nagging tugging at their souls.

"Cornelius gets to save the day. What do we get?"

"I don't know. Another job? You know we aren't going to last here."

"Been thinking about that. I don't think Beth is going to get this project."

"Cornelius is going to figure out how to take it."

"And even if he doesn't, if that vote passes and she gets control, she'll fire us just because."

Jacob didn't disagree with Daniel. They drove around Summerhill. Jacob pointed out Sherman's office, showed Daniel all the places Sherman had shown him. By the time they finished, Jacob had a good feeling. They'd formed an alliance to help Auggie and his family, which, in turn, would benefit Sherman, Cornelius, and Elsie Grace, and the sum of that would rescue the two of them.

Beyond the window, emerging moonlight danced through the weeds on Daniel's side of the car. There was still enough light for Jacob to notice that the usually sharp cut of Daniel's fade was a light covering of curls. His goatee needed to be trimmed.

"So that maybe is a yes?"

Across from where they parked, Daniel motioned to the remains of a house. "I used to live in that house. Me, my sister, my brother, my mother, and her husband—my sister and brother's father. There used to be a whole bunch of those little houses up and down this street. Look at it now."

The house was about twenty feet wide, about the length of a car and a half. The frame of a single front window remained, the light pouring through the roof illuminating a crumbling interior. Jacob could see to the back of the house, about fifty feet from the front window. He imagined more of those same houses on both sides of the street, imagined children playing in what once must have been a decently paved road. No yards, no driveways, no fanciful places for kids to escape. Daniel's house and a few others had porches, if they were that: four-by-six-foot spaces where chairs may have sat, a table for people to talk over a cold drink. A neighbor may have stopped by to share a bit of news. But those porches didn't look like places to linger. So what happened? It seemed like progress collapsed, turned upside down, and went backward. There was one streetlamp shining mid-block, and beyond that, one or two houses with what looked to be signs of life. A fire hydrant sat a few yards from where they parked. Dirt festered through fissures in the worn tarmac. On the other side of Daniel's window, an awful racket of bugs erupted in the weeds like a chorus of rattles. Daniel said they were katydids.

Daniel watched Jacob silently surveying the place he had lived. "Yeah. If we don't help Auggie, anything can happen."

"So, it's decided, then? We're together in this?"

"Yeah. Might as well do something good before getting out of there—or at least try." Silence again. Longer this time. "So tell me about you and this dude Sherman."

"Nothing to tell. Just another activist giving us a headache." Jacob checked his breathing, kept his voice even. In the close space of the car, he avoided Daniel's eyes. He ignored the vision of Daniel's package he had seen in Beth's office, reminded himself that they worked together. Jacob slid his seat back a few notches.

Daniel smiled—smirked?—moved closer. "So why am I just hearing about him now?"

"No reason." Despite his concentration, Jacob's voice caught. He coughed to clear his throat.

"You keeping secrets." Daniel poked him playfully, and Jacob jumped.

"What do you mean?"

"I mean I've been pouring my heart out to you—giving you my guts, showing you pieces of my life, telling you my dreams, showing you this place—and you haven't shared nothing."

"I've been listening."

Daniel's face was a brazen look of wild-eyed want. He leaned close to Jacob, licked his lips, and Jacob's dick throbbed in response. Daniel was too pretty and too distracting, and it was too warm in the tight space of Jacob's little car. It was time to go. Jacob reached to start the ignition, but Daniel stopped him, pushed him against the seat, kissed him hard instead. Daniel's kiss was desperate. A kiss that said afterward, they'd each go their separate ways. A searching kiss, grabbing but not knowing for what. It was a finite kiss with a limited emotional scope. Jacob was as familiar with Daniel's kiss as he was unfamiliar with Sherman's. Jacob knew that wasn't what he wanted, but he let Daniel finish. His breath was hot in Jacob's ear, teeth on his neck, then he started undoing his pants.

"No." Jacob pushed him off and sat up.

Daniel's buckle was undone, zipper down, the outline of his erection starting to wear at Jacob's resistance.

"What? Nobody out here to see us."

"I didn't know you were gay."

"Who cares what the fuck I am?"

"No." Jacob heard the question, realized Daniel was a stranger to himself. That's not what he wanted.

"I see the way you look at me. You want this as much as I do."

"No I don't."

Daniel sighed a long, labored breath, did his best to arrange himself back in his pants. "So you one of them romantic-type motherfuckers. You need a meal first? Some clean white sheets under your back?"

"Fuck you, Daniel."

"Yeah, that's exactly what I was planning to do."

"That's not going to happen."

Daniel looked at him. "We been driving around all day. You just let me put my tongue all down your throat and we both sitting here with hard dicks and now you're telling me no?"

Jacob shrugged. "Don't you ever want more?"

"I know this is what I want right now."

Jacob started the car. "Sorry, I can't help you."

"Yeah, I got that." He reached for the door.

"Where you going?"

"I grew up around here. You think I don't know how to take care of this?"

"I don't know how to get back."

"You should have thought about that before playing hard to get."

"Are you fucking serious?" But Daniel started laughing before Jacob finished.

"Calm down. I wouldn't do that—things would be too awkward at work. Make a left at the corner and keep straight. You'll start seeing signs for I-20 in about ten minutes. Then you'll know where you are."

"Okay. And you and me at the office . . . ?"

"Let's just focus on this project and Auggie. Things don't have to be awkward."

"Okay. So we're good?"

"We're good. You know where you're going?"

"Yeah. You be careful."

"I'm home. But if you're that concerned, you can help me out right now. . . ." His hand back on his crotch.

Jacob shook his head and waved him out.

"Thanks for the blue balls."

"I think you'll be alright."

As Jacob drove off, he looked at Daniel through his rearview mirror, standing in the middle of the street, maybe hoping Jacob would change his mind as he watched the little white car turn the corner.

THIRTEEN

DANIEL

Daniel stepped off the path into the grass, the crunch of dry leaves a loud, sharp sound cutting through the quiet. Swore he'd never be out here again. That fucking Jacob. Maybe if the man spoke more and thought less, Daniel would have figured out Jacob wasn't looking for just a quick and easy nut. Problem was Jacob always caught Daniel off guard. Like when they toured those houses and Daniel was going on and on and Jacob just stood there looking at Daniel like he was stupid. Like he figured out something about Daniel the man didn't already know himself. *I didn't know you were gay.*

Daniel wasn't interested in starting some kind of life with another man. Holding hands. Cuddling. Displays of affection that revealed an emotional connection. But the mechanics required just to stand, watch a man bent over in front of him while he slammed into him over and over? That Daniel could do and he'd looked forward to doing exactly that to Jacob ever since they agreed to the tour. Jacob had gotten so animated by the suggestion, Daniel had to relieve himself in the bathroom afterward. Daniel had intended to enjoy every moment. Intended to make sure Jacob felt every word he ever uttered again. Wanted to feel Jacob lose control, make him forget that background he projected, separate him from that security he took for granted. And when they finished, they'd each know something about the life of the other. Daniel listened to the way Jacob said Sherman's name—like there was a secret between the two of them that excluded everyone else. He had intended to enjoy making sure Jacob knew he wasn't Sherman.

One step after another, down a path more remembered than seen, Daniel heard himself breathing. The hour of the night was thick black magic, pierced through by the milk-white light of the moon and the twinkle of starlight. Daniel listened beyond the rhythm of his walk, beyond the rough, ragged flow of his breath. Listened for the labored, breathy invitation of leaves being crushed under the weight of another. He looked for forms in the dark. If Daniel was able to see himself, to look down from the stars and the deep black night through the tops of trees to where he stood on a carpet of leaves, he'd see that he was part of the world and see the person in front of him, that they were both part of the great expanse of the universe. But that wasn't his perspective—he just looked down at something that looked up at him. He felt himself being gulped and swallowed, then Daniel was thrusting, deep and hard, listening to huffs and grunts at the ground. That was always the case, as it just happened now. There were no words once they finished, nothing said as they adjusted their clothes. And for Daniel, once was usually enough. Usually, the voices shouting in his head didn't sound so loud.

The night looked down on Daniel as his breathing returned to normal. There was a body kneeling in front of him. There was the moon, the stars, the trees, and leaves scattered all around. There was the pulse and rhythm of the world, expansive and moving and knowing. A ruckus no longer echoed in his head; now it was a silent strobe light flashing: Jacob, a brown-colored cherub; Mama, doubled in half, holding her gut laughing; Marty, a ten-foot giant; Lilah and Ray, two haunting, frozen ghosts. The body in front of Daniel moved, whimpered. He hit it. Once and then again. And again and again until it didn't move, until it didn't make a sound, but the flashing in his head wouldn't stop, and the voices shouting became even louder. He got up slowly and started to walk, faster and faster, until his momentum turned into running. Daniel ran. He ran over the leaves, through the trees under the stars and the moon, ran through the park and out into the night and the world. He ran and didn't stumble. He ran without looking back over his shoulder. He ran, wild-eyed, stared straight ahead and sucking in huge breaths. He pumped his arms, his fists to his chin, his torso leaning forward, his shoulders giving him arch and angle through the air. Daniel ran, his legs covering the ground in great, wide strides, and he knew he wasn't a man running toward something; he was a man being chased.

FOURTEEN

JACOB

In late July, the *Atlanta Journal-Constitution* published a series of articles, "Olympic Village: What's Happening?" The first two were about Summerhill. They told the story of the neighborhood being the working-class cousin to tonier Grant Park. Summerhill was a decent place to raise a family with its quiet, tidy blocks and neighbors who looked out for one another. The first article described various local places to shop, the ways in which Summerhill supported its residents. When the neighborhood was still intact—before the 75⊠85 interstate highway connector was built in 1962, followed by construction of the Atlanta–Fulton County Stadium in 1965—the neighborhood hosted a month-long BBQ fest each July. The entire neighborhood competed to show off which block had the best secret family recipe for grilling or smoking or frying chicken or catfish or ribs or brisket. Nobody remembered exactly when it started or how it grew from simple backyard cookouts to an elaborate, thirty-day contest for the distinction of becoming the best neighborhood BBQ. Folks next door in Peoplestown and Mechanicsville judged the contest. The block that attracted the biggest crowd was declared the winner. Which meant there was always disagreement about the winner, but everyone always had great fun. It reminded Jacob of the African Street Festival back home. Every summer, usually kicking off on the Thursday right before the Fourth of July, hundreds of people would gather at Boys and Girls High School to buy African art, kente, or other African cloth. Artists displayed all types of beaded, hammered, or cowrie-shell-adorned jewelry. The air was thick with incense and African oils. A Tribe Called Quest, De La Soul, and Digable Planets all played there—and performances also featured African drummers and dancers. People stood in long lines for oxtails, jerk chicken, jollof rice, callaloo, fried chicken, fried whiting, and shrimp. Jacob and his best friend, Alex, bought daily tickets to the event. It was the official end of school, the start of summer vacation. It carried on through Sunday, and for those four days, Boys and Girls High School on Fulton Street in Bed–Stuy became a destination for all of Brooklyn.

The second article was published two weeks after the first one. It documented the impact construction of the 75⊠85 highway connector and stadium projects had on the neighborhood. Idyllic homes were destroyed and bucolic blocks vanished. The city shut off water without notice. Electricity was knocked out for days when trees that were being cut fell on power lines. Families who had lived in Summerhill since its founding after the Civil

War lost property to eminent domain. The highway connector project cut the neighborhood in half. Literally. Filth came with it, along with increased noise and traffic. Construction workers parked on sidewalks or blocked driveways and didn't care. Of all the jobs created, no one from Summerhill was hired. State officials said residents lacked the required training and experience. The stadium project finished what the highway connector project started. Eminent domain was used again to confiscate more property. Angered by the civil rights protests and demonstrations happening in other areas of Atlanta, white construction workers reacted against Summerhill residents: they drove into fences, destroyed gardens, broke car windows. The stadium project was a relocation scheme to get the Milwaukee Braves to move to Atlanta. Summerhill paid the price of the ticket. That second article set the tone for the third, which focused on Beth, an interloper—from the seat of the Confederacy, no less. Did she have the professional chops, the requisite intellectual heft and emotional sensitivity to help shepherd in this age of an International Atlanta? The writer quoted Cornelius as being familiar with Beth "in passing." Elsie Grace cited weeks of back-and-forth with Beth's office about the community-benefits agreement, the status of which remained unknown. Her comment ended with, "Let us not forget the chaos of that riot," a reminder that the community didn't support the project. Those articles helped Jacob secure a meeting with Cornelius—Beth sent the third article attached with a note, *Get in front of Cornelius and Elsie Grace before it's bye-bye to all of us.*

Cornelius's hands danced in front of Jacob's face. His fingers were long and skinny for someone so fat, and tufts of hair grew above each knuckle. Perfect half-moon cuticles nestled in the pinkest nail beds, and his nail tips were so white they could have been acrylic. He wore a ring on his right pinkie finger—gold topped off with black onyx and a square-cut diamond in the center. Dark, heavy lines creased the centers of his palms. Jacob was surprised at how quickly the meeting with Cornelius was scheduled. Thomas had been disappointed when Jacob told him he didn't have an update on the community-benefits agreement.

"You listening?" Cornelius's palms were down, fingers spread wide and flat on the table. It took a moment for Jacob to focus. He nodded at Cornelius, reached for his water.

"So here's the problem. . . ." Cornelius continued, his pinkie bent to touch his thumb as he tapped his ring on the table. The sound was loud despite the noise of the diner. Cornelius was on a soapbox about how Black folks forgot one another when integration happened, the masterstroke that pushed forward and set back at the same time. Suddenly there it was: access to everything Black folks ever wanted. Made them believe they were getting somewhere. But where did Black folks spend money? How good were the schools in Black neighborhoods? How did Black folks influence decisions? Integration was really the institution of their mass underclass status. Even with their little political clout, the real power was in economics—the power to shape growth and development, to define where and when money flowed, to determine on whom and how it would get spent. Integration was a parlor trick, just the next step in divide and conquer. Black folks should turn back the clock, remember themselves in their decisions about their future. Look how every ethnic group that came to America eventually got ahead—the Irish, the Italians, Jewish people, and all manner of Asians getting ahead, and soon Spanish-speaking folks from Caribbean and Central and South American countries would have more of an established economic foundation than African Americans.

"None of those other people have a history of slavery and Jim Crow."

"So?"

"None of those other people have experienced massacres like Black Wall Street or Rosewood or the years and years of lynchings and active government-sanctioned aggressions against their entire existence."

"Tell that to Indigenous Americans. And more reason Black folks should have one another's backs. Ain't nobody else going to look out for us. We need to close ranks—African American, African, Caribbean, whatever, who cares? We all *Black*—come together against our common enemy now. Fight among ourselves later."

Jacob listened politely. Cornelius hadn't convinced him as to the identity of their common enemy. He listened for a chance to introduce Sherman and Auggie. He recalled Sherman kissing him in the parking lot, still felt Daniel's kiss in the car. They were so different—Sherman, a comfortable cradling invitation; Daniel, groping, grabbing, grasping. Jacob listened to Cornelius, his belly tight, his shoulders hunched up and stiff. His most recent confrontation with Beth haunted him, and he felt a monster inside him stirring in agreement with Cornelius. It was the unspoken permission granted by power coupled with the knowledge that Beth couldn't do anything about it. How long before Jacob became Cornelius? When would this work become too much? Leave him exhausted? Could he just walk out? Tell Beth to fuck off. Tell Daniel he's not offering enough. Tell Sherman he's ready for their life together. Leave all of this behind—Beth and her houses, Daniel and his craziness, Cornelius and whatever he was plotting, even his mother and father and their expectations for his life. Leave all of it and find somewhere quiet to discover life according to his own expectations. But Jacob was stuck, rooted to a predetermined understanding of his existence. He sat and listened, watched Cornelius eat and talk—or, more accurately, watched as he maneuvered talking to Jacob around eating his breakfast and the people always coming to the table. Toast in one hand, coffee mug in the other, his black-onyx-and-diamond pinkie ring twinkled. Someone said hello. Mid-chew and mid-sentence, Cornelius stopped, put down his toast, swallowed, smiled, clasped another hand, talked about another empty lot or another children's event or another growing pothole. Another old folks' home to visit. A neighborhood rally. He would be present at the basketball game of the nephew of yet another neighbor who knew his mother (goodness how we miss that woman, but what a send-off, all those people, you know you did her proud). Jacob was always introduced afterward. "Here, say hello to Jacob Jenkins—give him your card. Good brother. Pay attention to him. He's different." People regarded Jacob cautiously, their eyes wide with unasked questions. Who was he—potential ally or an impediment? Native Atlantan or outsider? What was he doing with Cornelius? Cornelius introduced Jacob to people from the Atlanta Housing Authority, the Department of City Planning, a few utility companies, and a journalist. He was the village chieftain, pounding a tom-tom message. Eventually Morehouse entered the conversation, and that brought smiles and nods, and the air hovering between Jacob and the latest stranger became less lively with unasked questions. But those people didn't really see him; he existed only in their periphery, only to be watched and monitored, another element to ponder. The caravan to the table dwindled. Cornelius finished his breakfast, wiped his mouth, and pushed back.

"Let's walk."

Jacob hesitated. They were thirty minutes past the sixty-minute meeting Jacob had agreed to, and he still hadn't figured out how he was going to introduce Sherman and Auggie.

"Let's hurry. I have a meeting with the mayor in an hour."

The shine on his wing-tip shoes gleamed as Cornelius walked with Jacob. It was warmer than inside the diner, but not stifling yet. Thomas walked a few steps behind them—far enough not to be intrusive, but close enough to hear Cornelius if he barked a command. Cornelius nudged Jacob while they walked, a friendly gesture to emphasize something he thought was funny. To make sure he had Jacob's attention. Jacob stumbled, almost tripped, but Cornelius was quick, reached to keep Jacob from falling. His grip surprised Jacob, quite firm for someone who looked so soft.

"Thank you."

"Not a problem. You hurt my feelings with all your wandering attention, and here I thought my magnetic charm and personality was keeping you engaged."

"I like listening, Cornelius. It's hard not to pay attention to you." That sounded less friendly than he'd intended.

They turned down a street with a few abandoned houses, a few cars, and what looked like the beginnings of a small renovation project. Cornelius stopped, assessed Jacob with a long, measured look. His mouth twitched. He stroked his goatee, pulled out a handkerchief to wipe his face. Pulled a pair of shades from his pocket. Thomas stopped a few steps behind them.

"I like the way you say my name. Brooklyn, right?"

Jacob nodded.

"Umm-hmm. It has four syllables and the accent is on the second one, but something new comes your way every day, huh?" He walked away and Jacob's face got hot. Thomas still stood where he'd stopped. Cornelius took a few more steps, turned back to Jacob. "You coming?" But it wasn't a question. They started walking again, and Thomas resumed following.

"You married?"

Jacob felt like Cornelius just shoved him again. "No."

"Girlfriend?"

"No."

They walked quietly for a few seconds more, footsteps against concrete the only sound between them.

"I like you, Jacob—I like smart young brothers coming up, trying to do something. You have a lot of potential. But you need to be somewhere different. That woman you're working for isn't going to make it." Jacob heard Cornelius's declaration, feared the monster he felt stalking his future. "What all did you see back there in that diner?"

Jacob thought about what he'd witnessed. Cornelius held court and they came on bended knee, kissed his ring, and pledged their allegiance. He was indeed the minister tending to his flock. It was the function of everything he talked about at breakfast. They finally arrived at the construction site.

"This disgusts me." Cornelius surveyed the site.

If Jacob closed his eyes, it could have been Daniel standing next to him. Except that what he and Daniel saw was different from what was in front of Cornelius. Jacob saw the lives that were lost, and dead flat space yawned back at Daniel, who saw the limits of his own existence. Cornelius had spent years cultivating his vision, and what looked like seven houses was actually an economic development biosphere to him: seven microorganisms grown into good-paying jobs for local people. Local employment for local people translated into loyalty that secured his future. Loyalty of people like Elsie Grace. That loyalty was currency recognized by his colleagues at city hall. That currency leveraged more opportunities that increased the yield of his objectives. The cycle repeated itself over and over, the microorganisms of those seven houses evolving into a being of its own. That vision satisfied Cornelius. Jacob wondered if Cornelius saw individual people working on this site. If he saw the lives they might live; that they might be him or his family or someone he loved. If he saw each individual possessed of his own history, working for his own future, living his own highs and lows. Cornelius grunted, shook his head, said Beth had made this so easy for him. What Cornelius saw had a beginning and no end, was filled with the blunt, brutal truth of his experience.

"I'm going to take this project away from her, and dear God I hope she fights me for it. Challenging me. As if she can understand who I am. I will break that woman. I will break her in half in front of all of Atlanta." Jacob kept quiet, aware that Cornelius was talking out loud to himself. A few more minutes passed before Cornelius repeated his question about what Jacob saw at the diner.

Jacob thought about what Cornelius had asked. It wasn't an inexpensive question, but neither was it daunting. It was the same question those people had asked themselves before they saw him at the diner that morning. During their tour, Sherman asked the same question. Cornelius looked from Jacob to his watch. Construction cones and stanchions were stacked on porches. Demolition equipment stood where work crews had started, then stopped. A backhoe. A bulldozer. A half-filled dumpster.

"Okay, I'll go first, so we can move this along, but I told you already: I like what you're doing. I like what you represent. This is an advance courtesy warning: the developer of this project won't be Beth."

It was warm. Jacob felt the wind, heard bugs and birds and people, all confirmation of being alive. He knew fear—of the dark, of things in his closet, of monsters under his bed. He experienced pain—of falling off his bike, of his father's belt, of a cramp in his stomach. His parents had always turned on the light or showed him just clothes in his closet or swept under his bed. And even the pain of his father's belt lasted only for moments. But Cornelius was different. His parents never said people like him existed; Cornelius was something that crawled out from the dark corners in his closet and beneath his bed. He was a different type of monster. Jacob was beginning to understand accommodation had a breaking point. It was an end to supplication, when patience hit its limit, when the most eloquent appeals to decency were pointless. The purpose of accommodation had shifted, evolved, understood its initial undertaking—to articulate in high-minded tones and language, to engage with a spirit of truth and compassion, and to assume that spirit was a singularly unifying experience shared by all—was wrong. The shifting wasn't personal or specifically individual, it was universal and communal. It was four hundred years and more of evolution. Evolution crafted by torture, rape, murder, fire, ripping families apart, theft of bodies, theft of land, theft of hope, theft of decency and possibility and the robbery of legacies, violations of womanhood, manhood, childhood, physical and emotional and spiritual transgressions all met with grace and prayer and protests steeped in the grief of generational suffering, yielding to loud screams and marches and sit-ins and legislation and entire whole movements to educate, enlighten, and engage. And still the refusal. But the years of pleading, praying, marching, singing, protesting, crying, shouting, fighting, dying were not to request the return of what was taken; they were advisories informing that what was stolen shouldn't have been taken in the first place. Notice was being made that the ongoing refusal to relinquish what had wrongly been possessed would no longer be tolerated and was endangering us all. Jacob processed everything he had just witnessed while he sat with Cornelius. This was different from Dr. King and Malcolm X, consecrated by beliefs as fundamental as those of Mother

Teresa and Gandhi, was as demanding of justice as Denmark Vesey, Nat Turner, and Toussaint Louverture. Carefully, slowly, Jacob answered Cornelius's question, crafted for himself a lifeline anchored by Sherman and Auggie. Maybe helping them would help placate the monster. Cornelius smiled as he spoke, and the monster haunting Jacob's future stirred with recognition.

FIFTEEN

DANIEL

I found out by mistake about Mama and our landlord."

Marty talked about their life before Daniel. Daniel and Lilah already knew most of what he said—that they moved from one neighborhood to the next because investors prospected for real estate as though looking for gold and Mama's local budget didn't compare with the money those landlords saw coming to Atlanta. They cleaned Mama's apartment while they listened to Marty, boxed and taped or bagged and discarded; gradually, things disappeared.

"Life was bleak for us, you know? Just didn't expect nothing, so you can't half blame Mama for trying anything she could. That's what she knew to do, that's what she was supposed to do." A small, practical woman, not given to fanciful or whimsical tendencies, made mean and crooked, hardened by memory and the angles of life, wronged and broken, suddenly straightened, softened, became right, molded into a mother's love, her willful strategies, her forced manipulations. Mama's history in Marty's mouth.

"I skipped school once and followed Mama to work. That car kept dropping her off, and I had to know where it was coming from, why it didn't come pick her up in the morning. The house we were living in wasn't bad, but I was still hanging on to us moving somewhere nicer, and I had to know about that car. Every time I caught Mama tipping out that car gave me new hope. She never knew I saw her—or at least she never let on that she did. But when it got so I couldn't stand it, I followed her. And what I found out was that that car wasn't nothing."

Marty paced the story, was careful with the presentation of Mama, the revelation of what he knew about Daniel's father. Mama was never a haphazard woman, given to sudden urges or inexplicable impulses. Marty had rehearsed what to tell his siblings, especially Daniel. He wanted his brother to know that he wasn't an accident, that he was the result of Mama's predicament. And when he finished, Marty hoped Daniel would understand his father too.

"Now imagine my eight-year-old ass on a bike, chasing a bus. I managed to negotiate traffic, kept the bus in sight, maneuvered around cars, used the sidewalk when there was one, and saw Mama stepping off it forty-five minutes later—all of that without getting caught. I was kinda proud until I looked around and encountered my first problem—I couldn't follow Mama inside the building. One of those old factories up on East Ponce De Leon Avenue. Low to the ground—only three floors—but kind of wide, maybe covered half a block. Typical factory-looking type place: redbrick, chain-link fence, a parking lot. Looked just like the other buildings around it; other factories, warehouses, storage places. Decently busy. Traffic passing by with people going to work. Cars rolling into the parking lot. Folks arriving by bus. I stood far enough away so I wouldn't attract attention to myself.

"All kinds of people worked at that factory. Ray used to always grumble about that, said that was why he couldn't get a steady job—women and Blacks creating too much competition. He was always mumbling about the sit-ins, the protests going on all over Atlanta, equal rights this and equal rights that, and how all of that was keeping him back. Mama would say, '*Bullshit. It's your fat ass in that chair in front of that goddam television.*' And that would be the start of it.

"'*Who you talking to?*'

"'*You listening.*'

"'*You been getting beside yourself lately. Been getting real mouthy.*'

"'*I'm tired, Ray. I'm tired of busting my butt all week long for this nothing we got and all you do is sit on your ass. Seems like if you would get up and do something, we could get somewhere. I'm tired. Just tired.*'

"'*So what you tired. I'm tired too—tired of fighting with everybody out there in the world, then coming home to all this mouth.*'

"'*Yeah, well I'm tired of repeating myself. Seems like I'm always saying the same damn thing.*'

"'*So leave. Take your mouthy ass and walk.*'

"'*Maybe. Maybe one day I will. Maybe one morning you'll come in from one of your all-nighters and I'll be gone.*'

"That place was too small, their voices too big, and I was

always scared. Scared that Mama would leave us with Ray, that the day she left, Ray would not come home, and me and Lilah would be in this world alone. That's how our walks started; I was following her, making sure she didn't leave us.

"*Where you going, Mama?*'

"*Walking.*'

"*To where?*'

"*Nowhere. Just walking. To think.*'

"*Can't you think here?*'

"*Don't cross me, Marty.*'

"*You could, Mama, you can go back in your room and think there. And I will go in the room with Lilah, and I'll be quiet so she don't wake up, and then you can think.*'

"*Marty. Marty. My sweet boy. Thank you, baby, but I need some fresh air. I need to be out in the open to get my thoughts flowing.*'

"*Can I come? Can I walk with you?*'

"*Well, I was trying to be alone, have a little time to myself.*'

"*Don't leave us, Mama.*'

"*What?*'

"*Please.*'

"*Oh, honey. Honey. I'm coming back. Honest.*'

"*Can I come?*'

"Mama made me wait I don't know how long, and when she finally spoke, it was to tell me to get my sneakers and to make sure I didn't wake up Lilah." Daniel and Lilah were listening to the grown man talk, saw the little boy still hanging on.

"That first time we didn't walk far. A block or two, maybe, couldn't have been more than fifteen minutes. Mama didn't want to go too far from the house, in case you woke up. I was just content to be walking with her, making sure she kept good on her promise not to leave. And I was prepared to stay silent, let her have all the fresh air and thinking space she needed, just so long as I was there. But Mama wanted to hear herself out loud, and since I was there—since I insisted—I guess I became her witness.

"'This is not the life I wanted. Not at all. Not at all. But here we are, so what to do, huh? What to do?'

"'Huh? Mama—'

"'Grew up in a shotgun house. Still living in a shotgun house. Children born in a shotgun house. Be damned if I'm gonna die in one too. Be double damned. Be damned if that's the legacy I leave you and your sister.'

"'Mama, you not—'

"'Just listen. I'm telling you something.'

"I quieted and we walked while Mama kept talking.

"'Marty, stretch out your arms.' I did that. 'Close your eyes.' I did that too. 'Breathe in this air—you feel that, Marty? You feel that?'

"'Yes, Mama.'

"'No you don't, not yet, but you will. I feel it, though. Yes I do. I feel it. And I hope when you feel it, you feel it different. And I hope when your sister feels it, she feels it different from me and you. That's what I hope. I am thankful for what I'm feeling now, Marty. Thankful. But I want that feeling to be different for y'all, you hear me? I want you to feel what I'm feeling one day and for that feeling to be different.'

"'Yes, Mama.'

"'It's this feeling, Marty, this little small feeling I thank God for. Yeah, my life is hard. Yeah, this is not the life I expected. Did *not expect to get pregnant so young and have two children. I'm not working the job I wanted. Not living where I want to be living. I thought I would've been somewhere different. But here I am. I'm not sorry for where I am. Angry, maybe. Disappointed. Frustrated even, unhappy about the choices I made, but not sorry. You know what I'm saying, Marty?'*

"'Yes, Mama.'

"'Not yet. You will, though. Just listen. I don't see no ending, how all this can change into something different. But all that don't matter. I'm working at it. As long as I can feel this, I can work it. And when I can't feel it no more, well. Look at your father. That sorry ass. Don't know why I can't leave him. Don't know why I can't just shut him out and cut him off. I don't and I can't. But he sorry. Don't be no sorry ass, Marty. Don't.'

"'I won't, Mama.'

"'Hold on to that: Don't be sorry. Take care of your sister. Have a family. Take care of your wife. Take care of your children. Don't worry about me. I can take care of myself. Your daddy is walking around pissed for no reason. Pissed with women. Pissed with Blacks. Pissed with rich people. Pissed with whoever. Always thinking that somebody's taking something from him. But it's him, Marty, it's all him. Remember that. He ain't a woman and he ain't Black and he damn sure ain't rich. He don't know what none of that means. He ain't nothing. Don't be like your daddy, Marty. Be something to yourself. Be something more than him.'

"'I will, Mama.'

"'Will you?'

"'I will.'

"'Good. That's it. Hold on to that feeling. Hold on to it, and

when it blossoms, full and thick, when you feel it way deeper than your gut and you know, work with it, Marty. Make it work for you. It will give you what you need. Look at what we in, look at where we at, and I feel it, I know it: We moving beyond this place, beyond this ghetto, beyond poverty, beyond Ray even. Beyond all this we stuck in. This place is nowhere and we going. I know it. I feel it. I know. Hold that feeling, Marty. I want you to despise what we stuck in. I want you to hate this place we at, this nothing place of poverty. Hate it. Be angry with it. Fear it. Don't make my mistakes. Don't be your father, you hear me?'

"'Yes, Mama.'

"'No you don't. You don't know what I'm saying.'

"'I do, Mama, I do. But you're angry. I'm scared. Let's go home.'

"'You're scared? Why you scared?'

"'Because you're angry.'

"'I'm not angry. We're talking. Are you listening?'

"'I'm listening.'

"'Don't mumble.'

"'Okay.'

"'Speak up.'

"'Yes, Mama.'

"'What you scared of? Tell me.'

"'You're angry. I'm confused. I don't know.'

"'But you're scared?'

"'Yes.'

"'Maybe angry yourself?'

"'A little.'

"'And you know you don't want to be here no more?'

"'Yes.'

"'Hold on to that. Hold on to that feeling, Marty. That's enough. Let's go home.'"

Marty had disappeared, collapsed into the past of Mama's words, Mama's voice, Mama's conviction. Daniel and Lilah waited for him to resurface. No one stirred. No sound interrupted the silence until Marty decided to start talking again.

"Those long walks that both of you were so jealous of? That's how they were. 'Testifying,' Mama called it. Telling the truth of her existence. They were sporadic at first, happening just here and there whenever Mama got really stressed. Mama said she was toughening me up against the world. And all that started around the time that car began dropping her off. All Mama's talk about feeling it and hating poverty and fear and moving beyond where we were living. I thought that black car was a way she'd found, and even though she said she wouldn't, I still thought she might leave us, what with everything she was saying. The mystery of that fancy black car didn't help. That's why I had to follow her. I had to know.

"I stood outside the factory for a while, thinking to myself, trying to figure out what to do. There was no way for me to get inside that building to spy on Mama, find out what she was doing, see if whatever she did could explain a car like that and a driver. Mama looked like everyone else walking in that factory. So I thought I should just ride home and come back around the time Mama got off. Then I'd probably find out something. Maybe that car would be there to pick her up and I would see it and I could see what it meant. It was midmorning by then, and once I decided to leave, I hopped up on my bike and started to ride away. A block away from the factory were a bunch of two-story brick buildings that had space for stores downstairs with offices above. All types of businesses had opened up there—lawyers, accountants, real estate offices, barbershops, hair salons. I was on the sidewalk riding by when I saw what looked like the car I'd see Mama in, sitting in front of a property management office. It didn't look so fancy there, parked on the side of the street. I wished I could remember the type of car it was. I got off my bike, walked around it. I pressed my nose against the window, looked inside. I looked at it from the front, then walked around to look at it from the back. Maybe it was my imagination that made that car look like more than it was when Mama was getting out of it.

"*'You're Sue Milton's boy.'*

"A man standing in the doorway of the property management office was talking to me. I was startled to hear Mama's name come out his mouth, then I realized he was the landlord Mama had met when she signed the lease for the place we was in. I kept quiet, just watched him silently.

"*'What you doing over here? Shouldn't you be in school?'*

"I shrugged, then he noticed my bike.

"*'You going to see your mother?'*

"I wondered how he would know where Mama worked. Then I thought to myself, she probably had to tell him when she applied for the apartment.

I shook my head no, I wasn't going to see my mother. "*'Please don't tell her you saw me.'*

"I was thinking about the ass-whipping I'd surely get. He chuckled, walked a few steps closer to me.

"*'Okay, I'll keep your secret.'*

195

"He put an index finger up to his lips. I laughed when he did that; he looked like a big kid, and I felt like I'd just made a new friend. He was tall—bigger than Ray—a dark-skinned Black man, and muscular. I felt tiny next to him. I remember his voice being deep and loud, although when he spoke to me it didn't seem like he was shouting. He had one of those military haircuts—cut down to the skin on the sides and flat on top—and he wore a white, short-sleeved, collared shirt with dark-colored pants. He stuck out his hand.

"*'I'm Ralph Reid and you're Marty.'*

"He smiled and I laughed again. There was an easy familiarity about him. His deep voice and the way he grinned made me feel like I didn't have anything to fear from him. He gestured to my bike.

"*'You ride that all the way over here?'*

"*'It's not so far.'*

"*'Well, I'll do a better job keeping your secret if I know you got home safely. Let me give you a ride.'*

"He unlocked his trunk, helped me to lift my bike.

"*'Hey there, young fella, you okay?'*

"Neither of us noticed the three white men who'd pulled up on the other side of Mr. Reid's car. They looked from me to him suspiciously, started climbing out their car, clearly looking for trouble. Mr. Reid didn't look bothered.

"*'Why wouldn't he be okay?'*

"*'I wasn't talking to you.'*

"*'But I'm talking to you. Marty, stand back over there away from the curb.'*

"Them three guys were so frail-looking. One of Mr. Reid's

biceps was bigger than the head of the guy mouthing off. I felt sorry for the ass-kicking he was about to unleash on them. The three of them were coming around Mr. Reid's car onto the sidewalk when a police car pulled up.

"'*Ralph! Everything going okay here?*'

"A red-haired cop was calling out his car window to Mr. Reid. He and his partner had pulled up directly in front of the white guys' car. He had a Black partner who was already walking around their car, looking in the windows. The three guys looked like they were trying to figure out what was happening.

"'*Officer Dunham, everything's fine. Me and my young friend here were just about to be on our way when these boys here pulled up with some questions.*'

"Officer Dunham stepped onto the sidewalk directly in front of the guy standing closest to Mr. Reid.

"'*Jackie, how everything looking to you?*'

"He was talking to his partner, staring directly in the guy's face. He made a motion, popped the strap on his holster holding his gun in place. The other officer came walking from the front of the car to where the other two guys were standing. He'd already popped the strap on his holster, his hand rested on his gun.

"'*I don't know, D. How everything looking to y'all? We got a problem here, or y'all going to move your car, let this gentleman and his young friend be on their way?*'

"He stepped onto the sidewalk, so close to one of the guys that he backed up a few steps. By this time, a few other business owners were standing in front of their shops, watching. The three of them did a round-robin of stares—at me, then Mr. Reid, then to each of the officers.

"'We was just—'

"Dunham cleared his throat.

"'You're addressing an officer of the law.'

"The other officer's hand was still on his gun; he shifted his weight, jingling his utility belt. The guy who'd been talking opened his mouth, closed it, turned to his friends, then shook his head. His friends looked uncomfortable. Officer Dunham had moved them from the sidewalk to standing with their backs against the building, hands on their heads. From the clothes they wore and the condition of their car, if I had to guess, I'd say they were in their early twenties; they'd come into town from somewhere not too far from Atlanta, on what they thought would be a joyride, but they took a wrong turn. They looked helpless, like they were about to start pleading with Officer Dunham. His face was grim. Jackie snapped his fingers, directed attention to the name on his badge. The guy standing next to Mr. Reid was the one who'd been talking. He grunted.

"'Officer Henry. We was just making sure the young fella was okay.'

"'Why wouldn't the young fella be okay?'

"Me and Mr. Reid had moved back to the entrance of his office. Officer Henry closed the few feet of distance between him and the man who'd been talking; the three men were boxed in by the wall of the building, Mr. Reid's car at the curb, and an officer with a gun on either side of them.

"'Boy, did you hear me?'

"'Yes, I—'

"'Yes what?'

"'*Yes, Officer Henry, I heard you.*'

"'*So answer me, then. Why wouldn't the young fella be okay?*'

"'*I just— We just—*'

"He looked down, stopped talking.

"'*Young man, you doing okay?*'

"I told the officer I was doing just fine.

"'*How 'bout you, Mr. Reid?*'

"It was clear Mr. Reid knew those officers. A few of his neighbors had wandered over to assess the situation. They acknowledged the officers, looked at the guys, shook their heads. One remarked about what it took for Atlanta to get ahead of its history: How was a Black man supposed to safely run a business with all the little punk white bitches running around? Another neighbor told the three white boys they were an embarrassment to the good decent white people of Atlanta. He spat on the ground, told them they should keep their asses crawling around the rocks and caves out at Stone Mountain. Murmurs of agreement rippled through the little crowd. Mr. Reid still hadn't answered. He told me to stay put, walked over to the man Officer Henry was questioning. The top of the guy's head barely came up to Mr. Reid's chest.

"'*Why wouldn't the young fella be okay?*'

"He didn't utter a word, just stared directly into Mr. Reid's chest.

"'*Mr. Reid, you want to press charges against these boys for harassment?*'

"'*We didn't—*'

"'*You shut up. Mr. Reid?*'

"I was young, but I knew what was happening. I'd listened to Ray always arguing with Mama about the changing times. Made me remember everything Mama said on our walk. Who knows what would've happened if those cops hadn't shown up? Yeah, they might've gotten some licks in on Mr. Reid, but believe me, they would've definitely gotten hurt. I kept thinking to myself, why? What was the point? They saw this Black man with a white kid and thought they'd make him a target, just because? But the stars aligned that day—for them and Mr. Reid. He decided not to press charges. He said they weren't worth the time or headache. Officer Henry wrote down their license plate number. Officer Dunham told them that if Mr. Reid's shop windows were suddenly busted out or if his store suddenly caught fire or if his car was vandalized, they'd know where to look.

"'*You backwards-ass country fucks might do you what you want out there wherever you're from, but it's a different day here in Atlanta. And trust me, everyone round here ain't holding hands singing church songs while you hooligans go around busting people in the head. Now go on and get the fuck outta here.*'

"Once we were in his car, I asked Mr. Reid why he didn't press charges. He said the moment wasn't right for that yet. He said Atlanta might be a little oasis in the South, but just barely.

"'*Imagine me accusing them of harassment and the involvement of the police. Imagine the press it'd get. Imagine all the lawyers, all the politicians, all the television cameras. Wouldn't be nothing but a spectacle. The only thing that would happen is I'd become a different kind of target for a whole new set of the same kind of people. I'm working too hard for that. Me and those officers handled it correctly. We spoke exactly the kind of language those assholes understood.*

Maybe not today, Marty, but one day those three and all their kind of people will be extinct. Or something close to it.'

"He didn't drop me off right at the house—we both agreed that it was better for me to get out where no one would notice, where we wouldn't create a spectacle that might cause other problems. That's how I've come to understand all of what he said—that there are consequences attached to the choices of our actions, that we should evaluate the range of those consequences in the context of the direction we see our life heading. That's what he did. And so did Mama. I biked home thinking about what Mr. Reid said, wondering if he had these kinds of conversations with his children—he didn't mention having kids of his own. And all this because I was chasing down Mama riding in a car."

It was a loose framework from that car to Mama to Mr. Reid, but it was more information than Daniel had ever known. Pride stirred in Daniel, just like he heard the pride in Marty's voice. Admiration for a man who lived the life he was dealt, who didn't complain about the equity of circumstances, who charted his way forward based on his dominion over what was presented. And Daniel had a new appreciation for Mama, who tried her best to surmount the conditions in which she was trapped, but the best she could do was plot a path for her children. Mama's love was never a soft thing, never some light, feathery, gentle cooing to carry them off to some dreamy fairyland where it made magic and mystical things happen; it was thick and tangible and definite, existed always in the present. And so they sat in Mama's apartment, contemplating the sheen of a shiny black car, feeling the disappointment of the promise that it wasn't. Lilah moved first, bringing them back to the present, picking up loose somethings, adding them to a box, filling it to the top. Daniel moved next, bringing the tape and closing it. Marty moved last, lifting the box and stacking it with other boxes full of Mama's stuff. They did this in the quiet, their thoughts as chaotic as the growing emptiness in which they sat.

SIXTEEN

JACOB

Jacob lay in bed, stared at the blank white space of the ceiling. He waited for the chime of his alarm clock. Sunlight streamed through the blinds. A click cut through the silence as the air conditioner whirred on. A car alarm chirped, the car's door slammed, the engine sputtered before it finally turned over, the motor gunning high and loud as the car pulled away. Footsteps hit the floor on the other side of the wall in the apartment next door. He listened as they faded, moving farther away.

Sherman haunted Jacob, and his parents bothered his sleep. Trapped inside a picture in a folder, a little boy with a set of bright, big eyes smiled at the world. Jacob thought about his parents and the place he came from, their expectations for his life. Never thought things would turn out so differently from what they all expected. Lying in bed, staring at the ceiling, Jacob felt a hard, uncomfortable churning in his gut. He didn't have any answers, wanted only to be seen as the son his parents had always known.

There is this boy.
Small.
Dark.
Floating...

Except that as he swam in the blank white space of the ceiling, Jacob wasn't a small dark boy anymore. His arms spun hard, his legs kicked furiously, his breath came quick and short, but his transition into manhood had made it only harder for him to see himself. The calm, fluid current that was his life had been disrupted by the unexpected. What would it feel like to wake up next to Sherman? Did he snore? Did he sleep nude or in a T-shirt and drawers, or just bare chested with some long-legged pajamas? Did he top or bottom, or was he versatile? Was he one of those chatty morning talkers—a night of intense lovemaking and he was off the next morning to conquer the world, chart the new and undiscovered? Or was he a moody grumbler—sex just a restful escape from a difficult day, a mechanized distraction from the daily effort of living, a fantasy role-play in which each participant drowned himself in imaginings he dared not let occupy his mind when vertical? The coming of a new day wasn't the promise of a new, fresh, invigorating beginning, but a reminder he had yet to successfully renegotiate the terms of an unsatisfactory existence.

The first nick is a scratch.
He will ignore it.

He will concentrate.
He will start paying attention.

Tears blurred his vision as Jacob watched himself swim in the ceiling. He blinked. His mouth went dry. His tongue worked up saliva for him to swallow. Once. Twice. Three times. Why couldn't he see himself? There was a little blue house with a white picket fence and Sherman stood on the porch, smiling, holding little Auggie's hand. They waved. Jacob thought they waved at him, but when he looked to find himself, he expected to see his fingers and hands, his arms and legs, his torso, but there was nothing. They kept waving. Jacob's parents appeared, hovering high above the house, holding hands and looking down. Sherman walked off the porch, yelled Jacob's name. His father let go of his mother, unzipped his pants, and pissed. Sherman stood in the piss raining from the heavens, his smile turned to a grimace. He yelled Jacob's name again. Jacob saw him, yelled back, but he still couldn't see himself. His father's torrent of urine became a golden-hued puddle that expanded larger and larger until it was a rough, living body of water with a current running strong and deep. Yellow waves slapped against the house, pushed the little blue building farther and farther away. Sherman tried to swim, but the waves and the current were too rough. There was no wall for him to grab hold of, no firm place on which he could anchor himself. Jacob tried to swim to Sherman, but when he moved his arms and legs, he felt nothing. The current started dragging Sherman under; the waves rocked the house back and forth. Sherman yelled Jacob's name louder. Beth and Cornelius appeared, walked on top of the water; Beth squatted, took a piss, and Cornelius bent over to shit. Jacob's parents had disappeared, and no more urine fell from the sky. Jacob still couldn't see himself, and Sherman had vanished. Jacob yelled louder and louder until he felt himself shaking all over.

"Jacob. Wake up."

Sean sat on his bed, shaking him, and Rodney stood at his door. His alarm clock chimed.

"Turn off your alarm."

He hit the snooze button.

"You're crying."

Jacob put his hands to his face.

"Sherman is that good already?" But Sean sounded too grave to be joking.

"What?"

"You were calling his name—but you sounded more like you were having a nightmare than a wet dream. Who's Auggie?"

Jacob stared at Sean, until his alarm clock chimed again. He climbed out of bed, didn't answer Sean's question.

|| SEVENTEEN ||

DANIEL

Daniel felt betrayed. He watched Jacob. Heard him talk. But now he doubted the two of them ever went on that car ride together, ever spent time getting to know each other, ever agreed they'd both help Auggie and his family. Jacob had told Daniel about his talk with Cornelius. He explained that the opportunity had just presented itself, so he had to take advantage of the moment. Daniel heard the conflict in Jacob's voice, trying to justify a decision he made himself that the two of them should have actually made together. He wondered if that's how it happened between Mama and his father: one of them had made a decision that forced the other to follow.

"I know Cornelius is a politician, but I think we can trust him. He said this new developer will hire us as soon as he takes over."

"We? You're the only one who spoke to him. I don't have the kind of backup you got. I need a job." They were at the construction site, reviewing the progress of the demolition before it had stopped: deep gashes in the ground, piles of red-brown dirt heaped next to the houses, backhoes and bulldozers sitting dormant. From its lofty perch, the sun scowled down, the heat and humidity threatened suffocation. If Jacob understood Daniel's predicament, if he could feel Daniel's conflict with the world, he might show some contrition. See that from Daniel's perspective this was backroom maneuvering and double-dealing at its worst. They had made a promise, but now something was broken between them. Daniel wondered what had broken between Mama and his father. If it was something one of them tried to restore or if it was all just too much, if that was the situation he now found himself in with Jacob.

"Cornelius will come through for us. That's the way this works."

"And if he doesn't, I'll just move in with you." Daniel tried laughing, but it came out flat.

Jacob had wanted to know if Daniel heard what those houses were saying, if he understood what was happening. Daniel knew that dreams could be murdered, that there were places sacrifice didn't matter, that the only thing that survived was persistence, crawling, twisting, looking for a place to take root and begin. A place where God finally rewarded the value of hard work and the toll of sheer effort. Mama was that proof. Before Mama got out of bed, she lay quietly each morning. But even in silence, noise interrupted the quiet—the body of Ray lying next to her, for one; the heavy, lazy sound of his snoring. How he rested so easily bothered her. When he crawled in bed, tried to mount her, the gelatinous, veined mass of his belly made her violent. That Ray could sleep so peacefully while his family lived in a house like the one they lived in was nothing less than a disgrace.

A child's cough was another disturbance. Mama listened for the nature of the cough—did it come from deep within the chest? Or was it merely a slumbering body trying to clear a blocked airway? Mama strained to hear past Ray's rumble—hoped, prayed— then came a second cough, lighter, easier, the child stirred, turned, took an easier breath. That second cough was a glorious sound breaking through the silence, and Mama took a breath herself, relieved. Ray snorted, as though agreeing with Mama in his sleep. He stirred, rolled over, threw a pale, fleshy arm around her torso. Farted. Coughed. Returned to snoring. Mama wished his cough was deep and sick—one less mouth to feed would be a mercy. Especially the mouth of a full-grown man who couldn't even hold a job. One less meal to cook, less food to buy, less clothes to wash, less house to clean, less hours to work, one less human being on this planet to account for and accommodate. But with Mama's luck, any illness of his wouldn't be quick, it would be long and inconveniently indecent, just like his sloth and slovenliness were indecent inconveniences blanketing over her life.

Mama gazed down the length of Ray's body. She used to yearn for his touch, quiver and moan as his lips roamed her throat and his taut abdomen moved rhythmically against the suppleness of her belly. Their lovemaking had never been an all-consuming passion, but at least it used to be satisfying. Mama would forget the boundaries of expected behavior when they were together.

Their coupling was steady and reassuring as they moved against each other, fingers and lips, tits and asses, breasts and chests, arms and legs, penis to vagina, all of it harmoniously organized for their pleasure. Their sex was relief from that which plagued them that they could neither control nor forget. The frequency of it lessened after Marty was born, became sporadic after Lilah arrived. Then it stopped. Looking at the mass of Ray lying next to her, Mama would like to believe she was the same woman, but where she used to be soft, the curve of her hips inviting a nibble or kiss, she was now lean and sinewy, muscle hard and toughened by years of factory work and waiting at bus stops and carrying bags (or boxes or children) and cleaning and worrying (about payment plans and final notices) and taking care of her mother and wanting a day of rest but always working working working. She looked at Ray again, and it was as if they'd traded bodies—his belly, the lack of definition in his arms, the extra chin, the curvature of his ass. She turned away in disgust. How does a white man end up like him in this country? How did she end up marrying him? She knew when they married that Ray wasn't the kind of man who was going to take on the world. But Mama never wanted a savior; all she wanted was a partner. And was there a difference between what Ray expected and what Mama had become? Maybe they'd both become difficult, lazy, and stubborn, and staying together was just easier because she didn't lose desire for him so much as they'd lost desire for each other.

Dawn brought the chirping of birds, and the disquiet of Mama's thoughts roused her from bed. Her persistence, insistent and dogged and of such rabid constitution that it wouldn't allow

Mama to give up. She kept pushing, waiting for a place for her dreams to sprout stem and leaf. In the meantime, there were children to feed, a house to clean, her mother to look after, and the day stretching out ahead of her. . . .

Sweat covered Daniel. This was like their face-off behind the houses. Daniel wanted to believe Jacob was a good person, that he should also trust Cornelius. But the evidence of his life was different. Daniel wondered when Mama knew she was pregnant, if she even bothered to tell Ralph Reid; if she'd considered abortion. Standing hot and sweaty, Daniel and Jacob confronted each other. The heat bombarded them—it came up from the tarmac on the street, out from the red-brown gashes in the ground, down from a brazen sun in the naked blue sky. Daniel was stuck where Jacob had broken them. If he hit Jacob, would the man defend himself, or would he think Daniel was justified? Daniel recalled the press of Jacob's body underneath his, the taste of his tongue, the labored sound of his breathing. Maybe Daniel could beat Jacob. Maybe. Fucking him would be so much better, for Daniel to make Jacob buck and moan, instigate his loss of control. And when they finished, they'd know the control Jacob lost was the control Daniel took. That seemed like adequate recompense for the violation Daniel felt. In the heat he began to smell himself, the thought had made him so excited. It wasn't a funky smell, not one that required a bath. It was a smell that reminded Daniel there were thick tufts of hair under his arms, that a steady, certain girth swung between his legs.

Thinking became hazy in the heat. There was Mama with

the landlord, trying to orchestrate her future; there was Jacob and Daniel, trying to manage their present. Something would be built on the red-brown construction site where they stood, whether by Beth or another developer. But that future was too far for Daniel. He was focused on the moment: Jacob's violation; his dick lengthened down his leg; the heady smell of himself in his nose. Jacob waited for Daniel's acknowledgment that they would still work together to help Auggie and his family. Maybe. But Daniel still felt like Jacob owed him more than an apology for his talk with Cornelius. Daniel turned, started walking. Jacob followed. He stopped at Jacob's car.

"If you're really that sorry"—Daniel had one hand on Jacob's car door, while the other suggestively caressed himself—"maybe that's what we should discuss."

EIGHTEEN

JACOB

When Jacob was thirteen, he hovered at newsstands, tried to figure out which adult magazine titles meant naked guys were inside. He didn't know there were entire stores that existed that sold the kinds of magazines he wanted. The probability that two men could sleep together was as much a possibility to him as traveling to Mars. Still, he kept looking. Then back home at night in bed underneath the covers with his penlight, dick in hand, anxious to discover, it would just be page after page of vaginas and breasts.

His father was the nosy parent, always searched through his stuff, always asked questions, listened for the missing parts of Jacob's answers. Jacob used to think it was his mother when he came home and found pieces of his room out of order: a box of love letters from girlfriends opened on his desk, the dates all mixed up, double creases where they'd been unfolded then folded back again wrong; his bed pushed away from his wall, sheets pulled out from under the mattress, a parent's search for the nudie magazines he kept hidden.

When he'd finally had enough of the snooping, Jacob confronted his mother, and that's how he found out it was his father and not her. His underwear drawer was open. He and Alex had challenged each other to a dare: buy a pack of condoms. They wanted to see how they looked. Jacob got excited when he thought about putting them on, he and Alex showing each other (and then what?). In the rec room at his house after school, after they each took their turns at the corner-store counter, after the clerk looked at them and smirked and took too long to put their separate purchases each in its own bag, after Jacob's being so careful not to appear too eager, not to sneak a peek at Alex's crotch to see if they both were equally excited. After all the unfulfilling trips to newsstands, Jacob thought, *This is it, here it goes, finally it's going to happen.* He was anxious, his heart raced, and he had to concentrate to keep his breathing even. Alex pulled out a zucchini, a cucumber, and a banana from his book bag, threw his pack of condoms on the coffee table. They put the condoms on each one, spent what felt like hours comparing curvatures and widths and lengths, wondering what kind of men were able to fill up an entire condom. The latex was smooth and slick, had a rubbery smell like when opening a can of new handballs, and left behind a powdery substance. Alex kept grabbing his crotch and making lewd comments, said if Jacob were a girl he'd stretch him out right there on the table. Jacob thought, *I'm not a girl, but do it anyway.* He was trying to figure out the right combination of words that would turn their thoughts into actions, take them to Mars right on Earth. But nothing happened. Alex left with his fruit and veggies and his condoms. Jacob put one on to see how it felt and jerked off thinking about him. He flushed the condom down the toilet—or so he thought. He found out condoms hold air like balloons; if you threw one in the toilet, you'd better make sure it's flat when it hit the water. His mother told him that when he came home, saw his underwear drawer open, his two remaining condoms sitting on top of his T-shirts instead of where he had hidden them at the bottom of his drawer.

"Ma, why do you keep going through my stuff?"

His mother was at the kitchen table reading and drinking coffee. She put her magazine down.

"Excuse me?"

He asked about the letters, didn't mention the mattress, said his underwear drawer was wide open, figured there was no need to say anything about the condoms.

"You keep the iron and ironing board in your room, and your father irons his shirts for work in there after you leave for school."

Jacob panicked. He saw stars; his eyes opened wide. His bowels shifted on an empty stomach; his nostrils flared; his ears popped and he got dizzy.

She gestured toward a chair.

"Is there something else? You want to sit? Really, it's okay, Jacob. I guess it is time for us to talk."

The "us" to which his mother referred probably included his father, but Jacob was not about to have that conversation with either of them. If his father was the nosy parent, his mother was blunt and direct. Any situation prompted her to talk to him and his brother about their penises and fast girls.

Jacob shook his head no.

His mother sighed. "Okay. Your father does keep asking you to put the iron and ironing board back in the laundry room after you use them." His mother calmly regarded him. Maybe she saw this all the time—kids in her classes growing out of one phase and into another, trying to manage the transition. Maybe she had it marked on a calendar: *here* is where my sons will start; *there* is when we'll need to have *this* conversation. The room spun, Jacob's stomach twisted, and he took in all the air he could through his nostrils.

"You sure you don't want to talk?"

Jacob shook his head a second time. "No, Ma."

"Okay." She went back to her magazine, and Jacob turned to walk away. "Oh, and honey?"

"Yes?"

"The bathroom downstairs? Condoms are like balloons. Hard to flush down the toilet full of air. It's good you know what they are, but you're at an age now where you can't have girls over if we're not home. I know you don't want to talk to me, but please talk to your father."

Jacob ran from his mother, left her sitting right there at the kitchen table. He ran through the dining room, through the living room, took the stairs two at a time, and slammed the door to his bedroom.

Stroke, stroke, kick.
At the wall, flip.

Push off.
Again.

Daniel had Jacob cornered. His gesture was as familiar to Jacob as the expression on his face. Jacob knew he was angry, but he could tell Daniel was also scared. Jacob thought back to their kiss. He'd been kissed like that a few times, had kissed a few brothers like that himself. It wasn't a sharing, romantic experience; it was masturbatory and selfish. Just moaning and sighing in the dark. Pretense, those shortcuts were an easy way to a life too frightening to accept. Sherman changed that for Jacob. Jacob felt them reaching for each other; meeting Sherman was the permission he'd granted himself to confront a life he'd been ignoring. Jacob explained to Daniel that yes, he'd made a mistake and should have included him in his talk with Cornelius—he apologized once more—but the encounter Daniel wanted with Jacob wasn't going to fix what he was feeling. What he wanted was bigger—they both wanted something bigger—than a few heated moments in the back seat of a car. Jacob said they deserved more, that for the men they were, they were writing the manual for the lives they wanted, and that meant they shouldn't make each other pay for things that weren't their fault.

"Look, after all this, we're still helping Auggie. That's something to be proud of."

"Yeah. Then you and Sherman go off running through daisies. What do I get?"

Jacob shook his head.

"I'm just saying."

"I honestly think Cornelius will come through for us."

"Okay. But for real, your parents are the kind of fallback I don't have. Maybe I can lean on my brother and sister for a little while, but that's not gonna last."

"All this happening in Atlanta, even if Cornelius screws us, we'll find other jobs. But I really don't think it'll come to that."

"You say so."

"I do."

Daniel caressed his crotch again, gave Jacob a sly smile. "But just in case...? I can even give you a good review for Sherman...."

Jacob laughed, swung in his direction. "Boy, get away from my car."

The interaction with Daniel pushed Jacob to tell his parents—how could he preach all that to Daniel and not challenge himself? But he had no idea how. Freshman year, Jacob had his first male sexual encounter with a junior from Fort Valley State. Ever since Sale Hall, Sean had been showing Jacob the ropes around campus. There were those who liked to live on the edge—skipped Tuesday Freshman Orientation and Thursday College Assembly to have sex in their dorm rooms. Or the brothers who had late-night hookups in the showers. Those were campus-wide scandals that made a mess when they were discovered. Jacob avoided those, kept to himself except once when he and his next-door neighbor played peekaboo in the shower. A quick jack session was all that happened and neither of them ever mentioned it afterward. Sean said the dude was probably more curious than anything else and being away at college gave him the chance to explore. One day he'd maybe have a very brief gay affair, but he'd live his life with a wife. Jacob and the junior from Fort Valley State met at Loretta's one Friday night. By then, Sean had already figured out Jacob had little sexual experience coupled with a low threshold for alcohol, so when the guy introduced himself by handing Jacob a drink, Sean spilled it on purpose.

"Oops."

The guy looked Sean up and down, pissed. "What's up with that?"

Having two older brothers, Sean knew how to handle himself. "No drinks from strangers we didn't see get mixed." He said that to Jacob. "You're welcome to try again," to their new acquaintance.

Dude laughed, said his name was Conrad and that he liked Sean's style. "It's true—never know if someone handing you a drink with a lil' something in it." He ordered rum-and-Cokes for all of them. Conrad was from New York—uptown—said he always managed to end up meeting brothers from Brooklyn, must be how his vibe flowed. He was dressed New York from head to toe: fuzzy black-bucket Kangol; champagne-colored, gold-rimmed CAZALs; baggy jeans so starched they could have stood up by themselves; and black-striped, fat-laced, shell-toed Adidas that looked like he'd just taken them out of the box. Jacob loved the way he danced—Conrad stepped in close, wound his hips against Jacob, then stepped back, turned around, closed in again, his butt to Jacob's crotch, wiggled his torso, his back brushed up against Jacob's chest. He laughed, spun back around, put his hands on Jacob's waist, ground into him again. "You clean-cut Brooklyn brothas drive me crazy." Conrad professed to be a hip-hop head, although Loretta's spun mostly house music. But when the DJ rocked "The Humpty Dance," Conrad went crazy, waved his hands, jerked back and forth, rapped to the lyrics as he shook his head from side to side. Jacob doubled over with laughter. Sean interrupted their third trip to the bar.

"I think you've had enough." Sean, his arms crossed, stared at Jacob.

"Dude, you killin' me. Don't you got a man somewhere?" Conrad wasn't happy.

"Sean, I'm cool." Jacob was trying hard not to look like the novice that he was.

"No you're not. You look like you're about to fall over." Sean shook his head.

"I got him if he does. I'll take good care of him. Promise." Conrad smiled, licked his lips at Jacob.

"Yeah, I bet you will." Sean stepped between them, steered Jacob by the shoulders. "We gonna bounce." Jacob tried to protest, but Sean wouldn't let go.

"Damn, can I at least get his number?" Conrad winked, puckered his lips and blew Jacob a kiss.

Sean relented long enough for Jacob to write his number on a napkin. "Maybe we can grab lunch tomorrow."

"Bet."

On their drive back to campus, Sean told Jacob to slow down, tried to explain the rules of this new world he was just getting to know. "For real, Jay. There's a lot. You need to just chill."

Conrad called the next day, wanted to hang out before he went back to school that Sunday. They had lunch, which turned into a trip back to his hotel. Conversation turned into kissing, and that turned into getting naked. Jacob thought the good time they had at Loretta's, lunch, the talking, the kissing, the romping around in bed that hadn't been too heavy, their exchange of phone numbers, both of them being from New York, that the sum of all that meant the beginnings of something significant.

"Fort Valley is just about two hours away. Check you out next weekend?"

"Dude. That was just a nut. Don't go all gay on me, act like we dating."

That's what Sean meant when he told Jacob to go slowly: the difference between a one-nighter and a brother who wanted more, where he found himself on that spectrum.

There is this boy.
Small.
Dark.
Swimming.
This is what he knows:
The place from where he swims.
The strength of his limbs.
The certainty of his muscles.
What keeps his body afloat.

Jacob didn't see flags in his future or protests or marches. He wasn't interested in slogans or bullhorns or soapboxes. Whenever he saw gay-rights protests on TV, Black people were absent. It made him feel hidden and forgotten. That wasn't the future he wanted, living a life of the unknown, a life filled with secrets. He saw it all the time—gay brothers with girlfriends or wives, hooking up in the club, the excuses they made, the way they wore coward-ice like badges of honor. *I'm basically straight. . . . I don't do this all the time. . . . What I do is my business.* An undercover brother who didn't have the courage to live the truth of his life. When Jacob told his parents, he wanted them to remember the son they raised. To remember bedtime stories and riding bikes and Jacob learning how to swim. He wanted them to see the proof of his character, that he could stand tall, make his declaration in front of them with respect and confidence, not be ashamed or broken. He wanted them to know that the person he loved might be someone like Sherman, but that didn't make him different from the son they'd always known.

Stroke, stroke, kick.
At the wall, flip.
Push off.
Again.

Sean sat next to Jacob on the couch. "Okay, Jacob. When you tell your parents, remember it can go one of two ways: they could be fine, or they could say they never want to hear about this again."

Jacob nodded. He didn't know what it meant to be in this world without his parents. He lived under his own roof, had his own money, fed himself, paid his bills, bought his own clothes. But there were things for which he still needed his parents; they were his guides for whatever lay ahead. He was back in the kitchen, in front of his mother, asking questions about the things for which he thought she searched.

"I'm not saying you shouldn't tell them. I'm asking if you're ready. I want you to feel what it feels like to turn your whole world upside down. Once you tell them, you can't take it back."

Jacob nodded again.

"Remember that story you told me about when that white boy called you 'nigger'?"

A scrawny little white boy from Bensonhurst called Jacob that one afternoon at swim practice. Jacob was eleven. The coach and all the parents heard him, and so did all the other swimmers. Jacob alone and them, his Black body swimming against all of them, swimming with them, swimming in spite of them. *Swim faster, nigger.* Jacob alone, shocked by the wild way that word sounded; it sent a jolt of anger through his body. He punched the boy in his mouth, dunked his head underwater, and held him there until the coach threw them both out. When his father picked him up that night after practice, Jacob asked him for an insult of white people equivalent to the word "nigger."

Why would you ask me such a question? What happened?

And Jacob told him: They were doing a set of 50-meter freestyle on the clock. Struggling to swim faster than Jacob, the white boy held back the entire lane that swam behind the two of them. Jacob had given him five extra seconds on the clock, but he still caught the white boy. Jacob decided to go in front of him, but instead of the white boy giving Jacob the same courtesy of space, he pushed off directly behind Jacob, started scratching his ankles. Jacob told him to stop. *Swim faster, nigger*, was his response. The coach didn't do a thing, neither did any of the parents.

Jacob's father drove silently. As they navigated home through Brooklyn traffic, the evening turned to night. Jacob didn't feel sad; he didn't feel like he was going to fold up and die. If anything, he felt embarrassed. He felt weak in front of that white boy, the coach, and those parents. He felt like he needed power, something to make him feel strong.

What did you do?

He told his father he punched him, dunked his head underwater. Called him a honky and poor white trash, but that didn't feel strong enough, because that's what they called each other.

I need something with power.

Jacob's father didn't look at him, kept looking straight ahead, driving.

Dad?

There is no equivalent, Jacob. There is no word. His father sounded so distant. Maybe he had returned to the Jim Crow South of his childhood. After all these years he thought he'd come so far just for his son to end up exactly where he started. Arms locked, he gripped the steering wheel with both hands.

Jacob, listen to me.

Yes, Dad.

There are all kinds of people in this world. That white boy and those people on that swim team are just a particular kind of people. I'm sorry to have put you in that environment. I'm sorry, but there is no equivalent to that word. Do you understand what I'm telling you?

No.

You said you want something with power. You want something to make you feel strong?

Yes.

Well then, forget those people, Jacob. Forget them—you just keep swimming, but that doesn't mean you have to go back and swim there with them.

The father stared at the son, waited for confirmation of understanding. Jacob shook his head; he still didn't.

There is nothing I can tell you to make you feel what you're asking. There is no word that exists. Sure, you can call them all the names you can think of—"honky" or "poor white trash" or "cracker" or "redneck" or "peckerwood," but why would you do that? If you do that, you become just like them. And look at you, Jacob, look at you, my son. You are so much better than them. Look at you, alone in a room full of those kinds of people, and what did you do? You kept swimming.

Jacob nodded, his father's meaning finally clear. Their ride the rest of the way home was quiet.

Stroke, stroke, kick.
At the wall, flip.
Push off.
Again.

Sean and Jacob held each other's hands. The room stopped spinning, Jacob's stomach settled, his breathing returned to normal.

"Remember that, Jacob. Remember that your parents love you. Remember they're trying to protect you from things they can't control. Remember what your father said about swimming and power and what he told you about that white boy and that word 'nigger.' Remember there are other words just as powerless."

Jacob listened to Sean, heard what his father said again. He felt the smooth, even flow of his breath, the steady, calm pace of his pulse. He knew what he didn't want for his life. He'd never been anyone's nigger and wasn't about to become anyone's punk or sissy or faggot. He was his parents' son, the man they raised him to be. He hoped they understood. Wasn't sure what he'd do if they didn't. A kiss and hug to Sean and Rodney, then he was off to call his parents.

NINETEEN

DANIEL

Daniel knew Jacob was right—that he wanted Jacob to pay for the anger, anxiety, and fear he felt, the same way Daniel made people pay in the park. Jacob was also right about what he didn't say—that Daniel was fooling himself, thinking his park visits cost him nothing because he wasn't the one kneeling or bending. There was a cost to everything. Daniel felt that now.

Boxes stacked next to the door to Mama's apartment had disappeared with each of Marty's and Lilah's visits. Bags of garbage were in the dumpster out back. Her apartment was almost bare, only a few items of furniture remained. He needed a new place to live, a fresh start at a new beginning. The memory of his last park visit was foggy, but the bruises on his knuckles were reminders it happened. Daniel had run until his lungs hurt and his calves throbbed, and when he got home, he stepped into the shower with all his clothes on. He let the shower flow down over his body, the water mixed with the sweat and dirt. When his clothes were soaked, he peeled them off, then he scrubbed until the spaces between his toes tingled and his armpits hurt. He thought that would make him forget. He thought that would lessen the panic. It didn't. He heard the moans, felt the press of bodies. He lifted his head, closed his eyes against the rushing water. There was a body, sprawled out, spread-eagled in front of him. Again, the cost of his park visits: how something so joyful could be so sorrowful. The emptiness that poured out of him was more sadness than relief. Maybe Mama's lesson to Daniel was this: pay attention to what's possible. Help Auggie and his family. That was also present in what Jacob hadn't said—the power of family. The way Marty took his time presenting Ralph Reid and Mama, how he avoided turning them into monsters.

And there it was a third time; the truth of what love costs.

The sky darkened; shadows crept across the living room's emptiness. A merry-go-round cycled through Daniel's head. Of history and current stories and things yet to come. After he found an apartment, he would have to find Ralph Reid. Or at least try. Someone knocked at the door, and he opened it to his sister carrying packages, the smell of food filling the air.

"Hi." She stepped inside, went to the kitchen. "Have you eaten?"

"Not really hungry."

Lilah returned to the living room with two plates anyway,

set one in front of Daniel. "It's just a little something." Stir-fry chicken with veggies and rice. Shrimp egg rolls, his favorite.

"Thanks." He was hungry. "Just checking on me?"

Looking down from where she sat on the couch, she nodded yes, and the siblings chuckled acknowledgment, a fragile, delicate sound that would break if it got any louder.

The night outside intruded on their silence: crickets' songs whirled in the moonlight; leaves rustled in a breeze; bugs tap-tapped as they flew into the window screen. They ate, listened to the bugs' frustrated tapping, attracted to the lamplight that streamed out the window. Eventually, they either flew away or were caught in the mesh and died. There were more sounds—sirens in the distance; the thumping bass of music; nearer, their shallow breathing, waiting. They both started at once, sudden, verbal leaps forward.

"No, you go 'head," Daniel offered.

"I wasn't going to say nothing—you first."

He looked at the floor, at his plate, anywhere but at his sister, where he knew the truth of what he was about to do looked back at him. "Okay." Then, "What you think of what Marty's been telling us?"

Lilah played with a forkful of food. Scooped, chewed, swallowed, twisted her head, her hair falling over her shoulder. "It's the life we got. It's the life she gave us."

"Is it? Or was she just trying to rescue herself?" Daniel's thoughts still looped, one into the next. He thought about life, his conversations with Jacob. He was going to tell Lilah about himself; he wanted to be completely known by his sister. Marty too. He wanted to be as visible as possible to the only two people who were his family. As for the park, he'd say it was a secret he kept hidden, just like Mama kept hidden the secret of his father. But that the park was also a place where he discovered a part of himself. When he told them about Auggie, they would hear him talking about himself. The innocence of his smile, his dancing eyes, the unrestrained sound of his laughter. They would all agree that Auggie should be older before he discovered the true nature of danger. He'd tell them the part about his attraction to Jacob being new, a part of himself he just discovered. And just like Marty, he was learning the art of revelation. It took time to select the elements, construct the parts, understand the overall presentation, so that what finally showed—the whole with its missing pieces, the falsehoods and the truths, the aspirations to beauty for which one hoped, the messiness with all the misperceptions— was an organized exhibition, even if only to oneself. And so Daniel began. Sometimes he paused for long minutes, sometimes one sentence tumbled, tripped into the next. He was overwhelmed when he finished, as though unable to relieve himself for hours, then, finally, everything came out in one torrential rush.

Lilah reclined against the pillows, feet up, looked down at her brother. Her hair was gelled and pulled back. She had arched eyebrows, and what little makeup she wore accented the strong points of her face: blush, eyeliner, lipstick. She was a striking woman; every day looked more like Mama.

"I think we've all come to a revelation, each of us in our own way. I think what Mama was saying was that it doesn't matter.

It was different the way she said it, but that's what she meant: it doesn't matter, and all we have is each other."

"But I still want to know how it happened, Lilah. I still want to know how Ray didn't end up being my father. And I think I'd like to find Ralph Reid, if I can."

Lilah walked to the window. Lightning bugs danced around bushes, their bright yellow flashes ignited dark shadows. The headlights of cars moved eerily through tree branches. Framed by the blackness of the night in the window, Lilah turned back to the room.

"What will you do about Auggie?"

"Jacob made an arrangement with that council member. He's going to take over the project. Get rid of Beth. There'll be a new developer. Hopefully we'll both have jobs when it's all over."

"Over? Looks like things are just getting started."

Silence intruded again. Lilah returned to the couch; Daniel moved from the floor to join her. They could sit like this for minutes, for hours, each of them in a different place than the other but joined by this couch, the past, their mother.

"Well, at least you get to help, Auggie. And you're right; in some way, it's like helping yourself."

"I know."

They ended up stretched out on the couch, sleeping side by side in a room where the bugs tap-tap or die, and a lamplight's bright circle grows sharper, deeper into the night, until it fades and shrinks smaller with the coming of dawn.

TWENTY

JACOB

I t was simple the way they started. Jacob's father answered his
call. It was his regular check-in to confirm happenings of the
everyday life they expected him to live: that all his bills were
paid and he was saving money; that he kept food in the refriger-
ator and ate a decent meal every so often; that he and his roommates were fine. That first part was easy, sprinkled with laughter
and jokes about little habits and ticks that reminded Jacob and
his dad about the role of father and son. Then they moved to
deeper fare, and Jacob gave his father an update about work. He
diluted the story: Sherman was just a social worker helping Auggie and his family. Cornelius was still an overly ambitious and
intimidating politician whom Jacob hoped he could trust. Beth,
who started out as the neighborhood champion in their earlier
conversations, had turned into a villain. He and Daniel were

finally figuring out how to work together; he felt like a colleague becoming a friend.

"Be careful, Jacob," his father said. "This council member sounds like he doesn't have any ethics, and Beth has proven herself to be nothing but an opportunist." Jacob heard his mother ask what happened, before she picked up the line.

"How's work going, honey?"

"*I'm* talking to Jacob about work."

"So? I can listen. I'd like not to get secondhand information."

There was a brief pause, and Jacob imagined his father sitting in the living room shooting a look at Jacob's mother where she sat in the kitchen.

His father continued, "The thing about these people, Jacob, is that everything is changing and they're trying to figure out how to hold on to what they have or how to get more of what they want and ..." Gentrification was no longer just about the displacement of Black people. Open the paper and there was just as likely to be news of some young, up-and-coming Black person struck down by scandal as there was about some corrupt white politician. And when it came to real estate, Black developers and investors were using the same tricks and legal maneuvers that whites have used for decades in order to swindle good, hardworking, decent people—Black and white—out of property that took some honest person too many years to buy. "Be careful, Jacob. Be very careful. The kinds of decisions you make right now will follow you for the rest of your life." His mother said truer words were never spoken, and Jacob imagined the smiles now exchanged between the living room and kitchen. "Anyway. Enough talk about the world's problems. Tell us something fun—how's your dating life?"

Well. That was the question. Jacob thought of how to say to his father that the condition of his dating life wasn't what any of them expected. That he'd been trying to figure out how to execute the vision his parents presented, but it wasn't working for him.

"Jacob? Are you still there?"

"Yes."

"Did you hear my question?" his father said in a tone that was less a question and more a demand: they anticipated confirmation of things they thought were already known. "Well? Are you dating anyone?"

"I don't know."

His father paused, and Jacob heard him thinking. He heard both his parents thinking, listening for him to say something that would remind them of the little boy they'd always known. They wanted the skinned knees of bike rides and bright, dark eyes inquiring about the future. They wanted talks about manhood and womanhood and how to build a family. They even wanted Black versus white, how good always surmounted evil. Those were the conversations they had, and they traveled a distance, his parents getting him through childhood to the brink of adulthood, knowing he was prepared to go forward. But his hesitation, that was different.

"I don't understand," his father said after a few moments.

"I'm going to hang up now and let the two of you finish." His mother's voice sounded far away and frightened.

"Oh no you don't. You wanted to listen, now listen." His father's voice was steady. His mother sniffed, made sounds like she was crying. The fear in his mother's voice reminded him of the MTV premiere of Michael Jackson's *Thriller* video. A cheerful night between Thanksgiving and Christmas, the house lively with the noises and smells of the holiday just ended, the one yet to come. An uncle dropped by with his family to watch the premiere. Michael and his musical wizardry—his hit songs, his dance moves, the fashion trends he started. Everyone was a fan, Jacob's father and uncle included. And *Thriller* was mesmerizing—Jacob and his cousins sang, laughed, danced along. Near the end, when Michael looked at Ola Ray and said, "I'm not like other guys," Jacob's uncle snickered and his father said, "We know." They sounded dangerous, like they had suddenly become people Jacob didn't know, and he vowed never to become whatever they were laughing at.

"Jacob, what are you talking about? You don't know if you're dating anyone? What are you saying?" His father's voice was loud, but he wasn't shouting. It was the stern authoritarianism of a parent speaking to a child. Except that Jacob wasn't a child anymore, and he was confronted with a decision. That was what Sean meant: to be confronted with the entirety of a life that had been laid out before him and say, *I've discovered something different about myself, but I'm still that same little boy pulling, kicking, swimming. I'm still that same little boy learning to ride his bike. I'm still that same little boy, wide-eyed and looking at the future. Little boy that I was, I've become a man, and there are things that I know. I know that little boy swimming who someone called a "nigger," who someone else might call a "faggot," wants to be happy. I know that little boy is a man because of you, his parents. That little boy who is a man must define his own future.*

Yes, this was different from what they all expected.

"Dad. Ma. I want you to listen to me. I'm okay. I'm healthy and strong and sane. I have a job and clothes on my back and food in my belly and money in my pocket. I have the two of you to thank for all that. I have the two of you to thank for the life I have. I know how much you love me and I know that I'm blessed."

Silence.

"My life is going to be different."

One second. Two seconds. Three.

"And you know this because of someone you're not sure you're dating?"

"I'm gay, Dad. I'm gay. I've met a man who's confronted me with what that means."

His father was quiet, and Jacob's mother exhaled a long, shuddering sigh.

"I want my chance at happiness. I'm going to live a life I can recognize, however different it might be from what we expected. I'm going to live a life I can respect." Jacob heard the sound of his parents breathing on the other end of the phone, but they were too silent. He heard Sean and Rodney moving around, getting ready for bed. Beyond that, the quiet of the neighborhood—fewer cars going by on the street, fewer voices of people out for a walk. Beyond that still, Atlanta settled down for the night. Jacob heard it: Husbands kissed wives. Children were tucked in. Lovers sighed after sex. The world spun. A clock ticked. Somewhere the sun rose on a new morning.

"This is a surprise for which we are entirely unprepared. We understand that you're an adult and you'll make your own decisions about the kind of life you're going to live. We do love you, but this is a disappointment. This is beyond anything we could have ever expected. This is the first and last conversation we'll have about this."

"But—"

"Jacob, we're not going to argue. Your mother and I are going to hang up now." Then the line went dead.

The room folded in on Jacob sitting alone on the edge of his bed. He heard what his father said again. There was no shouting, no anger, no words that spoke of hatred, no condemnation. Maybe somewhere Jacob was ready for that. Maybe he had all manner of eloquent arguments to counter an unloving, outright hateful rejection. But he was unprepared for his parents' silent, sudden withdrawal, their loving, unyielding refusal to accept. He felt himself slowly going numb.

TWENTY-ONE

DANIEL

Beth was unprepared to lose the project, because she doubted the brutality of Cornelius's ambition. To him, she was just another white woman in an unending history of white people who fed off Black people with parasitic intent. They didn't have a care in the world of what happened afterward. After people lost their homes and livelihoods and dreams because the community in which they had lived their entire lives, in which the greater society had always been uninterested, was suddenly valuable to someone else. Beth's problem with Elsie Grace was that she never took the woman seriously, Beth found her activism fascinating. As though it were a fetish to be trotted out and displayed solely for entertainment. She didn't understand the trust Elsie Grace cultivated, that her work was actually a passion of the spirit. Didn't understand the woman had witnessed the death of a million tomorrows; she refused to witness a million more. And Beth thought that being Jacob's and Daniel's employer was enough to command their allegiance, her master-slave mentality morphed into a modern context. The synergy between the four of them was a deadly brew concocted against her.

Cornelius produced legislation that stated Summerhill was part of a federal renewal area. He rallied federal and state legislators, the mayor, and the governor to support his cause. The city council established the Summerhill Redevelopment Authority, then ceded control of it to Cornelius and the mayor. Everyone agreed the Olympics was a good start, but this project was more. The federal and state governments arranged an elaborate scheme that used tax credits to increase profit margins for the developer and all contractors involved in the project. But only if companies opened Summerhill offices, hired from the Summerhill community, and could get their bids through the city council's approval process that was controlled by Cornelius and the Summerhill Redevelopment Authority. It was exactly what Elsie Grace wanted. Beth was bewildered by the speed at which she'd lost control. She asked her investors to help her fight, but once they adjusted to the new requirements, their investments were protected. They told Beth she was aggressive and smart, but picking fights with Cornelius and Elsie Grace was stupid. Her attorney advised her that she'd either be broke or dead by the time the lawsuit she threatened was reviewed for its merits, delayed, and reviewed again. All this and Jacob had given Cornelius the reason: the dreams of little Auggie and his family. Cornelius said better publicity couldn't be bought. Big government and big development coming together to make sure there was something better for the people impacted by the

Olympics. Atlanta's housing office would provide low-interest, forgivable loans to returning families for the down payments to buy new houses in Summerhill. And with the benefit of homeownership, the families would end up paying less to buy the new houses than they would have spent if they'd continued renting.

The seven houses were only the beginning. The creation of new living-wage jobs. New, affordable housing. A nationally recognized grocery chain would open a thirty-thousand-square-foot grocery store. The operators guaranteed they'd stock fresh, healthy food options, even gave a twenty-five-thousand-dollar grant to PSGM to implement the Summerhill Farmers Market until the grocery store opened. The Center for a Progressive Atlanta would control five thousand square feet of retail space for the development of local small businesses. Cornelius gloated, lamented that the next mayoral election was a year away—coordinating successful collaborations between federal, state, and local governments, orchestrating private partnerships, said he'd win without even campaigning. And he stayed true to his word, secured new positions for Daniel and Jacob: they'd both be project managers working with the Summerhill Redevelopment Authority, making sure all the items in the community-benefits agreement were implemented and assisting the Fund for Atlanta in identifying families for the affordable housing. They'd also be assisting with the management of the new developer, Ralph Reid Development Partners, Incorporated.

Daniel thought about the coincidence of their new employer. He wouldn't have to go looking for his father after all. He checked himself, slowed his breathing, closed his eyes a moment before he went back to packing. Beth tried to prevent them from returning to the office. Cornelius had even taken care of that—armed with a court order that gave Daniel and Jacob access to the office until they had packed and removed all of their belongings, Detectives Wilson and Kennedy escorted them back. Daniel watched Jacob as they packed, decided something was wrong with him, something was off. He dragged the whole day, went listlessly from one task to the next. His eyes were red and he looked as though he hadn't slept. Daniel wanted to ask how much Jacob knew about their new employer. They were in the bathroom now, washing ink off their hands.

"Funny how that toner exploded," Daniel ventured.

Standing side by side at the sink, they saw each other in the mirror. Jacob didn't look up, just shrugged and continued washing his hands. He was distant, far away, and preoccupied with things that were not there. But Daniel was overwhelmed with thoughts about his father.

"You know anything about this developer?"

Silence.

They finished washing their hands, and Jacob was still too quiet, still lost in his thoughts. They stood face-to-face, dried their hands. Jacob looked up, and Daniel was shocked by what he saw. The sadness. The fear. The questions. This was a new and un-known Jacob who made Daniel stop. This wasn't the same man with whom he worked, full of bombast and swagger, the confi-dence to accomplish any task, ignorant of failure. This wasn't the same man he kissed in the car. This Jacob looked hollow, had an emptiness in him trying to get out. Jacob saw Daniel staring at him, realized Daniel recognized the hurt evident all over his face. Jacob hesitated, then he plowed ahead, gulping, grabbing, gnawing, and Daniel followed, the two of them stumbling into a stall. Daniel pulled back first, to look at Jacob again, to see if he could identify what he usually saw whenever he looked at Jacob.

"Hey, what's wrong with you?" Daniel caught Jacob's chin, concentrated, peered deeply into the other man's eyes. Jacob jerked his chin away, ground harder against Daniel's leg, decided he liked hearing Daniel whimper surprise, and kissed him again. If the Daniel who had taken the tour those few months ago stood here with this Jacob, what started at the sink would be approaching an energetic and vigorous climax. But Daniel was listening to whispers that warned him of the consequences that came with certain actions. He thought of Mama and his father. He remembered his conversation with Jacob about the betrayal he felt, Jacob's admonishment that they shouldn't require each other to pay the costs of someone else's expenses.

"Jacob, what are you doing?" This Jacob was off, desperate and different and out of order. Something happened. "Are you okay?"

Jacob unbuckled his pants. "I thought this was what you wanted."

"Like this? Here in the men's room at work? And those detectives out there might hear us."

"We don't work here anymore. And is a car really that different? Or the park? And maybe we should invite those detectives to join us. Especially that Detective Wilson."

Jacob's pants and underwear were down, he leaned over the toilet with his ass aimed at Daniel's crotch. His ass was as pretty as Daniel knew it would be; two brown mounds of chocolate perfection, peeking out from underneath the tail of his shirt. Daniel heard their conversation and knew this wasn't right. Whatever was hurting Jacob, he only thought this would be easier—his ass turned up, straddled, wide legged over a toilet—if just for the frenzied few moments it'd take them to finish. But Daniel knew from his experience in the park that Jacob would only end up feeling worse. He thought back to their talk about how much small things cost, how they sometimes took a back seat to the big things they actually want. Daniel saw Jacob, saw that they truly might be friends, but if this happened between them like this, their friendship would never develop. He had to do for Jacob what Jacob had done for him.

Daniel reached, pulled up Jacob's underwear and pants. Gently, with the tenderness of an attentive lover, tucked in his shirt, buckled his belt together. "Not like this, Jacob."

Daniel pulled Jacob close, hugged him around his waist, his chin resting on Jacob's shoulder. What was only minutes could have been hours of them standing in front of that toilet, Daniel holding Jacob, feeling him shake and shudder until Jacob suddenly bucked against Daniel, pushing them back and out of the stall.

"You're a real bitchified cunt, you know that, Daniel?" Jacob was crying. "A fucking lost, sometimey, confused little faggot." Then he slammed his way out the bathroom, out the office, out the building and into the world.

TWENTY-TWO

JACOB

Jacob felt outside himself, like he was looking at himself backward. The conversation with his parents had him frozen. Sean had said to expect "either/or" from them, but he forgot to mention the possibility of "and," a mid-space nether place of nothing. *We love you* and *We're disappointed. You're an adult making your own decisions* and *We never want to hear about this again. We will not argue with you, Jacob,* and *We're done talking.* Absolutely numbing. Jacob was ready for anger. He had prepared himself for shouting. He had readied explanations of why and when and how. What he hadn't thought about was the purgatory of a truce, a yielding, languishing suspension. And then to be bent over a toilet in front of Daniel, wiggling his bare ass. Jesus. Jacob wanted to erase that from happening, ignore the feeling of what he needed. He wove his way through traffic, pressed down hard on the gas. City lights streaked by—blurs of yellows and reds and greens—as he picked up speed, cut between cars, and took corners too sharply, the benign appearance of his little white car taking on the edge and aggression of a predator. Jacob wanted to feel something. Wanted to feel like he belonged somewhere with someone. He should have gone home, but he knew where his little car was taking him and he didn't care. He just smiled when Sherman opened his door to see him standing there.

"Think, and the man shall appear." The solid form of Sherman filled up the doorway, the sharp corners of his shoulders tapering downward to his narrow waist. Jacob felt a familiar swelling beginning to stir in recognition.

"Hey, back at you. What you doing?"

"I just told you. How was your day?"

"Difficult."

"Come here. Sit down. Tell me about it."

They sat on Sherman's couch, Jacob's back to Sherman's chest, Sherman's hands magic on his neck. Jacob melted under the steady, sure certainty of his touch. Sherman asked what happened again and Jacob mumbled a response, appreciated the gentleness of his touch, but wanted his touch to be something else. Sherman asked Jacob to repeat himself—he hadn't understood—and Jacob thought to himself it didn't matter, because conversation wasn't what he wanted. He wiggled, shifted against Sherman, and they were eye to eye at a different angle; another moment and they were kissing.

Somewhere beyond the veil of the numbness Jacob felt, he saw what he was doing. He thought, *This maneuvering I'm doing is unfair, and it might even be wrong.*

On the side table, next to the couch, the phone rang, and Jacob kissed Sherman before he could answer. By the time they finished it had stopped ringing. Jacob knew it was Rodney or Sean—he hadn't spoken with either of them since his conversation with his parents. The phone ringing gave him a moment's pause. He thought to himself, *Maybe I should try harder not to do what I'm feeling. Maybe we should take our time. Maybe I should remember what I told Daniel.*

"I'm hungry. You want to go out?"

"You should've said that before you came in here and started all this." Sherman looked down at his swollen crotch.

"I'll make it up to you later."

"Really?"

Jacob didn't answer, just leaned in and kissed Sherman hard, urgent, and not gentle.

Sherman pulled back, stared like Jacob was a new person. "You okay?"

"I'm fine." He gave Sherman another kiss, a light peck on the lips. "You ready?"

After dinner they went to Traxx, a gay club that catered to an all-Black crowd on Friday and Saturday nights. It was in an old warehouse building on Luckie Street and had three levels—a bar and pool tables on the first floor, hip-hop and reggae played on the second floor, and the third floor was divided between a dance floor for house music and a sitting area. Strippers worked the sitting area, and there were lots of dark corners. Friday nights were always the best; the place was packed with brothers. After a few drinks at dinner, Jacob was worse: his lips were loose, his eyes glazed over. The hurt had become an aching pulse, and he was losing his fight with himself. When Sherman asked after him again, and Jacob made a remark about his parents being in New York, Sherman just stared and Jacob looked down, pretended the flashing club lights shone in his eyes. He reminded himself about caution, looked up, pulled Sherman close for another kiss. Sherman reached for Jacob's hand, interlocked their fingers, said he liked the way their hands looked, one pressed against the other. Sherman kissed the back of Jacob's hand, rubbed it against the side of his face. They kissed again, long, exploring, and slow. The strobe lights, the loud music, the alcohol coursing through Jacob's system. Jacob squeezed Sherman's hand, and Sherman squeezed back. Jacob got another rum-and-Coke from a passing barhop that was gone in two swallows.

"Jay. What's going on?"

"Nothing. You want something?"

"No."

In the blinking club lights Sherman studied Jacob more closely. This time when Jacob tried for another kiss, Sherman wasn't so quick to kiss back. *Caution*, Jacob reminded himself. *Go cautiously and slow.* But the hurting ache made it difficult. Another barhop, another drink gone in two swallows, and Sherman let go of his hand. Jacob stopped himself from grabbing Sherman back in panic.

They were on the second floor, a rockers tune blared across the speakers. Grinding hips wound to the hyped-up reggae rhythm, one brother going low, catching the heavier, underlying beat, his partner riding the alternating tempo higher. Hands on hips, thighs touching, shoulders against chests, the music was a wave making brothers pulse together. Jacob could feel the heat of Sherman standing behind him, his breath glazed Jacob's neck, a tingling sensation rippling down his spine. He stepped back, directly into Sherman, and when Sherman didn't move, Jacob leaned into his chest until

Sherman wrapped his arms around Jacob. The rum-and-Cokes continued to work their magic, had Jacob teetering on the edge of wildness. He grabbed Sherman's hand—"Let's dance"—and led them to the dance floor, picking up the beat and swinging into motion. Arms above his head, Jacob clapped to the rhythm, dipped his waist to the time, rocked left to right, gave another clap-clap, waist-dip again, this time rocked right to left. All the while he held Sherman in his eyes. Sherman only watched, didn't dance at first. The expression on his face hovered somewhere between a smile and a smirk, and after the conversation Jacob had had with his parents, and being in the bathroom with Daniel, he didn't need that look from Sherman. He was losing the fight. Jacob closed his eyes, another clap-clap, another waist-dip, and he rolled his head backward. He turned, backed firmly into Sherman, ground his butt into his crotch. Sherman moaned, steadied himself holding on to Jacob's hips, but he didn't pull away. A harder beat blared louder through the speakers, a faster two-quarter tempo, and Jacob kept pace with the upswing and the down cadence, rocking double time against Sherman. The heat of his breath on Jacob's neck came coarse and rapid as Sherman held tightly on to Jacob's hips, his excitement rubbing hard and steady with the rhythm.

"Jay, I don't know about all this right now," Sherman moaned, his declaration sounding more like a whimper. But Jacob was wild and warm and losing.

It was awkward. Jacob was more than a little drunk by the time they got back to Sherman's. He kept kissing Sherman and Sherman kept telling him to stop.

"In the morning we're going to talk," Sherman said. "In the morning when you're sober and you can tell me why all of this all of a sudden."

Sherman was trying to do for Jacob what Jacob had done for Daniel, and what Daniel had done for him in return. But Jacob's parents were too loud. The time he spent debating himself in preparation to tell them, and he had just been ignored. Somewhere deep inside, buried beneath the dazed, chilled effect caused by his parents, Jacob felt the cost of what he was doing to Sherman. Sherman was still talking, still asking questions, trying to figure out what happened. But he didn't know Jacob's experience, didn't know the number of brothers and bedrooms and the things he would barely allow himself to acknowledge. After a night of dancing, after a night of drinking, after being in a room full of men where they all desperately wanted to hear exactly the one thing they wouldn't say, the one thing that would help them hold on to something—to themselves, to each other, to their families, maybe even to life itself—but where they were stuck not knowing how to get from one thing to the next, the sex was easy, silent, and quick. Fumbling came first. Fucking next. And then there was morning. Sherman was trying to be different; Sherman was trying to prove they could be more joy than relief to each other. But Jacob was drunk and hurting and still hearing his parents. He needed the relief first before any joy could come. He needed to silence the voices of his parents. The situation became clearer the more Jacob listened to Sherman. He calmed down and stopped with all the kisses. Sherman made him drink water. He let Sherman put him in the shower. Sherman talked about the things they could do the next day, the next week, the next month. Sherman said the things Black men never say to each other. Jacob pretended. Jacob waited. Jacob listened. And when they were finally in bed and Jacob was comfortable and warm and entangled with Sherman under the covers, Jacob said more things Black men never say to each other: he thanked Sherman for taking care of him, for making him feel safe, for making him feel wanted. Sherman asked Jacob again if everything was okay, and Jacob thought about his parents. Jacob told him the next day, next week, next month all sounded fantastic. Sherman smiled, like it was the first thing he understood all night. They kissed lightly at first, then more passionately with mounting desire.

Their bodies were a song for each other. They rose and they fell, they rocked and they tumbled. Sherman cried, opened up a place in Jacob, cried and made Jacob think of his parents. Sherman whispered while he was inside Jacob, moaned for them to belong to each other. *We should be ours.* Jacob felt the rhythm of his words, *Belong to me. Be mine. I am yours.* Over and over. Jacob had never belonged to anyone for any reason except for his parents. And no one had ever belonged to him. *Belong to me, Jacob.* The way his parents belonged to each other. For Sherman to watch Jacob walk, for Jacob to listen to Sherman talk, for them to eat, make love, sleep, get up, and do it all over again. How does that happen? Was it time for that yet? When does that begin? To race home from work just to be together, to say what they're thinking and know that they'd listen, know that they'd understand. *We are each other.* How does Jacob say that he belonged to another man? *Belong to me, Jacob. I am yours.* Jacob tried not to listen to Sherman, tried not to hear his parents, tried to empty himself of everything but the moment. He couldn't. Sherman kept whispering, and there on the bed as they rode the waves of each other, Jacob thought about the little blue house with the white picket fence around it. He thought about holidays. Easter. Thanksgiving. Christmas. At whose house? With whose family? *Belong to me, Jacob. I am yours. Trust.* Jacob thought, men that they are, Black, beat-up, proud, scared, confident, insecure, angry, intelligent, hurt, hurtful, resourceful, threatened, threatening, honest, deceitful, masculine, feminine, human, what was left after the world finished? Would there be enough of them left for each other? For each of them to say, *Here, baby, rest, but don't give up?* "Belong to me," Sherman had whispered. Just loud enough to peek into the future, but not loud enough for Jacob to forget the cost of his parents. When they finished, there was no relief for Jacob; the hurt ached worse, and joy felt far away and distant.

———

The sun rose the next morning. Sherman was on his stomach, snoring a light sound that wasn't unpleasant, his head turned toward Jacob. One arm bent up under the pillow, the other disappeared under the covers. His bare back rose and fell with each breath, the sound of him sleeping so gentle. A muscle twitched; an arm moved as he rolled onto his side. Jacob wondered what he was dreaming about. If Sherman could imagine a hole in his future. If he would understand the panic Jacob felt. He had needed something familiar, something he knew would deaden the hurt. But it didn't work. Maybe Jacob wouldn't have to do anything, just stand there and Sherman would see it anyway, especially if he tried, and he'd understand, and then Jacob would say sorry and they could return to who they were before last night, and everything would be as it was. Sherman was right; they should have waited. In the morning everything would have been different—a different morning than Jacob was used to after the kind of night he'd had. A different morning would have made the future so bright. Stealthily, quietly, he tried to find his clothes.

"You're up."

"Yeah. I was trying not to wake you."

"You didn't."

"Okay." Silence.

"You leaving?"

"Yeah. I would have woken you up first." Even to himself, Jacob sounded like he was lying.

"Don't say what isn't true."

Jacob wanted to move, to vanish, but his jeans were missing and he couldn't find his underwear.

"You going to tell me what all that was about last night?"

He didn't answer.

"Look at me, Jacob. That's the least you can do."

Holding what clothes he'd found, Jacob stood in the middle of Sherman's room and felt lost, like he'd stolen something and gotten caught. Sherman sat up in bed, tears beginning to well in his eyes. He looked like as hard as he tried to hope otherwise, this is exactly what he expected. Jacob could still feel what Sherman whispered last night. He could still hear the voices of his parents.

"For not being the one who got fucked, I sure feel like it."

Sherman sat in the bed, bare chested and beautiful with the covers pulled up to his waist. Jacob tried to reason with himself, tried to form the words, *Sherman, I need your help*, but something stopped him. The hurt and anger came together, and he wanted to say to him, *Don't tell me you haven't been here before. How can you sit there in judgment?* and then again, *I need your help.*

"I seem to remember you having to apologize. Twice." Jacob's voice fell to the floor.

"You're really going to compare those moments to what just happened?"

Jacob didn't answer.

"I didn't fucking think so." Sherman climbed out of bed. "I'm going to the bathroom. Please be gone when I get back."

Jacob found the rest of his clothes in the living room. Sherman had folded his jeans and shirt, placed them in a neat pile on the couch. His car keys and wallet sat on the coffee table. The night was such a blur, and now everything had been perfectly ruined. He heard Sherman in the bathroom, the water running. Jacob had no idea what he might have said if he'd gone in to Sherman. An apology didn't seem like enough. Sherman deserved an explanation, but the more Jacob thought about telling Sherman about his parents, the more he couldn't think at all. His thinking became foggy and everything in his present seemed blurry. He took one step, then another, found his way outside to his car. The air felt like the end of summer approaching. Such an ordinary day for him to feel so different. He had woken up, breathing, inhaling and exhaling as expected. He still had his same ten toes, his same ten fingers, his ears, eyes, nose. But there were parts of him missing—the history of who he was, the future of who he would become. Jacob drove a few blocks before he pulled over and let the tears flow, steady and silent.

TWENTY-THREE

DANIEL

Daniel thought this moment should be bigger. That the clouds should part as a rainbow arced across the heavens and song from disembodied ethereal voices floated through the air. It was too quiet. Marty ushered in silence when he walked through the door carrying a taupe-brown shoebox, which he set on the kitchen table. Daniel and his siblings stared at the box. The sparkling gold stars on the surface of the plastic tabletop reflected small bits of light around it. That's the kind of fanfare Daniel expected to attend Marty's revelation. The kitchen was so clean: no dishes in the sink, just the gleam of stainless steel cradling rays of sunlight through the window; the stovetop brilliantly white, stripped bare of layers of grease; the linoleum swept, scrubbed, and mopped, free of its blackest spots. And all of this, too, seemed appropriate—a crisp, fresh, shining new beginning, heralding confirmation of

Daniel's father. Daniel stared at the box, wondered if its contents would align with his feeling—that the pieces of Mama's life that Marty'd been sharing would add up to more than what he already knew. His life of asking, of searching and looking for evidence of his beginnings, should amount to more than just a brown box sitting on a table. It should be heart-pounding, surprising, and unexpected, just like life with Mama.

Marty coughed, yawned, stretched. Sunlight hit the table, the stars dazzled even more brightly, the light twinkled warmly on Daniel's face. He stared at the box. The pieces of himself were beginning to settle, organize themselves into a coherent, recognizable whole. Daniel would like to know this Ralph Reid—the events that occurred between Mama and him that resulted in Daniel's existence; the reason they didn't stay together; if Ralph Reid even knew that Daniel existed.

"So you know what's in here?"

"I do."

"You think I should open it?"

"I do. Whenever you're ready."

There were news articles in the box—a few clippings from the *Atlanta Daily World*—about a local businessman, Ralph Reid, who'd begun buying single-family houses and small rental buildings in southeast and southwest Atlanta. The first article, dated March 1971, described how he'd moved to Atlanta from up North— New Jersey—before Maynard Jackson was elected mayor, the first Black man to be elected mayor of a major southern city. Reid had heard Atlanta was the place for Black folks to be, that Atlanta was going to be at the forefront of creating opportunities for Black Americans. A second article in April 1976 included a black-and-white picture of Ralph Reid, who looked to be a tall, well-built man with a head full of curly black hair. He was dressed in a light-colored suit, shirt and tie, standing near a small building he owned on Gordon Street. The article said he was a local landlord, quoted his excitement about the development of MARTA, that access to reliable public transportation was going to be a great economic boost to residents living in areas like West End. He was thrilled Jimmy Carter was on his way to the White House, that Maynard Jackson had proven himself a progressive advocate for the interests of Black Atlanta. The last article was from May 1984, and it was mostly a send-up trumpeting Reid's acquisition of a few vacant sites of land on Georgia Avenue in Summerhill. He envisioned building a project that would have restaurants, local shops that served the needs of neighborhood residents, and provide affordable housing—for renters, yes, but particularly for homeowners, because that was the way to build equity and security for a family. The reporter stated that Summerhill was an afterthought—not quite a ghetto, but almost—and it'd take years to amass both capital and political support for the project Reid proposed. "Real estate has cycles," was his response. "Today's down markets are tomorrow's gold mines. You watch—these few sites I just bought for pennies will be worth millions." The article went on to describe Reid as a community crusader, referenced his profiles in years past, said he'd never once evicted a tenant, nor did he believe in charging the highest amount of rent he could get. Daniel read all this, said it was nice to have this introduction to the man, but other than that, wondered why Mama even kept the articles.

"Maybe that was the point. Maybe she was trying to find him, if only just to tell him about you. Maybe she kept tabs on him through those articles—they might have mentioned somewhere he lived or where he worked or the address of one of the houses he owned."

Daniel looked at his brother. "But wouldn't she have known that already?"

Marty shook his head. "Well, Ray started to suspect something was going on. There were times she came home late. Said she'd stopped by the landlord's office to talk to him about fixing something, drop off the rent, or make arrangements for paying what was past due. It'd turn into an argument—Ray would say that's what the phone was for, and Mama would shoot back that if he had a steady income she wouldn't have to speak with the landlord in the first place. Ray wasn't buying it—said she was a married white woman with children, and Reid was a Black man, and even if this was Atlanta, this was still the South. Said he'd find us somewhere else to live or he'd cause problems. So we moved, and then you were born."

Daniel looked from one sibling to the other. "Why didn't Mama just leave Ray?"

Marty snorted. "And do what? Two kids, a newborn, and no money? Back then, this Reid guy was just getting started. And he was Black. And Mama was white. And this was definitely the South, Daniel. They were just trying to live."

Daniel nodded understanding. "Well, why did Ray stay?"

Lilah and Marty both laughed. "Where was he going to go? That one time he found us a new place was the only time I ever remember him helping with anything. He found the place. He paid the deposit and first month's rent. He made all the arrangements with the utility companies. He got his friends to move us. Mama didn't have to do nothing, and I'd never seen her so quiet. They did have more arguments—especially after you were born. I don't think she knew she was pregnant when we moved."

Lilah's voice trailed off, and the three of them sat, remembering their childhood as though it just happened. Daniel stood up, shook his hands, stretched. Looked down at the news clippings again.

"You're going to be working for the man. You are going to tell him, aren't you? You figure out how?"

Daniel shook his head. "I don't know. What if I tell him and he fires me? What if before I even open my mouth he can see who I am?"

The three of them looked at one another, their faces more questions than answers.

TWENTY-FOUR

JACOB

The second press conference was different from the first. Construction resumed as soon as Cornelius took control of the project. The Summerhill Redevelopment Authority supervised the completion of demolition and the start of work on the foundations. Cornelius arranged for Jacob and Daniel to meet the new developer, Ralph Reid. He wanted to meet them as well, to review plans for the initial site he took over and tell them about his vision for the larger project. They also suspected he just wanted to make sure they'd be a good fit as his new project managers. Ralph asked Elsie Grace to join the meeting, said it was an opportunity to establish a clean slate working with the community, so they met before the press conference to be sure that they'd be comfortable with one another when talking to the public. Jacob kept his distance from Daniel, responded only to

Ralph as he described how he planned to proceed. Elsie Grace had also invited representatives from community-based organizations to be Cornelius's featured guests at the press conference, which Ralph thought was a great idea.

"I don't hold the two of you accountable for how Beth Washington conducted herself. I just want you to know that. And we appreciate you didn't press charges, Jacob. Those people got out of hand and they're no longer affiliated with us." Elsie shook hands with Jacob and Daniel.

"It seems like we were all in the wrong place at the wrong time." The authority in his own voice sounded strange compared to how Jacob felt. There was so much happening around him that felt beyond his control.

Elsie Grace smiled, nodded at Jacob's youthful brown face, remembering when she had first started this work. What she heard in his voice was the tempering resonance of experience. "Indeed. But here we are now, moving forward. Having the groups at the press conference will be important. It'll let them know they're a valued partner in this project. I'll be sure to introduce you to the executive director of the Fund for Atlanta."

Later, Ralph said their first meeting had gotten off to a positive start. Said he understood Jacob and Daniel were employees of the Summerhill Redevelopment Authority, but that good communication between all of them would translate into project success. Jacob mostly listened. Studied this Black man for clues as to the kind of person he'd be working with. Ralph seemed different from Beth, more confident in his interactions, less insistent that he be recognized as the person in charge. Daniel was quiet, which made Jacob think they were both silent for the same reason—he too was stuck on what happened between the two of them.

"Do you think we'll get a chance to speak with you one-on-one?" Daniel asked Ralph.

Ralph looked at Daniel and shrugged. "Sure. We can set up regular meetings. What do you think—weekly progress meetings? Or would every other week be better?"

Daniel shook his head. "No, this would be about something outside of this project."

Ralph looked appraisingly at Daniel. "You not thinking about quitting on me? I've only heard good things from Cornelius about you two."

Daniel took a breath, held Ralph's steady, searching gaze. "I'm not quitting. It's not about this project."

"Have my assistant schedule a time for us to talk."

It was a late September day and the sun shone in a cloudless, brilliantly blue sky, the merest hint of fall in the air. Jacob and Daniel sat in the VIP section with Cornelius's featured guests. Ralph and Elsie Grace sat on the dais with the mayor and Cornelius. Little Auggie and his family were also on the dais, and Sherman sat with them. Elsie Grace introduced Cornelius, said that this project was being given a reinvigorated beginning thanks to him, proof that he was the neighborhood's champion. He had worked hard to make sure Summerhill became a true partner in the development of its future. When Cornelius spoke this time, he didn't start with thunder, and he didn't give a sermon about the history of the neighborhood. He quietly told the story of a single mother and her children; painted a vivid picture of that mother waking up every day in her little house in Summerhill to feed and clothe her family before sending them off to school and herself to work. That each night they returned home to a house full of love and a hot dinner. Cornelius said their house was small and clean and simple, and though it might be rented, it was theirs, they were comfortable, and in this quiet, simple home, this mother—who asked no one for nothing—did her best to take care of her family and prepare for their future. And because Cornelius was a theatrical politician, he picked up the cadence and volume of his voice when he described how one day, this mother and her family were told to get out, that they must make way for the future, that they must surrender to the coming of the Olympics. The house where she lived and raised her family, this house that no one had ever wanted, the home where they were comfortable and had dreamed of the future, this house and the land on which it sat had become prime real estate, and Atlanta must not falter. Atlanta must herald the arrival of a new era. No longer content to be the New City of the South, Atlanta must become an International Destination. This place—this house with this mother and these children—must be the focal point of Atlanta's evolution. . . .

As Cornelius spoke and the crowd listened, Jacob watched little Auggie sitting next to Sherman. He coughed, yawned, fidgeted, leaned his head against Sherman. He swung his legs back and forth, tapped his foot against his chair. Sherman leaned down, whispered in his ear, and Auggie straightened, sat up. Jacob's eyes found Sherman's for a few seconds, long enough to scatter his thoughts, and by the time Jacob remembered to smile, Sherman had turned his head. Auggie stopped kicking but went back to leaning against Sherman, who moved his arm so the little boy could lean in more comfortably. The ache inside Jacob still hurt. Sherman's whispered, *Belong to me*, still clashed with his conversation with his parents. Jacob wanted a do-over, to find a way to repair all the damage. He needed a way to make his own announcement, stand in front of a crowd, just like Cornelius, and make a proclamation about the future. To not just smile at the image of Sean and Rodney cuddled up, but also make that a part of his reality—the sum of all he'd be—his intimate connection to Black men. To recognize it as part of how he'd navigate the world, make it a part of his strength instead of treating it as a deficit. It would be a gift to himself, a true step into the future, a way to truly establish his independence.

Cornelius formally introduced Ralph Reid as the new developer for the project, an honest broker dedicated to Summerhill's future. A northern transplant who had developed strong southern roots, Ralph had become a native son of Atlanta. He was a benevolent landlord with numerous properties dotted across the southern crescent of Atlanta. That meant he understood the community in which he worked—its needs, its wants, its dreams for tomorrow. He wasn't an outside interloper, here to build for a minute then vanish with his profits. He was here to make an investment, and, as proof, Cornelius introduced Auggie and his family as the first residents who would become homeowners in Ralph Reid's new community. Ralph had even agreed to house them in one of his other properties until their new home was ready. Cornelius's speech ended to thunderous applause and a standing ovation. Ralph and Elsie Grace joined him at the podium, their arms raised triumphantly, all of them holding hands. Photographers snapped photos of Cornelius with Auggie and his family; microphones were pushed in everyone's faces. Cornelius waved for Jacob and Daniel to join him and Ralph, as light bulbs flashed and reporters clamored. He introduced the two of them as his new project managers working with the Summerhill Redevelopment Authority. He said they'd be monitoring the project's progress and would be working to keep his office and the community updated. Cornelius told them to smile, said the worst thing in the world to see first thing in the morning was a picture of yourself grimacing under a headline. The crowd laughed. Cornelius told them how Jacob and Daniel alerted him to the plight of Auggie and his family. Said they were project managers with the souls of community activists, a Morehouse graduate and a lifelong Atlanta resident. Couldn't ask for better caretakers than that.

As they congratulated one another for protecting the future of Atlanta, Cornelius posed with the mayor. They said taking care of Atlanta's own while preparing to host the world was the best preparation for the Olympics. Cornelius introduced Sherman as a future commissioner; it was his agency's vigilance that prevented Auggie and his family from slipping through the cracks. The mayor invited Sherman to take a picture, agreed that Sherman was indeed a future commissioner. Jacob experienced the activities happening around him from a different time and space. Sherman and Daniel introduced themselves, before Sherman said something to Auggie and his mother, and the little boy gave Daniel a hug. Jacob tried to join the merrymaking, but Sherman rebuffed his approach. The ache inside him became a hollow pulse.

Jacob headed for his car once the press conference was over, remembered six months ago there'd been a riot where bottles fell from the sky. The walk to his car was quiet now, but inside his head was chaotic.

"Hi, Mr. Sherman's friend."

It took a moment for Jacob to focus on Auggie. "Hi, Auggie. What are you doing by yourself?"

"I'm not." He pointed. His mother, sister, and Sherman were a few yards away, standing next to Sherman's car.

"Oh."

"You look like you're about to cry."

The frankness of children. "I was just thinking about something."

"Well, Mommie says you should come eat with us. She says she wants to thank you. She says you can't say no." He paused, puzzled through something. "And if you come eat with us, maybe you'll feel better and won't want to cry anymore."

Jacob smiled at Auggie, looked down the block to where Auggie's mother and sister waved. Sherman stared but didn't move a muscle.

"Is Mr. Sherman coming?"

"Of course!" Auggie said, and shrugged like Jacob was the dumbest person on the planet. Of course he knew the answer to that question.

"Well, Auggie, I don't know—" But Auggie grabbed his hand and dragged him toward his family.

"Mommie, Mommie! Mr. Sherman's friend said he doesn't know."

Jacob introduced himself to Auggie's mother and sister. Sherman acknowledged they knew each other, then stepped back.

"You will join us, won't you? It'll just be something simple—I'm a humble woman. Sherman told me how all this happened, and after all that back there I just want to let both of you know how much we appreciate this." Jacob listened to Auggie's mother, watched for Sherman's reaction.

"I really do appreciate the offer, but it's probably best for all of you to spend time together."

"For whom?" Sherman's interjection surprised everyone.

"Here these folks are trying to express gratitude and all you can do is think about yourself."

"Sherman, I was just thinking things might be less awkward if—"

"Less awkward? Did you say that to Rodney and Sean? Did you think about how what happened affects all our friendships?"

Silence.

"Children, why don't we wait in the car—let Mr. Sherman and his friend finish their conversation? Jacob, the invitation is still open. We're going to Paschal's."

After he settled them in the car, Sherman walked back to where Jacob waited. "Be a man about it, Jacob. It'll just be about an hour. That's only a little longer than we fucked. We can be cordial for an hour."

Jacob was trying to arrange an apology in his head, a credible, sequential explanation of what happened with his parents that resulted in what occurred between the two of them. But those moments of his standing there so silently took too long for Sherman.

Sherman exhaled, frustrated. "You think too much at the wrong fucking moments, Jay. And when it really matters, you don't think enough." He started walking toward his car.

Jacob caught him by the arm. "Wait."

Sherman's shoelace was untied. Jacob bent down on the street in front of him, kneeled underneath the shining sun, the hint of a cool breeze chilling the air, and tied Sherman's shoe. He looped the lace, tightened the bow, straightened the break in his pants. Checked his other shoe before he stood up.

His face softened, Sherman looked at Jacob. "You could've told me to tie that myself."

"Yes. I could've done that."

And then Jacob wasn't thinking, he kissed Sherman right where they stood. Kissed Sherman to tell him that was the best he could manage. Kissed him to tell him he was truly sorry. Jacob kissed Sherman to ask for a new beginning, to tell him that there would be mistakes and confusion and anger, but his kiss also asked for a future. Jacob kissed Sherman to say they could hold each other, to tell him he was willing to try, if Sherman was willing not to give up. Jacob kissed Sherman, and when Sherman kissed him back, salty tears seeped between their lips. Jacob wrapped his arms around Sherman to let him know he recognized all of him just as Sherman recognized every bit of Jacob, wrapped his arms around Sherman, not caring who saw them in this world where they lived, fighting every day to make visible the small parts and little pieces of themselves into one great big whole. They finished, held each other, their eyes closed, breathing easy and steady, Sherman's heartbeat a solid pulse beating against Jacob's chest.

TWENTY-FIVE

DANIEL

Daniel sat in the parking lot, debating how to reveal himself to Ralph Reid. He brought a picture of his mother, figured he'd hand that to Ralph as soon as they started talking. See if he remembered her, if that would make him look at Daniel harder. He thought about giving Ralph the box that Marty had given him. He would explain his entire childhood of wanting, tell Ralph Reid how Mama always kept him at bay. Daniel had so many questions. The more he debated with himself, the more he thought maybe he should just drive away. Or maybe he should just keep quiet. He had the answer he wanted, and, after all, this was his job and Ralph was basically his new employer. Did anything else really matter? Daniel leaned back, closed his eyes, and relaxed.

Startled, he woke up to tapping on his car window. He'd fallen asleep, thinking about his predicament. It took a moment for him to register Ralph peering at him. Embarrassed, he checked his watch, opened his car door, and apologized. He was thirty minutes late for their meeting.

"Not the best way to start a new job."

"I know. Really am sorry. I was here on time. Just took a moment. Guess I got a lot on my mind." Daniel climbed out of the car, stood in front of Ralph.

Away from the podium and all the people who surrounded them the last few days, Ralph seemed less imposing. Still a formidable man—tall and well-built, like Marty first described—but less the boisterous, fidgety, fussy personality that was Beth and more a thoughtful person. Like someone who made decisions after analyzing the facts laid out before him. The real-life color version of Ralph was more detailed than the black-and-white newspaper articles: what was a mass of black curly hair was cut close to his scalp, shot through with streaks of gray. His youthful look and buoyant smile tempered with the quiet reserve of experience. His eyes were still observant and sharp, gave Daniel a quick once-over as they stood by his car before he started toward the building.

"Either that or working too hard, huh? I'll give you a pass this time."

"Thank you."

But Daniel wasn't walking with him. The car door was still open, and he was still undecided about Mama's picture and the box of articles. All Daniel had to do was reach, grab, and hand them to Ralph. The rest of what happened would take care of itself. All the years of not knowing, the questions, the anger, and here was the moment. But what *would* happen afterward? Would the moment *really* take care of itself? Daniel thought about the decisions Mama made that had brought him to where he was now. Desperation had fueled her actions. He was still crafting parts of himself, figuring out which elements went where, what revelations were necessary, which details weren't so urgent. Here he stood with a range of options, with the possibility to actually plot the direction of his life.

Ralph finally noticed he was walking alone. He stopped, turned back toward Daniel. "Something wrong?"

Daniel hesitated, stood and watched Ralph, the car door still open, the distance of a few feet separating them. He took a breath, swung the car door shut. The heavy sound was the finality of a past closing, the end of an earlier life filled with guesses about a questionable path headed toward an inconceivable destination. "No. Just making sure I have everything."

Ralph registered Daniel's hesitation. "You sure you're okay?"

Daniel nodded, looked down at the ground before he looked up and stepped in Ralph's direction. The years from where he began to where they were stretched between them, then went beyond, and on and on. He would take his time; he hoped his father would understand.

"Everything is okay."

ACKNOWLEDGMENTS

My father said to me, "He's at the tip of your pen." He was responding to a question I asked about the lack of Black men writing fiction. He reminded me what Morrison said about writing the book I wanted to read. Always my biggest champion, my mother, Jacqueline Jones, urged me on. While there are aspects of my Life my parents and I have never discussed, I know they are proud of what I've accomplished. I am the man I am because of my mother and father. Their love and support are deep, evolving, and ever present, and I thank God He/She/It sent me to this world through them. Likewise, the love and support of my brother, Duane Jones, my sister-in-law, and my nieces, as well as my aunts, uncles, and cousins, is thick and whole and filled with ongoing opportunities for mutual understanding. Chadra Pittman and her sons, my nephews, James Carlton and Chaden Timothy, are the family I didn't have. Her sister (and mine too), Carlane Pittman, will never know how appreciative I am of her ability to share her sister with me. The love and selflessness of Amy Nickerson-Allen, Tayari Jones, Zelma Harrison, Kara Olidge, and Melanie Babb saved me from insanity and sustain me to this day. I count Jafari Allen, Alton Allen, Imar Hutchins, C. Todd Inniss, and Smedmore Benard among the men who have helped me cultivate the true meaning of friendship. Engaging myself with deep, soul-fortifying honesty has been an ongoing journey in which I've entrusted guidance from my therapist, Mona Lisa Ortiz-Rosa.

During high school, Mrs. Goldstein and Mr. Levy encouraged the young writer in me. For introducing me to the prescient writers of Other Countries, a debt is owed to Bill Crawley. That discovery led me to the brilliant work of Joseph Beam, Essex Hemphill, and Donald Woods. Dr. Melvin Rahming and Dr. Gloria Wade-Gayles helped me blaze a path to Columbia. For early recognition of my work, I'm appreciative of the Richard Wright / Zora Neale Hurston Foundation. I was thrilled to be included in the inaugural group of Lambda Literary's Writers Retreat for Emerging LGBTQ Voices. My writing is also lavishly informed by my experience working for almost three decades in economic development and real estate.

This book is the result of an incredible team of people. Haley Heidemann at WME is my dynamic literary agent, courageous, daring, and valiant. Editorial discussions with Yahdon Israel are filled with precise insights, challenging questions, and recommendations that expand my command of the work and constantly increase my confidence as a writer. Sophia Benz, Tzipora Chein, Yvette Grant, Chonise Boss, and Anna Skrabacz keep momentum moving productively forward with incredible skill and acumen. Shikeith is a visionary artist. I cannot imagine a more perfect book cover. The beautiful intimacy of the book's interior design is the result of Lewelin Polanco's attentive care. Abundant thanks to Sarah Dylla for her accessibility, willingness to share details about community planning and economic development in Atlanta, and her deft networking prowess.

I've created community and family with an intrepid group of men. David Malebranche, Marlon Hines, and Stephen Barr are truly my "brothers from another mother." My New York crew: Marcus Allen, Stefan Moore, Lloyd Boston, Eric Hall, Anthony Darden, Leslie Bowman, Somari Saeed, Chris Montgomery, Michael Hall, Henry Mitchell, Quincy Ballon, and Adrian Steward. My boys in Atlanta: Cedric Gilbert, Clarence Gabriel, Jerome Hoskins, James Davis, Wendell Blair, Chavez Phillips, Craig Washington, Richard Moultrie, Terry Hooks, and Tim'm West.

These brief acknowledgments can't possibly capture the full range of my gratitude and appreciation for the many people who've lent an ear, provided a shoulder, and offered the encouragement and inspiration that have resulted in this book. Thank you.

Doug Jones was born in Brooklyn, New York. An alumnus of Morehouse College, he received his MFA in creative writing from Columbia University. His work has been included in the anthologies *Black Love Letters* (Zando Projects / Get Lifted Books), *Role Call: A Generational Anthology of Social and Political Black Literature & Art* (Third World Press), and *Sojourner: Black Gay Voices in the Age of AIDS* (Other Countries Press). He has also written for *Black Issues Book Review* and *Venus Magazine*. An inaugural fellow of the Lambda Literary Writers Retreat for Emerging LGBTQ Voices, Doug's early work was recognized by the Hurston/Wright Foundation. An avid art collector who enjoys swimming and traveling, Doug is a proud pet dad to a lovable mixed-breed German shepherd, Baldwin. Doug lives in Atlanta, Georgia. *The Fantasies of Future Things* is his debut novel.